Love Between the Lines

The Lilac Lake Inn Series
Book 2

Judith Keim

BOOKS BY JUDITH KEIM

THE HARTWELL WOMEN SERIES:
The Talking Tree – 1
Sweet Talk – 2
Straight Talk – 3
Baby Talk – 4
The Hartwell Women – Boxed Set

THE BEACH HOUSE HOTEL SERIES:
Breakfast at The Beach House Hotel – 1
Lunch at The Beach House Hotel – 2
Dinner at The Beach House Hotel – 3
Christmas at The Beach House Hotel – 4
Margaritas at The Beach House Hotel – 5
Dessert at The Beach House Hotel – 6
Coffee at The Beach House Hotel – 7
High Tea at The Beach House Hotel – 8 (2024}

THE FAT FRIDAYS GROUP:
Fat Fridays – 1
Sassy Saturdays – 2
Secret Sundays – 3

THE SALTY KEY INN SERIES:
Finding Me – 1
Finding My Way – 2
Finding Love – 3
Finding Family – 4
The Salty Key Inn Series – Boxed Set

SEASHELL COTTAGE BOOKS:
A Christmas Star
Change of Heart
A Summer of Surprises
A Road Trip to Remember
The Beach Babes

THE CHANDLER HILL INN SERIES:
Going Home – 1
Coming Home – 2
Home at Last – 3
The Chandler Hill Inn Series – Boxed Set

THE DESERT SAGE INN SERIES:
The Desert Flowers – Rose – 1
The Desert Flowers – Lily – 2
The Desert Flowers – Willow – 3
The Desert Flowers – Mistletoe & Holly – 4

SOUL SISTERS AT CEDAR MOUNTAIN LODGE:
Christmas Sisters – Anthology
Christmas Kisses
Christmas Castles
Christmas Stories – Soul Sisters Anthology
Christmas Joy

THE SANDERLING COVE INN SERIES:
Waves of Hope
Sandy Wishes
Salty Kisses

THE LILAC LAKE INN SERIES
Love by Design

Love Between the Lines
Love Under the Stars – (2024)

OTHER BOOKS:
The ABC's of Living With a Dachshund
Once Upon a Friendship – Anthology
Winning BIG – a little love story for all ages
Holiday Hopes
The Winning Tickets

For more information: **www.judithkeim.com**

PRAISE FOR JUDITH KEIM'S NOVELS

THE BEACH HOUSE HOTEL SERIES – Books 1 – 5:

"*Love the characters in this series. This series was my first introduction to Judith Keim. She is now one of my favorites. Looking forward to reading more of her books.*"

BREAKFAST AT THE BEACH HOUSE HOTEL *is an easy, delightful read that offers romance, family relationships, and strong women learning to be stronger. Real life situations filter through the pages. Enjoy!*"

LUNCH AT THE BEACH HOUSE HOTEL – "*This series is such a joy to read. You feel you are actually living with them. Can't wait to read the latest one.*"

DINNER AT THE BEACH HOUSE HOTEL – "*A Terrific Read! As usual, Judith Keim did it again. Enjoyed immensely. Continue writing such pleasantly reading books for all of us readers.*"

CHRISTMAS AT THE BEACH HOUSE HOTEL – "*Not Just Another Christmas Novel. This is book number four in the series and my introduction to Judith Keim's writing. I wasn't disappointed. The characters are dimensional and engaging. The plot is well crafted and advances at a pleasing pace. The Florida location is interesting and warming. It was a delight to read a romance novel with mature female protagonists. Ann and Rhoda have life experiences that enrich the story. It's a clever book about friends and extended family. Buy copies for your book group pals and enjoy this seasonal read.*"

MARGARITAS AT THE BEACH HOUSE HOTEL – "*What a wonderful series. I absolutely loved this book and can't wait for the next book to come out. There was even suspense in it. Thanks Judith for the great stories.*"

"Overall, *Margaritas at the Beach House Hotel* is another wonderful addition to the series. Judith Keim takes the reader on a journey told through the voices of these amazing characters we have all come to love through the years! I truly cannot stress enough how good this book is, and I hope you enjoy it as much as I have!"

THE HARTWELL WOMEN SERIES – Books 1 – 4:
"This was an EXCELLENT series. When I discovered Judith Keim, I read all of her books back to back. I thoroughly enjoyed the women Keim has written about. They are believable and you want to just jump into their lives and be their friends! I can't wait for any upcoming books!"

"I fell into Judith Keim's Hartwell Women series and have read & enjoyed all of her books in every series. Each centers around a strong & interesting woman character and their family interaction. Good reads that leave you wanting more."

THE FAT FRIDAYS GROUP – Books 1 – 3:
"Excellent story line for each character, and an insightful representation of situations which deal with some of the contemporary issues women are faced with today."

"I love this author's books. Her characters and their lives are realistic. The power of women's friendships is a common and beautiful theme that is threaded throughout this story."

THE SALTY KEY INN SERIES – Books 1 – 4:
FINDING ME – "I thoroughly enjoyed the first book in this series and cannot wait for the others! The characters are endearing with the same struggles we all encounter. The setting makes me feel like I am a guest at The Salty Key Inn...relaxed, happy & light-hearted! The men are yummy

and the women strong. You can't get better than that! Happy Reading!"

FINDING MY WAY- "Loved the family dynamics as well as uncertain emotions of dating and falling in love. Appreciated the morals and strength of parenting throughout. Just couldn't put this book down."

FINDING LOVE – "I waited for this book because the first two was such good reads. This one didn't disappoint.... Judith Keim always puts substance into her books. This book was no different, I learned about PTSD, accepting oneself, there is always going to be problems but stick it out and make it work. Just the way life is. In some ways a lot like my life. Judith is right, it needs another book and I will definitely be reading it. Hope you choose to read this series, you will get so much out of it."

FINDING FAMILY – "Completing this series is like eating the last chip. Love Judith's writing, and her female characters are always smart, strong, vulnerable to life and love experiences."

"This was a refreshing book. Bringing the heart and soul of the family to us."

THE CHANDLER HILL INN SERIES – Books 1 – 3:
GOING HOME – "I absolutely could not put this book down. Started at night and read late into the middle of the night. As a child of the '60s, the Vietnam war was front and center so this resonated with me. All the characters in the book were so well developed that the reader felt like they were friends of the family."

"I was completely immersed in this book, with the beautiful descriptive writing, and the authors' way of bringing her characters to life. I felt like I was right inside her story."

<u>COMING HOME</u> – *"Coming Home is a winner. The characters are well-developed, nuanced and likable. Enjoyed the vineyard setting, learning about wine growing and seeing the challenges Cami faces in running and growing a business. I look forward to the next book in this series!"*

"Coming Home was such a wonderful story. The author has such a gift for getting the reader right to the heart of things."

<u>HOME AT LAST</u> – *"In this wonderful conclusion, to a heartfelt and emotional trilogy set in Oregon's stunning wine country, Judith Keim has tied up the Chandler Hill series with the perfect bow."*

"Overall, this is truly a wonderful addition to the Chandler Hill Inn series. Judith Keim definitely knows how to perfectly weave together a beautiful and heartfelt story."

"The storyline has some beautiful scenes along with family drama. Judith Keim has created characters with interactions that are believable and some of the subjects the story deals with are poignant."

SEASHELL COTTAGE BOOKS:

<u>A CHRISTMAS STAR</u> – *"Love, laughter, sadness, great food, and hope for the future, all in one book. It doesn't get any better than this stunning read."*

"A Christmas Star *is a heartwarming Christmas story featuring endearing characters. So many Christmas books are set in snowbound places...it was a nice change to read a Christmas story that takes place on a warm sandy beach!" Susan Peterson*

<u>CHANGE OF HEART</u> – *"CHANGE OF HEART is the summer read we've all been waiting for. Judith Keim is a master at creating fascinating characters that are simply irresistible. Her stories leave you with a big smile on your*

face and a heart bursting with love."

~Kellie Coates Gilbert, author of the popular Sun Valley Series

A SUMMER OF SURPRISES – "The story is filled with a roller coaster of emotions and self-discovery. Finding love again and rebuilding family relationships."

"Ms. Keim uses this book as an amazing platform to show that with hard emotional work, belief in yourself and love, the scars of abuse can be conquered. It in no way preaches, it's a lovely story with a happy ending."

"The character development was excellent. I felt I knew these people my whole life. The story development was very well thought out I was drawn [in] from the beginning."

A ROAD TRIP TO REMEMBER – "I LOVED this book! Love the character development, the fun, the challenges and the ending. My favorite books are about strong, competent women finding their own path to success and happiness and this is a winner. It's one of those books you just can't put down."

"The characters are so real that they jump off the page. Such a fun, HAPPY book at the perfect time. It will lift your spirits and even remind you of your own grandmother. Spirited and hopeful Aggie gets a second chance at love and she takes the steering wheel and drives straight for it."

THE DESERT SAGE INN SERIES – Books 1 – 4:

THE DESERT FLOWERS – ROSE – "The Desert Flowers - Rose, is the first book in the new series by Judith Keim. I always look forward to new books by Judith Keim, and this one is definitely a wonderful way to begin The Desert Sage Inn Series!"

"In this first of a series, we see each woman come into her own and view new beginnings even as they must take this tearful journey as they slowly lose a dear friend. This is a very well written book with well-developed and likable main characters. It was interesting and enlightening as the first portion of this saga unfolded. I very much enjoyed this book and I do recommend it"

"Judith Keim is one of those authors that you can always depend on to give you a great story with fantastic characters. I'm excited to know that she is writing a new series and after reading book 1 in the series, I can't wait to read the rest of the books."!

THE DESERT FLOWERS – LILY – "The second book in the Desert Flowers series is just as wonderful as the first. Judith Keim is a brilliant storyteller. Her characters are truly lovely and people that you want to be friends with as soon as you start reading. Judith Keim is not afraid to weave real life conflict and loss into her stories. I loved reading Lily's story and can't wait for Willow's!

"The Desert Flowers Lily is the second book in The Desert Sage Inn Series by author Judith Keim. When I read the first book in the series, The Desert Flowers-Rose, I knew this series would exceed all of my expectations and then some. Judith Keim is an amazing author, and this series is a testament to her writing skills and her ability to completely draw a reader into the world of her characters."

THE DESERT FLOWERS – WILLOW – "The feelings of love, joy, happiness, friendship, family and the pain of loss are deeply felt by Willow Sanchez and her two cohorts Rose and Lily. The Desert Flowers met because of their deep feelings for Alec Thurston, a man who touched their lives in different ways.

Once again, Judith Keim has written the story of a strong, competent, confident and independent woman. Willow, like Rose and Lily can handle tough situations. All the characters are written so that the reader gets to know them but not all the characters will give the reader warm and fuzzy feelings.

The story is well written and from the start you will be pulled in. There is enough backstory that a reader can start here but I assure you, you'll want to learn more. There is an ocean of emotions that will make you smile, cringe, tear up or out right cry. I loved this book as I loved books one and two. I am thrilled that the Desert Flowers story will continue. I highly recommend this book to anyone who enjoys books with strong women."

Love Between the Lines

The Lilac Lake Inn Series
Book 2

Judith Keim

Wild Quail Publishing

Love Between the Lines is a work of fiction. Names, characters, places, public or private institutions, corporations, towns, and incidents are the product of the author's imagination or are used fictitiously. Any resemblance to actual events, locales, or persons, living or dead, is coincidental.

No part of *Love Between the Lines* may be reproduced or transmitted in any form or by any electronic or mechanical means, including information storage and retrieval systems, without permission in writing from the author, except by a reviewer who may quote brief passages in a review. This book may not be resold or uploaded for distribution to others. For permissions contact the author directly via electronic mail:

wildquail.pub@gmail.com
www.judithkeim.com

Published in the United States of America by:

Wild Quail Publishing
PO Box 171332
Boise, ID 83717-1332

ISBN 978-1-959529-28-6

Dedication

For writers and their editors.

CHAPTER ONE
TAYLOR

In the rental house she shared with her two older sisters in the resort town of Lilac Lake, New Hampshire, Taylor Gilford sat at her desk in the room she'd set up as her "writer's cave" and stared in dismay at her computer screen. Outside the sun was shining, and purple finches at the nearby bird feeders were chirping happily, but she ignored both as she fought tears.

Addressed to Taylor Castle, her pen name, her new editor, Thompson C. Walker at her New York publishing house, had sent a message stating the author's work lacked credibility, that it was obvious she hadn't experienced a soul-baring relationship of her own. He'd even gone through and marked the first couple of chapters with numerous suggestions for changes and informed her that he wouldn't look at it again until extensive re-writing had been done.

Taylor had always been shy, but it didn't mean she was a pushover when it came to defending herself. She picked up the phone and called her agent, a smart, encouraging woman who was to retire soon.

As Taylor waited for her agent to answer, she stewed. How dare someone try to destroy her "word baby?" Just thinking of it made her want to cry. It was like telling a mother her baby was ugly!

The minute she heard Dorothy Minton's "hello," fresh tears blurred Taylor's vision. It took a moment to reign in her emotions, and after she'd calmed down a bit, she drew a deep breath and prepared to speak.

"Hello, Taylor, how are you?" Dorothy asked. The concern in her voice caused more tears to threaten.

"Not well. I'm upset by an email from my new editor, Thompson C. Walker. I'm furious that he would tear down my work as if I hadn't had a couple of successful book launches. I've never met or even talked to the guy before this. If push comes to shove, I can be just as ... rude ... as dismissive."

"Okay," said Dorothy. "Let's start at the beginning. He sent you an email?"

"Yes. But he didn't use my name, simply referred to me as 'the author'." Taylor's lips quivered, but she quickly gained control over them and felt a wave of new anger fill her. "He said it was obvious I'd never had a soul-baring relationship of my own. That really hurt, Dorothy. All my readers love my stories without so-called 'soul-baring' relationships."

"Well, let's see. For your last book, you wanted to write something a little longer, a little deeper. Maybe that's the problem." Dorothy's voice was gentle. "Why don't we let that email rest? Sometimes, no response is the best response. You've told me you've had trouble starting the next book. Why don't you take some time and enjoy your stay in Lilac Lake for a few weeks, and then we can discuss how to move ahead. By then, we'll have a clearer understanding of what's been said. Will you do that for me?"

Feeling like an overwrought teenager, Taylor swallowed hard. "Okay. But I'm still furious that he would be so rude about it."

"Understood," said Dorothy. "It's easy to belittle a writer when you've never published a book of your own."

"Right," said Taylor once again feeling the anger bubbling to the surface. "I'll do as you say and try not to think about it and just enjoy my time here." Even as she said the words,

Taylor knew she was lying. She'd never forget how a cocky new editor had shredded her work. Didn't he understand she put her heart and soul into her work, that writing was hard?

"Remember, Taylor, you have many readers who adore your books. Be kind to yourself," said Dorothy. "We'll talk later."

Taylor ended the call, got up from her desk, and went downstairs to the kitchen to fix herself a glass of soothing iced tea. She was glad her sisters weren't there. She needed to have time to calm herself.

Dani, her middle sister, was off meeting a building inspector at the cottage being renovated for the three of them. Whitney, the oldest at thirty-two, was spending some time with their grandmother, GG, who was living at The Woodlands, an assisted-living facility nearby.

As Taylor walked into the kitchen, Mindy, the black and tan dachshund Whitney had adopted, trotted over to her begging for attention.

Taylor picked her up and hugged her, laughing when Mindy's pink tongue swiped her cheeks. Setting the dog down, Taylor realized she was the only one of the three sisters who didn't own a dog or any pet, for that matter. Did that mean she didn't have a natural ability to love? Was that what her characters were missing?

Chiding herself for being foolish, Taylor slipped a treat to Mindy and fixed a glass of iced tea for herself.

She let Mindy out to the backyard and took a seat in one of the Adirondack chairs on the patio so she could watch her. She breathed in the cool morning air. Evergreens of many varieties were part of the landscape and added a subtle perfume. The last of the lilac blooms had faded ready to begin their annual journey to next spring when they'd dazzle once more. Marjorie Hight, the owner of the house she and her sisters were renting, had planted a lovely rose garden, and Taylor gazed at the colorful flowers, enjoying their beauty. This quiet moment, she decided, was more important than worrying about a nasty email.

She glanced over the fence at Brad Collister's white Cape Cod house next door. That was a story worth writing about. Dani and Brad had quickly fallen in love and were now engaged. Dani told her it was love at first sight, and that she and Brad were soulmates, almost as if their love was by design. As happy as she was for them, Taylor didn't believe that something like that could happen so easily for others.

She frowned. Was that another of her flaws?

It was a fluke that she and her sisters were now living together in a rented house in Lilac Lake, but then, she supposed, life was full of surprises. After being beckoned there by GG, the three of them had learned their beloved grandmother had sold the family's Lilac Lake Inn and had moved into The Woodlands. As part of the sale, GG had retained the cottage and three acres around it for her three granddaughters with the understanding that the house had to be occupied for at least six months of the year. It was a lovely gift, but first, the cottage, thought to be haunted, had to be renovated completely.

Not everyone believed the house was home to the rumored ghost of Mrs. Maynard, a woman who'd died in the snow outside the house in December 2002. On the other hand, no one could be certain that the strange occurrences there were only coincidences. Taylor just knew she didn't want to be in that house alone, not until everyone was sure the mysterious happenings had ended.

Her older sister, Dani, had a degree in architecture and was overseeing the renovation of the cottage after giving up her job at a prestigious architectural firm in Boston. No doubt, she'd soon be moving to Lilac Lake permanently because Brad and his brother, Aaron, owned Collister Construction and were successfully overseeing a big housing development in the area. As if her thoughts had conjured her up, Dani appeared on the patio with her black lab, Pirate.

"How's it going?" Dani asked, taking a seat in the chair beside Taylor. With honey-colored hair and light-blue eyes like GG, Dani was the tomboy of the group, the most outgoing. With her recent engagement, she radiated happiness.

Taylor looked away from Dani's probing glance and then faced her with a sigh. "I'm not doing very well. I received some terrible comments about my latest book at the publishers from my new editor. It's pretty devastating news."

A look of concern flashed across Dani's face. "I'm sorry. I know how sensitive you are. That must be very difficult. Especially when you're trying to start another book."

"I talked to my agent, and she told me to take some time off to regroup. She said to enjoy Lilac Lake for a while. And that's what I'm going to do."

"Okay, then, how about coming with me to the garage at the cottage? We need to go through all of the things left in there. After we get it cleaned out, we can store some of Whitney's boxes inside."

"Where?" asked Whitney joining them. She swept Mindy into her arms and pulled up a chair, forming a circle. The oldest sister, Whitney was a beloved actress on a popular television show, and after bad publicity, she'd left California uncertain whether she'd ever return. A blonde beauty, Whitney had loved to sing and dance all her life. Now, she was going through a hard time. Taylor hoped the stay in Lilac Lake would do her good.

"We can store some of the boxes you sent here in the garage at the cottage. We need to clean it out anyway. If we all work together, it shouldn't take too long to get the work done."

"Okay. I need to keep busy," said Whitney. "I'm so used to working that I'm at loose ends."

"But the rest is already helping you," said Dani. "You looked terrible when you first arrived."

"Gee, thanks," said Whitney, but she was smiling. She stroked Mindy's head and stared out at the yard. When she turned back to them, a look of determination filled her features. "I've decided to concentrate on our responsibilities during my time here and not worry about what's going on in Hollywood. It's time for me to stand firm on my beliefs, which don't include some of the things going on out West."

"Bravo," said Taylor. She'd always admired her sisters for their ability to stay the course in whatever decisions they made. They didn't mean to, but they'd often made her feel inadequate. With dark, straight hair, brown eyes, and the stronger features of her father, she looked nothing like her blonde half-sisters. Dani and Whitney had hung together without wanting a little sister around. Now, as adults, they were all close. But, as a kid, she'd turned to books as an escape from the feeling of being left out. Was that another reason her writing needed to be stronger? Oh, God! That email made her feel so insecure.

Dani stood. "If everyone is ready, let's go to the garage now. After it's cleaned out, we can store stuff for the house there as well as Whitney's boxes."

Happy to be able to do something besides stew about that horrible message from Thompson C. Walker, Taylor accompanied her sisters to Dani's SUV, carrying a bucket of cleaning supplies.

Each time she approached the cottage, she recalled the memory of her sisters teasing her, leaving her in the cottage alone after telling her a ghost lived there. When they learned how scared she'd been, they'd told her they were truly sorry, that all the kids joked about the ghost.

Now, the house, deconstructed in places, looked as if it couldn't hold any ghost. Interior walls had been ripped out, the kitchen was torn apart, and pieces of demolished wallboard, plaster, and other construction materials along with a few old, useless appliances sat in a dumpster beside the house.

Dani parked in front of the garage beside workmen's trucks. Taylor got out of her car and waited while Dani tried the old-fashioned lock on the garage door, then stood back as Dani lifted the door and a burst of dust exploded in the breeze and settled.

Inside the dark space, various shapes loomed.

Taylor snapped on the light and the shapes morphed into boxes, gardening equipment, and an old lawn mower that looked as if it was permanently damaged by rust and disuse.

"Okay, we'll pull everything out piece by piece. Items we know we don't want to keep we'll toss into the dumpster. Others will be left to inspect later," said Dani. "There's not as much here as I thought."

With the three of them hauling items out of the garage, it didn't take long to empty it. Most everything, including the lawn mower, went into the dumpster. A few garden tools were set aside.

"We need to wipe down the walls, sweep the floor, wash the one window, and get everything as clean as possible," Taylor said, gazing around her with disgust.

"I'm going to get a ladder to check the open shelf at the far end of the garage," said Dani.

"We'll be here working while you go see that fiancé of yours," teased Whitney. "I saw his truck here. Don't be gone too long."

Dani laughed. "It's not as if we'd be alone."

"When the two of you are together, it makes it seem as if it's just the two of you in the world," Whitney said.

Is that what my characters have been missing? Feeling all alone in the world? Taylor asked herself and then shook her head. She had to stop thinking of that horrid email.

Moments later, Dani returned carrying a ladder. She set it up by the shelf and climbed up to peer into the space. "Nothing here," she said. "Oh, wait, there's a box pushed back against the side wall."

Whitney walked over to the ladder. "I'm here. Hand it down."

Taylor rushed over to help her.

Grunting, Dani reached for it and then dragged the large box that looked as if it had come from a store to the edge of the shelf. "It's light, but be careful," she warned Whitney, lowering it to her.

Taylor helped Whitney struggled to hang onto the box before setting it down on the concrete floor.

Studying it, Taylor's imagination flared, creating all kinds of images in her mind. "It must be special to have been stored so carefully. What do you think we'll find?"

Dani got off the ladder and elbowed Taylor. "You're such a romantic. Let's take a look."

"Here goes," said Whitney. She lifted the lid and they all stared at the assortment of baby clothes inside. With shaking hands, Whitney lifted a tiny blue sweater from the box.

"Whose baby? And why are they here?" said Taylor. Her imagination was already forming a story in her mind.

"Maybe it has something to do with those birth and death certificates GG was keeping for someone," said Dani. When they were cleaning personal things out of the inn a few weeks ago, they'd found a tin box filled with GG's personal papers, a birth certificate for a baby boy named Isaac Thomas, along with a death certificate for him a day later. When they'd told GG about it, she'd had no idea what was inside the envelope a friend had given her for safekeeping.

Whitney handed the sweater to Dani's outstretched hands. "Brad and I want children," Dani said holding up the sweater. "But looking at this tiny piece now, I want to wait a while after we're married."

"It sure is small," said Taylor. She wanted children, too, but knew that time wasn't near. She hadn't even found a boyfriend, much less a "soul-baring" love.

As Whitney got ready to close the box, a flash of white caught Taylor's attention. "Hold on. I saw something we might want to look at."

Whitney handed Dani the baby sweater, a hat, booties, and a crib blanket, exposing a white dress. Carefully, so as not to get it dirty, Whitney stood and held up a sleeveless, white floor-length dress in a silky fabric.

Taylor clasped a hand over her heart. "It's a wedding dress."

"Do you think it's connected to the certificates we found?" asked Dani said.

At the thought of what she was sure was a sad story, Taylor sighed. "We'd better ask GG if she knows anything about it."

Whitney carried the dress outside. Dani followed with the baby clothes, and Taylor took up the rear with the empty box.

An unexpected breeze came up, ripping the box from Taylor's hands and sending it flying into the air.

Stunned, Taylor watched it swoop like a kite and come crashing down on the driveway, crumpling it into a useless mess from the impact.

"Wow! What was that?" asked Dani, giving her a wide-eyed

stare. "It was like a small tornado."

"I ... I'm not sure what happened," said Taylor, shaken. Whitney and Dani still held their items safely in their arms.

"Let's lay these things inside my car to keep them safe and clean," said Dani. "We still need to work on the garage. I'm expecting deliveries of appliances any day. We'll store them inside until we're ready to put them in the house."

Throughout the time Taylor helped to clean the garage, her thoughts remained on their discovery. There were stories behind the items, and she didn't think they were happy ones.

After they returned to their house, Whitney took a small suitcase from her closet. "Let's use this to store the things we found."

Whitney laid the dress on her bed, folded it carefully, and nestled it in tissue paper she took from a bureau drawer. "There. Such a lovely dress, so simple." The sleeveless dress was made of a satiny fabric and had classic lines.

"I'll put these baby clothes and the quilt underneath, so the dress doesn't get ruined," said Dani. "Like you said, Taylor, there's a story here. Maybe you can use it in the book you're writing."

"Maybe," Taylor said, but even as she spoke, a shiver crossed her shoulders. Some stories were not hers to tell.

CHAPTER TWO

TAYLOR

A couple of days later, Taylor sat with Whitney at an outdoor table at the Lilac Lake Café sipping on a diet drink while waiting for Crystal Owens, the owner of the café, to speak to them. Crystal had asked them to meet her to discuss a plan. Both were curious about what Crystal was planning, and Taylor was anxious to escape thoughts of the email that wouldn't leave her mind,

It didn't bother her to wait. It gave her a chance to study the small resort town that had become a favorite of tourists. The Town Hall sat across the street from the café. Its white-clapboard exterior matched that of the church a short distance down the street but lacked the church's steeple that rose to touch the sky with a promise of salvation. The red brick building between the two housed the police department, giving them a central spot from which to keep the peace.

Main Street was several blocks long and was lined on both sides by a variety of restaurants and store fronts to suit any tourist's tastes. Taylor sighed as she observed groups of people, mostly tourists, strolling along the sidewalks of the picture-postcard street. It felt fantastic to get out of the house where she wouldn't have to stare at her computer wondering if she could write again.

Crystal arrived, arousing Taylor from her uncharacteristically gloomy thoughts. A couple of years older than Whitney and with her purple hair and ever-present smile, Crystal was a cheerful presence. "Hey, there. Glad you could make it. I have a huge favor to ask of both of you."

She sat down next to Whitney opposite Taylor. "I'm in charge of creating a float sponsored by Collister Construction for the annual 4th of July parade. I know Dani is busy, but I would love for you two to help."

"What does that entail?" asked Whitney. "I'll be glad to work behind the scenes, but I want nothing to do with sitting or standing on the float." Since escaping her life in Hollywood, Whitney wanted to keep a low profile, especially in town, to avoid any unwanted attention. She needed a break from the glare of publicity and from people thinking they deserved to know her every move.

"No worries. I use girls from Linda's Dance School to ride on the float and throw candy and other goodies to the crowd. This year, the theme is Collister Construction's 5th Birthday. We'll make a birthday cake out of Styrofoam that we'll cover with paper flowers. There will be other decorations, of course: helium balloons, streamers, and other party trimmings. The girls are going to dress in jeans and hard hats and wear T-shirts with 'Collister Construction' on them. It should be cute."

"How are we going to make a cake out of Styrofoam?" asked Taylor.

"I've ordered custom-cut, circular pieces of Styrofoam that can be shaped into a big, two-layer cake," said Crystal. "The hard work will be covering the exterior with the paper flowers and doing the other decorations. The girls from the dance studio will help."

"And the float itself?" asked Whitney.

"We have one that we use from year to year. It's covered with a green cloth that has white fringe. Very practical. What do you say?"

Taylor glanced at her sister.

"Sure," said Whitney.

"When do we start?" asked Taylor. A project like this seemed a useful way to get involved with the community.

"The Styrofoam pieces are on their way. As soon as they arrive, we can start. We park the float in a storage area at the Beckham Lumber Company," said Crystal. "You can go there any time to work on it once the decorating gets underway. In exchange for storage there, we hang a big sign for the lumber company on the end of the float."

"Sounds fair. How many floats are going to be in the parade?" Whitney asked.

"Usually four or five," said Crystal. "We've become the place where neighboring towns come to participate. Two high-school bands, school clubs, and special-interest organizations in the area join in. The parade starts outside the downtown, winds its way right down Main Street, and ends at the state park on the other side of the lake. Some people anchor their boats and watch from the water."

"I remember doing that," said Taylor grinning.

"Me too," Whitney said. "What a slice of small-town Americana. It'll be nice to become part of it again."

That afternoon, at Brad and Aaron's invitation, Taylor and Whitney accompanied Dani to the new housing development Collister Construction was building at the far end of Lilac Lake. Called "The Meadows," it consisted of upscale, custom-designed single-family homes. As a new team member with her architecture training, Dani was proud to show it to them.

Two locals, Melissa Hendrickson, a chef at her parent's restaurant in town, and Ross Roberts, a former baseball star and now part owner of the Lilac Lake Inn, were buying homes there. Most of the rest of the homeowners would probably come from the New York and Boston areas.

"I'm so happy I get to show you the development. I'm proud of Brad and Aaron for making this happen. It's a gutsy move but one that's paying off already," said Dani.

She pulled up to the sales office and parked. "Inside, you'll be able to see a topical map of the area and the available lots. If we didn't have the obligation to the cottage, this might be the perfect place to have a retreat or a permanent home."

Taylor chuckled. "You sound like a real estate agent, Dani."

Dani laughed. "I can't help it. I'm excited to be part of this."

After viewing sales materials on display and the available lots on the map, Taylor followed her sisters to the first house, which had been sold but was being used as a model home.

Stepping inside the contemporary log structure, Taylor let out a gasp of pleasure. "Wow!"

She gazed around. The open space had a feeling of being outdoors with its views of the hardwood and pine trees behind the house. In its own natural way, with its subdued colors and textures, the woodland was just as beautiful as a bright, formal garden.

Taylor took in every convenience, every finishing detail of the house. "This is gorgeous."

"It's the same sort of feel inside that we're striving for with the cottage. The structure will remain pretty much as it is with maybe an addition of a screened porch or sunroom, but we have plenty of open space to play with after the walls were taken down."

"That will be beautiful," said Taylor, ashamed to admit she hadn't wanted to go inside the cottage. And with the discovery of the box in the garage, she was even more skittish. She'd always had a vivid imagination. Too much, her sisters said.

"So, what specifically do you do for this project?" asked Whitney. "They already have a number of building plans."

With a look of pride, Dani said, "They're using me to

personalize those plans. I already told them they needed more storage for active families. With skiing and lake activities close by, there's a need for storing equipment for different lifestyles."

"I'm so happy you're not working for that firm in Boston anymore," said Whitney.

"Oh, but I'm still working on Anthony Albono's apartment building in Providence, Rhode Island," Dani reminded her. "But, yes, here in Lilac Lake my work is appreciated. No "old boy network" games."

"Show me the upstairs," said Whitney to Dani.

They left, and Taylor stood in the kitchen looking out at the scene behind the house. She caught sight of a flash of red and smiled. She loved cardinals. They were such pretty birds with an easily identified call.

While she was standing there, Aaron Collister walked into the house and noticed her. "Hi, Taylor. Nice to see you here. What do you think about this one?"

She turned to him and smiled. "It's a gorgeous house. And the entire development looks like it's going to be a huge success. What a setting. The lake, the woods, and a view of the White Mountains in the distance are perfect."

He grinned and his dark eyes lit with excitement. "I think so too." With his tan skin, dark, straight hair, and eyes so brown they seemed black, Aaron was as different looking from his blonde, green-eyed half-brother, Brad, as possible. Yet they both were kind, hard-working men who'd taken a chance on developing these homes and were doing well.

Taylor pointed out the pair of cardinals to him.

He grinned. "There is a lot of bird life in this area." Aaron was part Native American and had been taught by his deceased mother to appreciate the beauty of nature from an early age. Taylor appreciated that part of him and his quiet manner. Watching the birds, enjoying a sunny moment, she felt at peace with him as she gazed out at the scenery.

When she turned to leave, she noticed Aaron's gaze on her and smiled. "See you later. I'm missing the tour of the upstairs. But I love what I've seen."

He dipped his head and went out to the garage, and she hurried up the stairs to rejoin her sisters.

Later, after touring the second almost-completed house and having seen the sites that Ross and Melissa had chosen for their homes, they headed back to their house.

For the next few days, Taylor answered email and checked social media and reminded herself that she'd promised Dorothy to step away from the writing process for a while. It was just as well. The few times she'd sat down to begin to make notes on a new story, the memory of Thompson C. Walker's crushing words stopped her.

When news came that the Styrofoam that Crystal had ordered for the float had come in, Taylor was excited by the prospect of working on the float. It would get her out of the house.

She drove to Beckman Lumber to the shed used to store the float. As she parked her car, she saw Bethany Beckman in the distance and waved. Bethany was married to Garth, one of the sons in the family, and ran the gift shop in the main building.

Inside, Crystal was talking to a young man dressed in jeans and a dark green T-shirt that said "Beckman Lumber" on it.

Crystal waved her over. "Come meet Brooks Beckman. And before you say anything, yes, his mother is a devoted Garth Brooks fan."

Taylor laughed and gazed into his smiling face. He had dark-auburn hair and gray eyes and cheeks scruffy with a light-red beard.

"It's hard to escape being a joke," said Brooks. "Thank God I love my mother."

She loved how pleasant, how laid-back he was.

"Brooks is going to do the final shaping and assembly of the Styrofoam for the cake. But I'm hoping you, Taylor, will unbox all the paper flowers and other decorations and get them ready to use. We'll give each girl from the dance studio a paper bag filled with flowers separated by color, so the colors need to be spread evenly in twelve different bags. It's a tedious job but it would be helpful if you'd do it," Crystal said.

"No problem. Better me than Whitney, who would want to bring Mindy here."

"Oh, yes. I thought of that," said Crystal chuckling. "I've got to go back to the café. See you two later. If you can make it, I want you both to be my guests at Jake's tonight."

"Thanks," said Brooks. He glanced at Taylor.

She gave them a thumbs up. It would be nice to get out of the house and have some fun. With Dani doing so much with Brad, she and Whitney had been hanging out together at the house. Whitney was keeping a low profile as rumors about the show being cancelled and her ex-costar, Zane Blanchard's life being out of control kept swirling in the entertainment news loop.

Taylor stood in front of a stack of brown boxes and stared at them, helpless.

"Here's a cutter to open them," said Brooks, handing it to her.

When their fingers touched, Taylor felt a jolt and stepped back as she accepted the utensil from him.

He grinned at her, and she felt her cheeks turn hot. Turning away, she faced the boxes and allowed her pulse to slow. *Is this what Thompson C. Walker meant? Some hot shock of attraction? Is that what he wants in the book?*

She cut open the box of flowers and began to work. Fortunately, there were seven different colors, which made it easier—red, yellow, orange, green, purple, blue, chartreuse. Taylor made a game of dropping the different flowers into the marked paper bags. Even so, she realized there were plenty of flowers left for Whitney and her to use.

As she worked, Brooks asked if she'd mind if he played some music. She wasn't at all surprised when country music filled the area. When a Garth Brooks song came on, she couldn't help laughing.

Brooks heard her, looked up from his work and joined in. "Too bad you don't have a sense of humor," he teased.

"Or you," she countered. "How are you doing with your project?"

"It's slow work trying to put the pieces together with enough tape so that it looks smooth and will hold. The pieces are well designed though, so it's not impossible. My brother tells me you're here for the summer and beyond."

"Yes, I'm a writer and can work anywhere. I thought a change from New York City would be helpful, but I'm struggling a bit."

"I can't imagine writing an entire book, but I like to write songs, which means I write lyrics," said Brooks.

"How interesting," said Taylor "I wish I could sing, but when I try, I sound like a mewling cat."

He laughed and shook his head. "Most people have some ability, but it takes training."

"Do you play locally?" she asked.

"I'm in a band, and we have gigs in Portsmouth, Concord, Manchester, and in Durham at UNH and other places within comfortable reach. But mostly, I play for myself. Sometimes, I'll play at Smokin' Joe's Fish Shack. They put on Saturday night shows featuring local artists during the summer."

"It all sounds cool. Let me know where you're playing next. I'd love to come and hear you," said Taylor. She could picture him with a guitar crooning to a crowd.

"Thanks. So, what kind of books do you write?" he asked.

"Stories with happy endings," she answered, careful not to use the word romance.

His eyes lit as he studied her, but he didn't make any comment. He simply nodded.

Relieved, Taylor said, "Guess I'd better get back to the flowers."

She'd been working for a while when Whitney showed up with Mindy on a leash. "Hi. I talked to Crystal, and she told me the project was getting started," she said to Taylor and turned to Brooks.

"Sorry, I don't know your name. I'm ... uh ...Taylor's sister."

Brooks' cheeks held new color as he gazed at Whitney. "I know who you are. I'm Brooks Beckman, Garth Beckman's younger brother."

"Nice to meet you," said Whitney. "It looks like we'll all be working together on the float."

"Looks that way," he said, and tipped his head in a little nod before going back to work.

Whitney came over to her. "What a hottie," she whispered in Taylor's ears. "Maybe he can help your writing."

Taylor gave Brooks a thoughtful look. But she wasn't sure about any future soul-baring relationship with him. What did that term mean, anyhow?

CHAPTER THREE
DANI

Dani could hardly believe how quickly her life had changed. A couple of months ago, she'd been working and living in Boston caught up in her routine of frustration at being left out of some interesting projects at the architectural firm where she worked. Now, she was using her training to work for a loyal client of the past and with the owners of Collister Construction. The brothers who owned the company were not only in charge of renovation at the Lilac Lake Inn her grandmother had just sold to three new owners, but they were also building a housing development at the other end of the lake and wanted her help. In addition, GG had made a deal with them to assist Dani in the renovation of the cottage she'd given her and her sisters.

But the most wonderful thing of all was that she and Brad Collister had quickly fallen in love and were now engaged. For Brad, it was a second chance at love after mourning the tragic death of his wife two years ago. For Dani, it was a dream she didn't realize she'd wanted for some time. Together, they were perfect.

Dani pulled into the driveway of the cottage and let her dog, Pirate, out of the backseat. At the front of the cottage, she stopped as she often did and stared out at the arresting scenery. The lake was a mirror to the blue sky and white clouds above. The large granite rock that emerged from the surface of the water close to the shoreline was as enticing as ever as the best place to sit or stretch out to catch the sun's rays. A gentle breeze came up and ruffled the surface of the lake sending tiny ripples dancing across it.

Pirate let out a happy bark and headed into the surrounding woods. She smiled and let him go. He needed to run, and she knew he'd come back when she called.

On the front porch, Dani hesitated and then sucked in a deep breath before she entered the house. Even though no one else was there, she felt as if she was intruding. She chided herself for thinking of the ghost, but after seeing the baby clothes and the wedding dress, she knew talk of a ghost could well be true. There was definitely a story behind that box.

Inside, the first floor was beginning to take shape. The removal of walls wherever possible had opened up the space for combined living and kitchen/dining areas that would hold enough nooks and crannies to be interesting as well as useful.

Even though all three sisters would probably not occupy the house at the same time, they wanted the house to be able to accommodate all of them, if desired. According to the agreement GG had made with the new owners of the inn, she and her sisters had a commitment to occupy the cottage for at least six months of the year.

Dani checked the electrical wiring to make sure it was all put in according to plan. The plumbing had already been installed, inspected, and approved. GG, she now knew, had set aside enough money for the project to carry out most of Dani's ideas. A screened-in porch or a possible sunroom was last on the list and would be built if all the sisters invested some money of their own. The cost of making the attic a comfortable family retreat was accounted for, but work would wait until the rest of the house had been completed. Neither she nor her sisters wanted to spend much time in the attic until they were certain there was no evidence of any unusual activity.

While she was working, Brad stopped in. "Hey, sweetheart,

what are you doing? Everything okay with the plumbing?"

"Yes." She turned to him, her pulse racing at the sexy smile he was giving her. "Well, hello."

He took her in his arms and kissed her, the kind of kiss that told her how right they were to be together. She closed her eyes and soaked in the smell, the taste of him. When she opened them, little sparkles of light danced around them and disappeared. They were nothing new. Dani accepted it was all part of the magic of his kisses.

They pulled apart and smiled at one another. "I'm going to miss you when you go to Boston tomorrow."

"I'll be gone only a couple of days," Dani said, torn between missing him and sharing the progress of the plans she'd designed with her special client. Her old boss, Herb Watkins, thought he could entice Dani to return to the firm, but that was never going to happen. After experiencing the freedom she had in her work with Brad and Aaron, she had no desire to be trapped once again in a job she hated. There was something to be said about New Hampshire's motto: "Live Free or Die."

He checked out the wiring with her and said, "It looks good. I'll call the building inspector and set up an appointment. Then insulation can be put in."

"That would be great. I don't need to be here for that. When I come back, we should be able to move ahead with the drywall."

"We'll work it out. The drywallers are busy at the development, but we'll pull them off that when it's needed."

"You and Aaron are fantastic about helping me with the renovation," said Dani, loving him.

"It's only right and we're happy to do it. If your grandmother hadn't helped us get the contract for The Woodlands, we might not have been able to get the business going."

"Then it's a win-win for us all," said Dani.

He winked at her. "It's always a win-win where you're concerned."

She chuckled happily and followed him out of the house.

CHAPTER FOUR
WHITNEY

Though tedious, Whitney enjoyed the work of adding flowers to the Styrofoam birthday cake designed for the float. It allowed her mind to drift from the world she'd left. Staying in New Hampshire was healthy for her after being pulled into a messy situation with her co-star, Zane Blanchard. After their initial love for each other had faded, she'd been foolish to pretend they were dating to keep interest alive in the television series they were doing together. She'd watched him go from a talented actor to one consumed by drugs. And when she'd caught him with two young women in a drug-fueled threesome, she'd ended any pretense of even liking him.

He'd been full of apologies for ruining their relationship, but she hadn't heard any remorse for some of his worst activities or a promise to try and clean up.

While she was working alone in the storage shed at Beckman Lumber, Nick Woodruff, the police chief walked in.

"How's it going?" he asked her.

"We're making progress."

"The 4th of July parade is a big deal in this area. It's nice that you and your sisters are going to be here for it. I remember when you all would come to Lilac Lake to see it." His smile crinkled the corners of his bright-blue eyes. The touch of gray in his dark hair at the temples gave him a look of wise authority.

"It's been years, but I remember how much we loved it as kids," said Whitney. A couple of years older than she, Nick was as sexy a cop as she'd ever seen. After the theater of Hollywood living, he seemed down-to-earth.

"Thought you might like a casual dinner out. A group of us are going to meet at Stan's, a bar and restaurant out of town specializing in seafood and beer. I'd be glad to pick you up."

Whitney smiled at him. "Thanks. That's sounds like fun. I've been sticking around home, but it's time I got out and did something like that."

Nick tipped his hat at her and walked away.

Whitney studied his ripped body and sighed. He was such a nice guy, but she had no interest in dating anyone seriously.

CHAPTER FIVE

TAYLOR

Taylor was sitting in Jake's with Crystal, Brooks Beckman, his brother, Garth, and Garth's wife, Bethany. The "thank you" dinner Crystal had offered them in exchange for work on the float had been postponed a few days ago and was now taking place.

Jake's was ideally located on Main Street in the center of town and was a favorite hangout for locals and tourists alike. Like most sports bars, several televisions were strategically placed around the space. But there was something intimate about the bar when the sound of the televisions was turned down during early dinner hours.

Taylor sat in a large booth next to Crystal facing Bethany, Garth, and Brooks. Since coming to Lilac Lake, Taylor had enjoyed meeting a lot of congenial people. It was as if the slower pace and the love of nature had made them more open, even kinder, to others.

She'd just finished swallowing the last of her chicken sandwich when she noticed a young man enter the bar and glance around. He was tall, with chocolate brown hair and wearing horned-rim glasses.

Crystal elbowed Taylor. "Who's the hottie? Someone new in town."

He turned toward them and then walked over with a confident stride.

"There you are, Taylor. Someone told me you might be here."

Taylor frowned. He knew her but she didn't have a clue to his identity. "Who are you? And what do you want?"

He smiled, showing straight white teeth. "I'm Cooper Walker."

Her frowned deepened. "Is that supposed to mean something to me?"

He shuffled his feet. "Ah, you might know me as Thompson C. Walker."

Taylor felt the blood leave her face so quickly she grabbed onto the edge of the table. She stood up shakily and faced him. "You bastard! What are you doing here?"

She knew her behavior was over-the-top, but his words had sent her into a tailspin she was still struggling with. How many other writers had he shredded with his comments?

Brooks got to his feet. "What's going on? Are you okay, Taylor?"

"No, I'm not. I don't want to be in the same room with him, and I certainly don't want to talk to him." She refused to let the tears that stung her eyes roll down her cheeks.

"Look, Cooper, or whatever your name is, you'd better leave now," said Brooks.

Cooper shook his head. "I can't. I'm here on business."

"What kind of business?" Taylor said narrowing her eyes at him.

"The head of the publishing house sent me here to try and fix things with you," Cooper said. "We need to talk."

"I have no intention of spending any time with you," said Taylor as angry as she'd ever been. "Leave me alone!"

Johnny, one of the bartenders, came over. "Are we having a problem here?" He gave Taylor a questioning look.

"I don't want this man anywhere near me," said Taylor.

Johnny turned to Cooper. "You heard her. Guess you'd better leave."

Cooper stared at Taylor. "I'll go, for now. But I can't go back to my job until you and I have settled things."

Taylor shrugged. "I don't care about your job."

"Leave," said Johnny, pointing to the door.

Walking away, Cooper's back was ramrod straight. Taylor and the others could see how angry he was.

Unable to stand on her quivering legs, Taylor sank onto the booth's bench.

Brooks and the others gave her worried looks.

"Are you okay, sweetie?" Crystal asked.

"I will be," said Taylor. "I just need to calm down. That man is the most irritating person I know. Well, actually, I don't *know* him. He's my editor at my publishing house and a real jerk."

"Okay, then, let's just relax," said Bethany, caressing her newly pregnant belly. "Don't worry, we'll all keep an eye out for you. But it sounds as if you're going to have to talk to him at some point."

"Not if I can help it," said Taylor. She might be shy and in some cases a bit naïve, but she was no puppet on a string.

After they broke up after dinner, Brooks said, "Why don't I drive you home? I know you're within walking distance, but I'd feel better if I drove you."

"Thanks. I'd appreciate it," she said, grateful for his support.

She found Whitney watching television with both Mindy and Pirate snuggled up against her on the couch.

"How was the celebration dinner?" Whitney asked.

"It was fine until Thompson "Cooper" Walker showed up," said Taylor gritting her teeth.

"Who's that?" asked Whitney frowning as she spoke.

"That, dear sister, is the editor who tore apart my book,"

said Taylor. "His boss sent him here to speak to me."

"You've got to be kidding," said Whitney, straightening, disturbing the dogs. "You must be a really important author to them, Taylor, for them to go to all this much trouble."

"I guess you're right." Whitney's comment gave her pause. "I think my agent, Dorothy Minton, must have talked to the people at the publishing house about that email. At any rate, he said he can't leave until he and I have fixed that relationship. But I have no intention of meeting with him. I don't think I can get past his words."

"At some point, you're going to have to talk to him. I understand how sensitive the situation is. Maybe you could make him sweat it a bit," said Whitney. "Perhaps he needs a lesson of his own."

"An excellent idea," said Taylor with a satisfied nod. "What are you watching?"

"A romance. Something to settle my soul," said Whitney. "It's cute."

Taylor sat down beside her and soon became lost in the plotting of the story, making mental notes of things to use in future books.

The next morning, Taylor woke up to the ringing of her phone. She checked caller ID. *Cooper Walker*. She ignored it and rolled over.

Thoughts kept whirling in her head as she lay in bed, making it impossible to go back to sleep.

Her cell rang again. She checked caller ID. *Her agent, Dorothy Minton.*

"Hi, Dorothy. How are you?" Taylor asked. She knew how lucky she was to have Dorothy on her side in the tough publishing business.

"Fine, thanks. I'm calling because I've just had a long talk with Grace Pritchard of the Pritchard Publishing Company. I've been friends with Grace for many years. She and I have decided this business with you and Cooper Walker needs to be resolved. I told her I would see that the foolishness at your end would stop. She's going to handle him. In fact, after some discussion we've agreed it would be best if he remained at Lilac Lake until you're both sure you can work together. Am I making myself clear?"

Taylor's jaw dropped. She'd never been at the receiving end of one of Dorothy's "declarations" as was known in the business. Before Taylor could speak, Dorothy continued in a gentler tone.

"You're a very fortunate young woman to have the interest of someone like Grace Pritchard. She's known for having an uncanny ability to spot talent and to promote it. This book and the one you are beginning will enable you to have a very secure future in the business."

"But ..."

"No 'buts,' Taylor. I would be remiss if I didn't ensure that you took advantage of this opportunity. My job is to help take you to the next level. Trust me. This is it."

Taylor sat back and let out a puff of dismay. She'd always listened carefully to whatever Dorothy suggested. This was no suggestion; it was a command. She thought of Cooper and wondered how he was taking these orders.

"What do you say, Taylor? Cooper Walker is a talented editor who can help you add depth and new levels to your work. I wouldn't say this if I didn't believe it was true."

"All right, but I intend to be true to myself when editing this book. I'm the writer; not he."

"That's fine," said Dorothy. "Both Grace and I feel it's a beneficial arrangement. Sorry, but I must go. Another call is waiting. You're a lovely young woman, Taylor, and I'm always proud to represent you. Now, do as I ask."

"Thanks," Taylor mumbled as Dorothy ended the call.

Grumbling softly to herself, she climbed out of bed and decided to walk to town and grab a cup of decaf mocha at Beans, the local coffee shop.

Since moving to Lilac Lake, she found that walking was a soothing way to conjure new ideas for books. Though she was on a bit of a break, there was no way she could stop thinking about her writing.

Striding through town, she felt the cool air of a New Hampshire summer morning was a pleasant way to start the day. Main Street in Lilac Lake was alive with colorful storefronts and opportunities to purchase everything one could desire. No need to rush about as she did in New York City. Here, everyone was comfortable with either a stroll or jogging.

She stopped in front of the Artists Collaborative shop and peered through the window at the arts and crafts featured there. Dani had talked about doing some of her watercolor paintings when she had the time during the winter months. This would be a great place for her to exhibit them.

Next door, the toy store was filled with all kinds of treasures for boys and girls. Here at Lilac Lake, where everyone spent so much time outdoors, kites were a big thing.

She moved along, gazing into store windows until she came to Pages, the bookstore owned by an older woman appropriately named Estelle Bookbinder. The window was full of enticing books. Taylor recognized several written by online friends of hers. Thinking of her situation, she grew angry. She's seen how self-assured Cooper Walker was. But that didn't mean he knew what he was talking about.

Taylor sat down on the front step of the bookstore half hidden by the awnings on both sides and drew a calming breath. She was used to critiques both good and bad of her books. Every reader had a right to his or her opinion. She knew that. But to have someone in publishing handle any author as Cooper had done to her was not only destructive; it was callous. She knew she was sensitive about her word babies, but every writer was.

She was about to get up when someone stepped in front of her, blocking her way.

"There you are," said a familiar voice, causing her to jump to her feet.

"You! What do you want?" Taylor faced Cooper with fisted hands. She couldn't help it. Just seeing him standing there as if he owned the world made her furious.

"I told you what I wanted," he said calmly. "I need to talk to you. Apparently, I hit some kind of nerve with you. I didn't mean it. I was just being honest. It's my job to make a book better."

"By destroying it? Is that how you usually introduce yourself to new authors? By picking apart their manuscript and destroying it?" Taylor told herself to calm down, but his attack still stung.

Cooper shuffled his feet. "I'm sorry if I was too tough. I'm trying to do an exceptional job for authors and for the company. The manuscript wasn't that bad, just not very realistic about real love."

"And you would know because?"

The tips of his ears turned red. "That's personal."

"You would judge me because of your experience?" She studied his ring finger and found it empty. "Where's the ring?"

"What do you mean?" he asked, frowning at her.

"If you know all about soul-depth love, why aren't you wearing a ring?"

Cooper glared at her. "Because I chose not to. That's why.

And that is none of your business."

"There's no use talking to you," said Taylor, crossing her arms in front of her. "I can see we're never going to be able to work together. You made a rude, judgmental call on me that can't be fixed."

He stepped forward. "Oh, but it can. Give me a chance. It's my job to see that it *is* fixed. That or lose the job I've always wanted."

Surprised by the anguish in his voice, she stared at him.

"Will you give me that chance, Taylor? I really need this to work out," he said, pushing his darkened glasses atop his head to gaze at her. His hazel eyes changed from brown to green as he waited for her answer.

Taylor remembered the earlier phone call with Dorothy and sighed. She had no choice. She had to make this business relationship work. Drawing a deep breath, she nodded. "Okay. We'll start by getting to know one another like my agent wants. With one condition. If we can't talk about your love life, we're not talking about mine. Is that clear?"

He gave her a half-smile and nodded. "Deal. Now, why don't I take you to breakfast? I hear the Café is the place to go."

"Okay," she said, suddenly hungry. She hated confrontation. Always would. Besides one didn't receive an order from Dorothy Minton and disobey it. And having the attention of a publisher like Grace Pritchard was a dream come true even if she had to deal with Cooper.

CHAPTER SIX

DANI

Dani's heart was full as she drove back to Lilac Lake. Her visit to Boston was everything she'd ever wanted—a client who was thrilled with her work, an ex-boss who wanted her back, and a chance to see a couple of her friends. But nothing could compare to the excitement she felt at seeing Brad again. Their relationship had developed quickly and strengthened to love, but it was deep and true.

She wouldn't sell her condo in Boston for a while. She liked the thought of spending time in the city every so often, and having a comfortable, convenient, and familiar place to stay in was important to her. She had yet to spend a winter in Lilac Lake and might need to get away.

Instead of pulling into the house she rented with her sisters, she drove into the driveway of Brad's house next door, where his truck was sitting. He'd promised to meet her there.

She parked beside it and got out.

Brad opened the door and swept her into his strong arms. Laughing with pure joy, she hugged him tight and lifted her face to kiss him.

His lips met hers, warm and wonderful.

She'd just started to respond when the sound of a car horn made her stop and turn.

A gray car pulled up to the house and a tall, blonde figure emerged from it. Smiling, she gave them a wave. "Just wanted the two of you to know I'm back in town for good. Thought we could get together for dinner."

Brad's body grew so tense Dani felt as if she was hugging a brick wall. "Sorry, JoEllen, we're busy," he said.

JoEllen's lips formed a pout. "Okay, then, we'll make it another night. I just wanted to celebrate being here. I'm sure we'll be seeing a lot of each other. 'Bye."

Dani turned to Brad. "I'd hoped her vow to return wouldn't happen." JoEllen was the sister of Brad's deceased wife. She'd thought she'd marry Brad as her dying sister had hoped. Brad had made it clear that wasn't going to happen, but JoEllen decided she liked Lilac Lake enough to move there. JoEllen had informed them it would be a way for her to keep an eye on Brad. Something both Brad and Dani resented.

"How can that woman be so dense?" asked Brad, threading his fingers through his blond hair.

"She has the twisted idea she would somehow be doing what her sister wanted," said Dani, as frustrated as Brad. "Let's simply ignore her." She threw her arms around Brad's neck and gave him a teasing smile. "Now, where were we?"

He grinned and lowered his lips to hers.

CHAPTER SEVEN
TAYLOR

When Taylor walked into the Lilac Lake Café with Cooper, Crystal gave her a wide-eyed look from behind the counter.

Taylor shrugged and continued walking to an open table. She was as surprised as Crystal that she'd accepted a truce from the man who'd made her lose her confidence in her writing. Time to get it back.

"Any suggestions?" Cooper said after they'd settled in their chairs.

She handed him one of the menus from the metal holder on the table. "You're in for a treat. Anything here is delicious."

He looked over the menu. "What are you going to have?"

"Just a boiled egg on sourdough toast. I sometimes splurge and have the eggs benedict. They're delicious too."

Cooper grinned and set aside his menu. "I think I'll have the eggs benny. Sounds great."

The waitress came, and they ordered coffee and their choice of breakfast.

Crystal walked over to them. "'Morning, you two. What a surprise to see you here together." Her sly smile hit home.

Taylor's cheeks flushed. "Cooper and I are trying to work things out so he can go back to New York."

Subdued, Cooper nodded. "I need to convince my boss that we can work together going forward." He beamed at Taylor. "Fortunately, Taylor and I have agreed to get to know one another better."

Taylor looked away to hide her tingling reaction to his

smile. The last thing she wanted him to know was how unsettled he made her feel.

"So, Taylor, what are you having?" Crystal asked. "The usual?"

She focused once more on the conversation "Yes, it's just what I need on this gray morning. It looks like it might rain. Heaven knows we need it."

"Nice, lazy day," said Crystal after Cooper had told her what he wanted. "Perfect for talking things over."

Taylor sent Crystal a warning look. The situation between Cooper and her was serious for many reasons and not for community consumption.

Crystal gave her a quick hug. "Enjoy. See you later."

"What was that all about?" Cooper asked.

"Just friends supporting one another," said Taylor.

"I have an open-ended room at the Lilac Lake B&B. As I told you earlier, I'm not going to leave until you and I agree we can work together on your book. How about a tour of the town?"

Taylor swallowed a groan and then recalled Dorothy's comment about needing to get to know him better. "Okay. I know you're anxious to get to work on the book but I'm not ready. I need more time to get to know you before I trust you enough to do that."

He lowered his head and let out a sigh. When he lifted his face, his gaze settled on her. "Look, I need to prove myself in this job. Somehow, we'll make it work. Will you trust me if I promise to go easy?"

She leaned forward. "Trust is something you have to earn. It's easy to say it, just like it's easy to criticize a writer's work if you haven't written a book yourself." She studied him. "You haven't done that, have you?"

"No," he admitted. "But I do know a good book when I read

one. Yours is not the first book I've edited."

"And how did that go?" she asked genuinely curious.

"Pretty well," he said. "We both learned a lot."

"That's interesting. Guess there's more to learn," Taylor said, and added, "for both of us."

Their food came, and conversation stopped as they dug into their meals. But as she ate, Taylor glanced at Cooper from time to time. He was trying to be pleasant.

They finished eating, and then she gave him a quick tour of the town. As long as he was going to be there for a while, he needed to know where certain things were. She was not going to babysit him.

Afterwards, Taylor turned to him. "I've got to go home and get cleaned up. I promised to work on a float for the 4th of July parade."

"Can I come along? If we're not working on the book, there's not much else for me to do."

Taylor shrugged. "Okay, I guess. You've already seen a couple of the people working on the float last night at dinner."

She gave him a wave and headed home feeling as if it might be easier to get along with Cooper than she'd first thought. But getting along was a distance from trusting him enough to work on the book he'd torn apart. Still, Dorothy was right. She had to make friends with him.

When Taylor picked up Cooper at the B&B, he gazed at her and smiled. "You look nice."

"Thanks." Taylor had showered and shampooed her hair, letting it flow straight to her shoulders. Out of jogging pants and a T-shirt, she felt better dressed in a denim skirt and flower-patterned blouse. She noticed he'd changed out of khaki slacks and a golf shirt to shorts and a T-shirt that exposed his ripped abs. For a man who worked inside at a desk all day, he obviously took time out for the gym.

As she drove Cooper to the Beckman Lumber Company, she explained about the 4th of July parade being a big deal in the area.

"Small town charm," he murmured. "I've lived in New York City all my life," he said. "Can't imagine living anywhere else."

"I still have a condo there," Taylor explained, "but I'm not sure I'll ever go back to making it my permanent residence. Now that my grandmother has given the cottage at Lilac Lake Inn to my sisters and me, I'm discovering a whole new lifestyle."

"Really? This town is attractive but it's ... I don't know ... so quiet," he said.

"There's more to it than I first thought," Taylor admitted. "I haven't spent a winter here yet, but I can always leave for a break."

"As long as you don't have a deadline at the publishing house," said Cooper.

For a minute, Taylor thought he was serious and then seeing his grin, she laughed along with him.

When they pulled up to the storage shed, Taylor saw that two other cars were parked there. They got out and headed to the shed. Hearing the chatter from inside, Taylor realized some of the girls from the dance studio were there.

Crystal met them at the door. "You're just in time. We need taller people to help with the cake."

Taylor turned to Cooper who must be at least 6' 2" and grinned. "You're perfect for the job."

He smiled. "Okay, where do you want me to start?"

Crystal led them inside and pointed to a bucket of flowers. "We need these placed along the third tier of the cake. Place them as close together as possible without crowding them and don't place the same color next to one another."

"Is that all?" he said, cocking a teasing eyebrow at her.

Crystal elbowed him. "Get to work."

"What do you want me to do?" Taylor asked.

The girls from the dance studio were busy making strands of flowers by weaving the paper flowers between the strands of twisted rope.

"Supervise the girls. I have to return to the café to get ready for the lunch crowd." Crystal lowered her voice. "The two of you look good together. Are you sure Cooper is the bad guy you think he is?"

"We're just getting to know one another in order to work together." Taylor glanced over at Cooper happily doing as Crystal had asked. "Maybe there's hope."

"He's the sexiest guy in glasses I've ever seen," said Crystal.

Taylor frowned at her.

Crystal shot her a sly smile. "Just sayin'."

"You're incorrigible. How did your date go with Ross?"

Crystal shrugged. "We had fun, but I don't know if he's into me. He's so ...serious-minded."

Taylor hugged her. "Give him time to know you."

"Guess I can be overwhelming," said Crystal. "Thanks. I needed to hear that."

Crystal left, and Taylor turned to the girls. "All right, where do I join in?"

A sweet-faced girl with a series of braids all over her head patted the ground next to her. "You can sit by me."

Taylor lowered herself to the ground and listened as all six girls gave her directions. Laughing she said, "One at a time, please."

Sometime later, Taylor was still helping the girls when Cooper came over to her. "I'm done. Want to check it out?"

"Sure," she said, struggling to rise.

He held out his hand. His strong fingers curled around her

palm sending heat through her as he drew her up toward him. For a moment, they stared at one another, and then Taylor quickly moved away, pretending to brush debris off her skirt. His touch was a serious shock to her system.

"What do you think?" he asked, startling her until she realized he was talking about his handiwork, not her reaction to him.

She stared up at the cake and saw that he'd done an outstanding job. "It looks perfect. Everyone will be so excited to see the float, especially Brad and Aaron Collister. The cake is to celebrate the 5th anniversary of the Collister Construction Company."

"Were they with you at the café the other night?"

"No, but I can introduce you to them. My sister Dani is engaged to Brad."

Dorothy materialized in her mind. Taylor shifted on her feet and said, "Dani and Brad are inviting my sister Whitney and me to dinner at his house tonight. I'm sure they won't mind having you as a guest. That way, you can meet my family and know a little better what my life is like while I'm writing. They're very supportive of me."

"That might be helpful to both of us," Cooper said. "I promised my publisher I'd do whatever it takes for us to learn to work together."

"Okay, then, if that will help our business relationship. I'll give them a call."

CHAPTER EIGHT
WHITNEY

Whitney sat with Dani in the kitchen talking about the color schemes of the bedrooms at the cottage when Taylor walked into the room with a tall, handsome man wearing glasses. *Ah, This must be the infamous Cooper,* she thought and smiled. The two of them looked adorable together. Not that she'd mention it to Taylor. Whitney could see from the strained look on her face that Taylor was in no mood for such comments.

Whitney watched as Pirate and Mindy greeted Cooper. They wagged their tails when he bent over to pet them.

"Hey, everyone, this is my editor, Cooper Walker," said Taylor in an overly bright tone. She turned to him. "And these are my sisters. Dani is engaged to Brad Collister, as I've already mentioned to you. And this is my sister, Whitney."

"A pleasure to meet you." Cooper nodded politely to each of them, but Taylor noticed his gaze lingered on Whitney. That's how it always was. No matter how casually she dressed, with makeup or without, Whitney was a star.

"Dani, thank you for having both of us for dinner tonight," Taylor said. She knew it wouldn't be a problem. Her sisters were dying to know more about the man who'd upset her.

"Yes, of course. Brad and I are learning how much fun it is to cook together." Dani smiled at him. "Anything goes. It could be delicious or not at all. So, if you're willing to take that chance, you're welcome to join us, Cooper."

"Thanks, I'd like that," said Cooper.

Whitney had been trained to be aware of people's reactions

and noticed the slight flush on his cheeks and the way he rocked on his feet a bit and realized he was shy. Something to remember to tell Taylor.

CHAPTER NINE

TAYLOR

Taylor and Cooper sat outside in the grouping of Adirondack chairs on the patio while the others finished work in the kitchen.

"To fill you in, Brad's first wife died of cancer a couple of years ago," said Taylor. "Dani and Brad recently got engaged. It's really heartwarming to see how much in love they are."

Cooper's light-brown gaze met hers. Taylor swallowed hard as the word "love" hovered in the air around them, emphasizing his criticism of her work. The suggestion that she'd never experienced real love was the issue. And what could she do about that? It was true.

Taylor thought about the guy she'd dated in college. She'd believed it was serious, had even made love with him, and then found out he wasn't ready to settle down. And, frankly, neither was she. It was a first-love situation after dating casually. That encounter had made her skittish about other relationships, so here she was without a soul-baring relationship.

"Nice backyard," Cooper commented.

The lilac blooms had come and gone, but the rose bushes along one side of the yard were in bloom adding color and the distinctive aroma of roses to the clean air. It would be a while before dark, but the evening held a quieter note to the normal sounds of the day.

Whitney joined them, and then Dani and Brad appeared.

Dani held a plate filled with crackers topped by a soft

cheese and a dollop of fig preserves. Brad carried an opened bottle of white wine in one hand and a tray of five empty wine glasses in the other.

He set the tray down and said, "Everybody okay with a chilled pinot grigio?"

Hearing a chorus of responses, he poured a tiny bit into a glass. "Why don't you give it a taste test, Cooper?"

Taylor wasn't surprised when Cooper nodded agreeably. He was, no doubt, used to a very social life in the city and knew the routine with the wine.

After holding up the glass to test its color, swirling it about, and then tasting it, Cooper said, "Very nice."

"We're learning more about wine, too," said Dani, giving Cooper a smile.

Brad handed out glasses of wine to everyone and then lifted his in a toast. "Here's to a wonderful life in Lilac Lake. For all of us."

Taylor saw the hesitation in Cooper and hid a laugh. He'd already made it clear to her that he'd never leave the city for a small town like Lilac Lake.

Dani offered the crackers, and they all took one.

"Delicious," Taylor said.

"Very simple, but tasty. For dinner, we're having a chicken and rice casserole with a wine sauce. I hope everyone likes it. As Brad's mother told me, hardworking men like Brad need a hearty meal at day's end."

"So that's why you're learning to cook?" said Whitney, giving Dani a teasing smile.

Dani laughed. "You know what they say about mothers-in-law who have sons they adore. You'd better do as she says. Seriously, Brad's mother is a lovely woman who's hoping I'll help them at the farm in addition to doing design consulting work for both the construction company and on my own. I was worried about not having enough to do. Now, I'm wondering where I'll get the time to do everything."

"Tell me about the construction company," Cooper said to Brad.

Brad eagerly told him about building The Woodlands where GG lived and how she'd helped them get the contract for the inn. And he talked about The Meadows, the residential development they were doing.

"A lot to do for a new company," said Cooper. "I know it's turning five because I worked on the birthday cake for your float in the 4th of July parade."

Brad chuckled. "I've been working with my brother for much longer than that. We formed the company as we grew our business."

"You worked on the float, Cooper? That settles it then," said Dani. "You're invited to be part of our 4th of July celebrations. In fact, it's more than an invitation; it's a demand."

Taylor hid her annoyance. Dani should've asked her first before she invited Cooper. Trying not to ruin the evening, she told herself to relax as Brad offered her another cracker.

Dani sent Taylor a sly wink as she walked by to check on dinner.

"So, tell me about your job," Brad said to Cooper.

Cooper glanced at Taylor and back to him. "I'm an editor with a New York publishing house. It's a lot of detail work, but I enjoy it. I especially like when a book comes together in a better way than it would have on its own."

Whitney caught Taylor's attention and gave her a warning look to be nice.

Taylor swallowed hard and decided not to comment. She couldn't ruin Dani and Brad's dinner party.

"Well, let's talk about what's happening in town," said

Whitney. "Did anyone else hear that the selectmen have approved plans for the next annual Christmas walk? That should be fun. For all the times I've spent here, we've never come for Christmas. GG always came to us."

"GG is your grandmother?" Cooper asked Taylor.

"Yes, she's the best," Taylor said.

"You'll have to introduce Cooper to GG," said Whitney, smiling.

"I'd like that. She sounds like a wonderful lady," Cooper said.

Taylor squirmed in her chair. Were Whitney and Dani up to something? Or was it just a coincidence that for the second time one of her sisters had maneuvered her into asking Cooper to do something she wasn't sure about?

Later, as they were about to leave the house, Brad said to Cooper, "As long as you're spending time here, have Taylor bring you out to see The Meadows. You're welcome to check on the Lilac Lake Inn, as well."

"Okay, thanks," said Cooper. "I'm not sure of my timing, but I'd like that."

Taylor remained quiet. She had no idea how long it would take for them to come to some sort of agreement to work together.

When she offered to give him a ride back to the B&B, Cooper shook his head. "No, thanks. I think I'll walk. That dinner was excellent."

"Okay, goodnight then," said Taylor. She walked him to the front door and waited while he exited and waved to her before taking off.

What an evening. Everyone else seemed so eager to be friends with Cooper. What was up with that?

The next morning, Taylor awoke and lay in bed thinking

about last night's dinner at Brad's house. It was, in retrospect, a nice evening even though Cooper's presence unsettled her. He could be so annoying one minute and so charming the next. Brad and her sisters seemed to like him a lot.

She got up and went to her computer. Scrolling through her emails she found the one he'd sent her and grew angry all over again. He had the right to critique her work—it was his job, after all. But the way he'd implied that she hadn't ever had or probably never would have a deep relationship with a man hurt.

Frustrated, she tried to decide if she could ever work well with him. Some of her author friends had self-published books. She wondered if she should try it. Then someone as destructive as Cooper wouldn't cause her to wonder if she could ever write again. She'd hire other editors. Editors she knew she could trust to be both honest and kinder.

She got dressed and went downstairs determined to get along with Cooper so she wouldn't lose the book deal. She hoped Cooper would be content to look around the area without getting into a discussion of the problems behind her book.

Whitney was in the kitchen when Taylor walked in.

"'Morning. You're up early. What's going on?" Taylor asked.

Whitney sighed and shrugged. "It's taking some time to get used to all the changes. You're busy with your writing, Dani is busy with her business, and I'm at loose ends. I'm helping Crystal with the parade, but that's it. I need a creative outlet."

Taylor sat down and studied Whitney. "Remember all those plays you made up and then made Dani and me act in? Why don't you develop a children's theater program for the area? You still have time to put on a play or two this summer."

Whitney's eyes widened. "Oh, that could be fun. We could

use the auditorium in the community center for productions." Whitney clasped her hands together and grinned. "Have I ever told you how much I love you? This is a fabulous suggestion. I'm going to research information and materials for plays online, then talk to Crystal about the best way to publicize this."

"Remember, there are camps in the area that would love something like this, too," said Taylor. "I got to play the Cheshire Cat in a play one summer. I thought I was so talented even if nobody else did."

Whitney laughed. "I remember that. You weren't half bad for a smiling cat. Thanks for giving me the idea. I'm going to see what I can come up with at such short notice. The girls from the dance studio might be a smart place to start. They're the kind of kids who might be interested. They're already little performers."

Taylor rose and gave Whitney a high-five. "Now, I need coffee to face my day hosting Cooper."

"He's very nice, Taylor. It might be helpful to work with him," said Whitney sounding more like her older sister.

"I don't know if I can. Every time I sit at my computer, I see those words in my mind about how unrealistic I apparently am about love. How can I continue to write sweet romances if nobody takes me seriously?"

"Whoa!" said Whitney. "You have readers who love your books. Don't let Cooper's negative comments change what you know is successful."

Taylor sighed. "We'll see. Right now, I can't even get started on my next book."

CHAPTER TEN

TAYLOR

After breakfast, Taylor did the dutiful thing and called Cooper to check if he wanted to see the cottage where she'd be living and working in the future. It was important for him to understand that even if she didn't stay with his publisher, she was going to continue writing. Once she got her mojo back, there'd be no way she could keep all those stories in her head from bursting out in written form, and the best place to do that might be the cottage.

"Thanks. I'd like to see it. Dani and Whitney seemed really excited about it. You're lucky to have a summer house like that," said Cooper.

"It's not going to be just a summer house. The house must be occupied by one of us for at least six months of the year," explained Taylor. "That's the deal my grandmother made with the new owners of the inn. If you're ready, I'll come pick you up."

"Sounds like a plan," Cooper said. "I'm set to go anytime at your convenience."

Taylor ended the call realizing Cooper was doing his best to cooperate. It made the fact that she'd been forced to be with him seem a little better.

Taylor picked up Cooper in front of the B&B, and they headed out.

"Is this where the inn is too?" said Cooper.

"Yes," said Taylor. She turned up the driveway. "As you can see, the original guestroom wings have been torn down, and the main house is being totally renovated. When GG owned it, the inn was quite small with a main building and two wings of rooms. The redesigned inn is much bigger. But with Dani's input, the new one will retain a compatible look with the natural landscaping and setting around it."

Tall evergreens edged the property adding deep-green color and texture along with the maples and other hardwood trees. Pine needles and other leaves carpeted the ground providing a nice, soft cushion beneath feet when walking through the woods.

"As kids, we always enjoyed playing 'hide and seek' around the Inn and in the woods," said Taylor.

She pointed out to Cooper how the inn sat on a rise, and lush, green lawn sloped gently to a flat expanse along the waterfront. A large wooden dock extended into the water; a long bench at the end of the dock provided a setting where people could sit and enjoy the scenery.

"From there, on a clear day, you can see the White Mountains where the White Mountain Hotel & Resort is just outside of North Conway. While not as grand, The Lilac Lake Inn has always had a certain upscale style of its own, and the new owners have said they intend to maintain the Inn's style and cachet."

Taylor and Cooper walked down to the dock and stood looking around. The water lapped in a soothing manner at the posts holding up the deck. The cries of birds around them added musical notes. And the quack of a mother duck trailed by her five ducklings made Taylor utter, "How darling!" as they swam past them.

"This is beautiful," said Cooper. "Very relaxing."

"Yes, except for the noise of construction when they're

working. But when, in the past, the inn was open and full, it still seemed peaceful even with guests swimming and sailing the inn's several small Sunfish."

"Are power boats permitted on the lake?" Cooper asked.

"No inboard or outboard motorboats, wave runners, or jet skis. But sailboats, canoes, paddle boats, rowboats, and fishing boats with very small trolling motors are allowed. That's one reason this lake is so peaceful. Larger lakes have plenty of motorboats, though, for those who want to use them."

"That makes sense," Cooper said, standing and looking up at the remains of the inn. "What about this flat space here?" He pointed to the lawn in front of them.

"That's always been used for events for family activities and special occasions like weddings."

"Nice," said Cooper. "I see why some people would want to spend time here."

"A lot of GG's customers were repeat guests who came year after year. I suppose the same thing might happen with the new owners."

"Someone mentioned three owners," said Cooper.

"Yes, a brother and sister and Ross Roberts, the retired baseball player," said Taylor.

Cooper's face lit up. "Ross Roberts? Really? I'd love to meet him. I'm a big Yankees fan."

"I believe he's out of town. He comes and goes," said Taylor, surprised by his excitement. "I didn't know you liked baseball. I'm a die-hard Red Sox Fan."

"Figures," said Cooper, shaking his head.

Taylor hid her amusement at his frown. "Let's go to the cottage. It's at the far end of the property in a space that will give my sisters and me privacy, and yet be close by if we want to grab a meal at the inn."

"The best of both worlds," said Cooper. "I understand why you like it here."

Taylor led him back to the driveway for the cottage, and they walked along the dirt road. Before they even reached the garage, shivers crawled across Taylor's shoulders. No matter how much she tried to calm herself, the thought of a ghost on the property made her want to turn and run away.

"Are you okay?" Cooper asked her, looking concerned.

Taylor nodded, unwrapped her arms from her waist, and straightened. She didn't want to give Cooper cause to make fun of her.

The garage door was open. Taylor noticed three appliances still in protective wrappings sitting inside. "This way," she said, leading him to the front of the house. All was quiet. No workmen around.

"Pretty view," said Cooper. "Look at that rock."

"That's our sunning rock," said Taylor. "It's a perfect place to come and think about things. Want to get closer?"

"Yes," said Cooper, walking down to it ahead of her.

They stepped onto the rock and sat down. "Ah, this is the life," said Cooper. He stretched out on his back and looked up at the sky. "This is almost as comfortable as a hammock."

Taylor laughed, and keeping her distance, lay back on the rock.

The sun above them played hide and seek with the puffy white clouds that floated by, looking like dollops of whipped cream or marshmallow topping, a favorite of hers.

Cooper turned to her and smiled. "I assume the rock is granite. It's hard but comfortable."

"A perfect symbol for New Hampshire where the tough New Hampshire spirit is such a proud thing. The motto of the state is: 'Live Free or Die.'"

Cooper propped himself up on one elbow. "Is that the way

you want to live? With no one telling you what to do? Is that why you were unhappy with my suggested revisions?"

She sat up and gazed at him. "I don't mind someone critiquing my book as long as it's done in a kind, constructive way." She took a deep breath and let it out. "Why did you think you could be so rude to me, demean me and my work? Is that how you usually interact with your authors? I make money for your publisher."

Cooper drew himself to a sitting position. "I know. That's why I'm here. I have to be able to prove that I can be more sympathetic, more understanding. At least, that's what I've been told."

"Are you always so hard on other people?" Taylor asked, wishing she could see his eyes behind the sunglasses he wore.

"No harder on them than I am on myself." Cooper stared into the distance and turned back to her. "Why were you so upset about my remarks?"

"You don't understand?" she said, raising her eyebrows with disbelief. "You were judging me and my personal life."

"That wasn't my intention," he said. "I can make your book better. Not in a big way like asking you to do a whole rewrite, but in smaller ways."

Like a sudden rainstorm, Taylor's goodwill was washed away. The editorial note he'd sent her was cruel. She could recite every word of it. God knows, she'd read it enough times. She got to her feet. "I'm not sure this is going to work. I still don't trust you. That makes the idea of us working together impossible."

Cooper scrambled to his feet and faced her. "I'm sorry if I've given you the wrong impression of me. You've got to give me another chance."

She stood quietly, her mind racing. If he didn't see how hurtful his words were, how they'd destroyed her self-confidence, she didn't think he ever would.

"Look, there's no point in my staying here if you've made up your mind. I'll leave tomorrow for New York. Your sister asked me to return for the 4th of July parade and I'd like to do that. But not unless you've decided to work with me. That gives you a week to decide."

Taylor heard the pleading in his voice, remembered Dorothy's warning. "Okay."

"Let's shake on it," said Cooper.

She lifted her hand.

He took hold of it and shook it once, twice.

The shock that went through her arm sent waves of alarm through her. *No, no, no!* She turned away and walked as fast as she could toward the cottage, praying he hadn't noticed her reaction to him. When it had happened before, she thought it was just a fluke, a case of nerves. If he knew about her feelings, he'd understand how inexperienced she was about relationships.

Taylor was already stressed when she reached the front door of the cottage, so she wasn't surprised when she felt a shiver of apprehension chill her.

Cooper hurried up beside her on the front porch. "Are we going in or what?"

"Yes. Even though things are still under construction, you'll get an impression of the open space on the first floor. My sisters and I love it."

They entered.

Cooper headed for the kitchen while Taylor stood by the front door, trying to decide if it was safe to follow him.

A burst of wind behind her made the decision for her and she stepped inside to be closer to him.

"This is going to be great," said Cooper emerging from the kitchen. "I like the openness and how you feel a part of the outdoors with so many windows strategically placed."

"Dani will be glad to hear that. She designed the space."

"Let's see the upstairs," said Cooper.

Taylor bit her lip. She didn't want to say it aloud and give Cooper something else to use against her, so she whispered, "We wish you no harm."

The atmosphere inside the house seemed quiet, so she followed Cooper up the stairs. It had been a few days since she'd seen what was being done.

The hall bathroom upstairs was ripped apart. The old fixtures had been removed and walls stripped to the studs showing the plumbing upgrades the plumbers had completed. But it was a sizeable room and would, she knew, be beautiful when it was done.

"The master bedroom is over here," said Taylor, leading him into the corner room with windows overlooking the lake. A skylight had already been placed in the roof, and Taylor stood a moment looking up at the sky. Feeling chilled, she clasped her arms around herself.

Cooper noticed and came over to her. "You're cold," he murmured and placed an arm across her shoulder as he studied the sky.

She looked up at him. Nearby she saw a cluster of small white lights appear and when she looked again, they were gone.

"We'd better leave now," Taylor said, stepping away from him. She had no idea what those lights might mean and had no intention of finding out.

"Wait! Isn't there a third floor?" Cooper said.

"Yes, but I never go up there," said Taylor. "I'm leaving now."

When they were once again on the front porch, Cooper gave her a steady look. "What aren't you telling me? Is this house haunted or something?"

Taylor shrugged. "We don't know. But sometimes strange things happen here." She couldn't help the quaver in her voice.

Cooper took her hand. "Don't worry."

Taylor saw those strange lights again. She closed her eyes, and blindly followed Cooper off the porch, her entire arm on fire.

CHAPTER ELEVEN
DANI

Dani sat in a meeting with Ross Roberts, Quinn McPherson, and his sister, Rachael, the new owners of the inn, listening as Brad and Aaron went over plans for the main building of the inn. She'd agreed it was best if both men spoke about the plans, not her, because they were the ones who'd signed the contract.

Silent as she was, Dani was proud of the way the three of them had worked to incorporate more suitable finishes for the main building. Gone was the stark, sleek, cold space they'd originally proposed. In its place, was a gorgeous room with beautiful woodwork that not only welcomed visitors to the inn but kept them comfortable and cozy during inclement weather. The new wings and spa building were contemporary like the original plans but now had finishing touches in keeping with the setting and the use of the space.

It wasn't just Dani's experience in architecture that led to these suggestions, but her years of coming to the inn to play and work under her grandmother's ownership and supervision.

"The foundations for the new guest room wings have been poured, and we're ready to start construction," said Aaron. "There's been a delay in getting the supplies, but now they're in."

"I like it," said Quinn. "Shall we celebrate at Jake's tonight?"

Aaron nodded. "We should. We'll begin the framing

tomorrow. But we need to make sure we have all the materials for the job. We're keeping an inventory of all we use for your records and ours."

Quinn got to his feet. "All right. My partner, Liam Richards, and I will host the party. Let's say six o'clock."

Dani stood by as Quinn, Rachael, and Ross left the small conference room at Collister Construction headquarters. Though not fancy, the building that sat outside of town near Beckman Lumber Company was well built, demonstrating the quality of work they did.

"I'll see you later," said Dani. "I'm having lunch with Taylor and Cooper." She was pleased to be invited because she was intrigued by those two working together. She loved her sister, but knew how introverted she was, how naïve, and she thought being forced to work with a sophisticated man like Cooper might help Taylor with further book projects.

She drove to the café, parked, and found them sitting with Whitney at a table under an umbrella on the patio. Whitney waved at her, and she hurried over, pleased they'd been able to find such a nice spot in the crowd.

"We've already ordered," said Whitney. "But our waitress knows to come for your order. Oh, here she is now."

Caught in a hurry, Dani ordered one of her favorites, a chicken Caesar salad and iced tea.

"It looks like another busy day for Crystal. I don't know how she does it—runs this café and does volunteer work and all," said Dani.

"I worked on the float doing last minute stuff," said Whitney. "It's going to be so cute. I'm also checking into forming a children's theater group, thanks to a suggestion from Taylor."

"Oh, that would be perfect for you," said Dani. "Great idea, Taylor."

Taylor's cheeks flushed. "Thanks."

Dani noticed the nod of approval Cooper gave her, making Taylor's cheeks even redder.

Damn! They were cute together.

Whitney caught Dani's eye and grinned.

Their food came—salads for the women, a sandwich for Cooper.

Dani had just swallowed a gulp of iced tea and almost choked when Cooper said, "So, is your cottage haunted?"

"Why would you say that?" she asked.

Cooper glanced at Taylor and then shrugged. "I don't know."

"Did you see anything that would make you suspect it?" asked Whitney.

"Uh, maybe some flashing lights, but I just figured it was because I'd been looking up at the sun through the skylight in the master bedroom."

Dani's stomach clenched. She'd seen lights like that there, too. She glanced at Taylor and knew by her wide-eyed look she must have seen them too.

CHAPTER TWELVE
TAYLOR

Taylor was shocked by Cooper's statement about viewing the sparkling lights she'd seen at the house. He didn't seem upset by them, simply curious.

Dani shot her a knowing glance. Whitney didn't seem to know what to think. One thing was clear. Before they moved into that house, she and her sisters had to be sure it was free from any paranormal activity, and that meant they'd have to investigate and understand what was going on. Was it somehow connected to the wedding dress and baby clothes they had found in the garage?

"So, will you come back here for the 4th of July celebration?" Dani asked Cooper, drawing Taylor out of her thoughts.

Cooper gave Taylor a steady look and then turned back to Dani. "Taylor will let me know if I should return. That depends on whether I can continue as her editor."

"I'm sure Taylor will work that out for everyone's best interest," said Whitney sounding like the big sister who liked to keep things orderly.

"Is anyone having dessert?" Taylor asked brightly, hoping to change the subject. She'd learned Cooper had a sweet tooth.

"The café is famous for their pies," said Dani.

Taylor knew Whitney wouldn't order dessert even if she was away from Hollywood. But she hoped Dani would split a slice of pie with her.

When the waitress came to their table, Cooper opted for

apple pie with ice cream, and to Taylor's delight, Dani agreed to split a piece of lemon chiffon pie with her.

"What are your plans for this afternoon?" Whitney asked Taylor.

"Cooper and I are going to visit The Meadows development," Taylor said. "At dinner, Dani and Brad wanted him to see it."

"What about a visit to The Woodlands to see GG?" Whitney asked. "She's the reason we're all here, and you know she'd be pleased to meet him."

Though she wanted to pinch Whitney's arm for suggesting it, Taylor knew Whitney was right. In the past, she'd often talked to GG about her books. She turned to Cooper. "Does that sound okay?"

"Fine," he said. "My grandmother and I were close, and I know you and GG are too."

Taylor couldn't help the smile that crossed her face. Cooper was really trying to be cooperative.

As soon as everyone had finished eating, Whitney rose. "I'm off to speak to a few people about a children's theater." With her baseball cap and dark glasses, it was difficult to see her well-known, beautiful face. Taylor could already see how much more relaxed Whitney was after leaving Hollywood an emotional mess.

On the drive to The Meadows, Cooper said, "It's hard to believe your sister is so normal when she's such a famous television star."

"Whitney's always been theatrical and active in productions. It's just that recently it's been on a much larger scale. She thinks she won't go back to Hollywood, but that doesn't mean she wouldn't ever do a movie or another series if it's right for her. Acting gives her joy. It's the behind-the-scenes foolishness she's uncomfortable with."

Cooper was quiet and then said, "Sometimes roles are given to you."

She turned to him with a questioning look. "What are you talking about?"

"Nothing," said Cooper. "Forget I said that."

They were silent as she drove into the development and got out of the car.

The sounds and smells of wooden construction work and the aroma from the evergreens blended in the air around them.

Inside the sales office, Kellie Yates, the young real estate agent working for Melanie at Lake Realty, showed them the layout of the development and handed them brochures of the two houses they were using as show homes. "Take your time looking. We're very proud of what's going on here. It's a beautiful development for the discerning buyer."

Dani joined them. "Hey, there. I'm glad you made it. I'm here to give you a private tour. I want you to see some of the new things we've added to the floor plans." She smiled at Cooper. "This is a chance for me to show off the excellent workmanship and to give you an opportunity to tell your friends about it. Several New York City people are looking here."

"Nice to know," said Cooper agreeably. "I'll take extra brochures with me and hand them out, though new editors don't make much money. But I have other friends who do."

Dani gave him a look of appreciation. "Thanks."

She led him to the first house, pointing out special features in each room, describing the relationship between setting and the interior and how they'd made sure they blended, and then Dani showed them the changes she'd suggested.

Taylor noted the pride in Dani's voice and smiled. Dani had

worked diligently to get where she was, and Taylor admired her for it. Both her sisters were successful in their fields, which was one reason Taylor worked so hard at her writing.

"What do you think?" Taylor asked Cooper when the tour ended, and Dani had gone on her way.

He gazed around them. "The houses are beautiful. I understand why everyone is so excited about them. And not bad to have a future neighbor like Ross Roberts."

"I know. And though they're not right on the lake, these residents will have access to a communal dock and beach at the lake."

"Nice addition."

Knowing she had no choice, she led him back to her car. It was time for him to meet GG.

Taylor's nerves did a little dance as she drove to The Woodlands. When she'd told GG about Cooper's remarks, GG's lips had thinned with irritation. At the time, Taylor had enjoyed that show of support. Now, she knew he wasn't the bad guy she'd thought. He just didn't get her at all. But then, how could she prove she understood the love he talked about if she hadn't experienced it?

She drew up to the front of the building. "Why don't you get out and look around. I'll park the car and meet you inside."

He nodded agreeably and got out.

She pulled into the parking lot, found a spot, and turned off the engine, wishing Whitney hadn't suggested Cooper's meeting GG. Her emotions were so tangled up when it came to him.

Inside, Cooper was chatting with the receptionist. Seeing Taylor, he smiled and waited for her to approach. She studied him, recognizing how handsome he was. Yet, there was a quietness about him that was even more appealing. Or maybe his horned-rim glasses gave him that effect.

"GG is down this hallway," Taylor said, leading him in that direction.

"The staff really likes your grandmother," said Cooper.

"She's a loveable person," said Taylor. GG might be her grandmother, but in other ways she was her hero. A strong woman who'd taken a family home and made it into a successful inn through hard work and creativity.

When they reached GG's room, Taylor knocked on the half-open door and called out, "GG? It's Taylor. I've brought someone with me."

GG got up from the couch and walked over to them with a happy smile on her lined face. "Ah, at last. Whitney told me you were going to drop by. I thought with the heat of the afternoon, it might be better for us to stay inside. I've ordered glasses of lemonade and cookies."

"Thanks. That sounds excellent." Taylor kissed GG and then turned to Cooper. "GG, this is my ... editor, Cooper Walker. Cooper, my grandmother Genie Wittner."

"Very nice to meet you," said Cooper, shaking her hand. "Your family often talks about you."

"And what things do they say?" GG asked, flirting with him.

He grinned. "Nothing but very nice things, I'm happy to report."

GG chuckled. "Excellent."

Taylor and Cooper followed her to the living area of her small suite and sat in chairs facing the couch.

GG lowered herself onto the couch, and after offering the lemonade and cookies to them settled her gaze on Cooper. "Did you know I'm one of Taylor's early readers for her books?"

"No, I didn't," said Cooper looking surprised.

"I take pride in my granddaughter's work, not only because

I love her, but because I believe, and her readers confirm, that she's a talented novelist."

"I see. Then we're in agreement," said Cooper.

"If that's the case, I don't understand your critique of her work. Is it just the relationship business?" GG asked, making Taylor want to disappear into the floor.

"Well, yes," Cooper stumbled. "My understanding was that this was to be a deeply-felt book."

GG's blue eyes bored into him. "So, I'm to understand that you've experienced such emotions?" GG held up her hand. "Forgive me. I don't need you to answer that. I just think you've unfairly accused Taylor of lacking them."

Cooper looked uncomfortable.

Taylor reached over and gave him a pat on the arm, shocked by her grandmother's attack.

Cooper swallowed hard and faced GG squarely. "I have no doubt that Taylor has emotion. She's kind and thoughtful. We just don't see eye-to-eye on the manuscript. I very much want to be able to work with her as her editor on her descriptions of how people relate to one another in a romantic relationship and perhaps some other issues. It's important to me."

"We're trying to see if we can work together," said Taylor.

"I see." GG looked from Taylor to Cooper and then said brightly, "Now that we have business out of the way, let's enjoy our refreshments. Please excuse me for being so outspoken, but when you reach my age, you don't have time to dance around issues. So, Cooper, what do you think of our town?"

Visibly relieved the inquisition was over, Cooper smiled. "Lilac Lake isn't New York City, but I can see why people might be attracted to it. It's a beautiful part of the country. And the cottage is going to be fantastic."

"Yes, I think so, too. My family has owned this land for generations. My grandfather, Taylor's great-great grandfather, used to bring people from New York City to go hunting and fishing, back when it was a journey to get here. Or so it seemed."

"It still has the feeling of being far away from city life, which I think, is its major appeal," said Cooper.

"It has always seemed a magical place for me," said Taylor. She didn't mention the ghost in the cottage.

"Sometimes we need a magical place, a special person to give life balance," said GG, staring into the distance for a moment before turning back to them.

"Tell me about your life in New York," said GG. "It's been a while since I've made the trek to the city."

"Well, as you know, I work as an editor. For Pritchard Publishing. It's the job I've always thought would be mine. I grew up with books and love escaping into them. I have since I was a kid," said Cooper.

GG gave Taylor a pointed look. "Like a certain someone we both know."

"I thought I wanted to be a teacher but decided after graduating from college with a teaching degree that I'd rather write," said Taylor. "Actually, that happened when I won a short story writing contest."

"Do you write novels?" GG asked Cooper.

"No. I tried once and though I'm an excellent editor, I realized I don't have stories inside me like true writers do. I'm not ashamed to admit it," Cooper said and winked at Taylor.

Taylor felt a flush rush to her cheeks.

"I understand you're leaving tomorrow but will return for the 4th of July celebration just days away," said GG, smiling at them.

Cooper looked down at the carpet and when he raised his head, he glanced at Taylor and then said, "My return is up to Taylor."

"Oh?" GG's gaze landed on Taylor, making her uncomfortable.

"We'll see," said Taylor, wishing she'd never agreed to bring Cooper here. It had been both pleasant and awkward.

"I'm glad you've had such lovely weather," GG said to Cooper. "Hopefully, if you return, it'll stay that way."

"Me too. Normally, I'm at the shore on Long Island. This would be something new for me."

They chatted about 4th of July celebrations in the past, and when Taylor saw that GG was tiring, she said, "We'd better go. I know you eat early, and I want to give you time to rest. We're meeting the gang at Jake's tonight. It should be fun."

They all stood.

GG shook hands with Cooper and gave him a steady look. "I'm very pleased to have met you. Perhaps, you'll return to Lilac Lake."

Cooper gave her a warm smile. "Thank you. I'd like to."

Taylor embraced GG, giving her a strong hug. "Thanks for always being there for me," she said softly into GG's ear.

"We'll talk later," GG said, hugging her back before stepping away.

Taylor and Cooper left the building without speaking.

After Cooper was settled in the passenger's seat, he turned to Taylor. "I like your grandmother. She's a straight shooter."

Taylor chuckled. "She certainly wasn't going to let you off the hook for daring to criticize me."

"It was fine. It got me to thinking about a lot of things," said Cooper.

Taylor waited for him to say more, but he just stared out the window even after they were underway.

CHAPTER THIRTEEN
TAYLOR

That evening, Taylor entered Jake's bar with Whitney, who'd finally agreed to accompany her. Taylor wasn't exactly sure what had happened in L.A. with Whitney's co-star. She just knew her sister had decided to rethink her career and her life. Taylor vowed to help her in any way she could. She'd sometimes envied Whitney's ability to be comfortable so quickly with other people and thought it was important now for her to be out among others instead of hiding out at home.

Walking inside together, she knew all eyes would be on her sister. Taylor didn't mind. She was here to have fun. Once Cooper was gone, she'd have time to herself to think about her future as a writer. As she'd thought earlier, indie publishing was a possibility.

Taylor's excitement about the evening disappeared when she saw Cooper standing at the bar talking to JoEllen Daniels. Brad's ex-sister-in-law was tall, thin, blonde, and very attractive. Her persistence in thinking that she would one day marry Brad after her sister's death had irritated them all. Even now, observing her, Taylor let out a puff of disgust. JoEllen was all but draped around Cooper. To his credit, he seemed uncomfortable with it, but he didn't make any effort to move away from her as Taylor approached.

"Hello," Taylor said to him, ignoring JoEllen.

He stepped away from JoEllen. "Have you two met? JoEllen was telling me about her nursing assistant work at The Woodlands."

Taylor gave JoEllen a half-hearted smile. "Yes, we know one another. But there are some other people I want you to meet, including Ross Roberts."

"Ross Roberts is here?" Cooper asked, his eyes alight. He turned to JoEllen. "Nice meeting you."

"I'll be here waiting for you to come back," JoEllen said, smiling and fingering her shoulder-length hair.

He gave her a little salute and followed Taylor. She led him to a corner of the room where Ross Roberts was sitting with four other guys, all wearing baseball caps displaying different sports teams.

When Ross saw them, he waved them over and stood. "Hi, Taylor. I heard you've been working with your editor." He looked at Cooper. "Hi, Ross Roberts."

Cooper's cheeks grew pink as he shook hands. "I've been a fan for a long time. How's the leg?"

"Still unplayable, but thanks for asking," said Ross.

"This is Cooper Walker," said Taylor. "He works for my publisher. It's complicated." She still had a lot to think about when it came to working with him. She realized he was a nice guy, but that didn't make him the best editor for her.

"Want to join us? There's room," said Ross.

Taylor glanced at Cooper. At his expression of pure joy, she said, "Sure."

Two of the guys sitting at the large round table got up and left, leaving plenty of room for Cooper and Taylor to sit.

When Taylor saw Whitney alone in the crowd, she rose and went over to her, and then drew her back to the table.

"Hey, everyone, this is my sister, Whitney."

The wide-eyed expressions of the faces of the men made Taylor grin.

"Whitney from *The Hopefuls*?" said a young man Taylor hadn't yet met.

"I'd rather it be just Whitney from Lilac Lake." She smiled at Ross. "You understand, I'm sure."

"Of course," said Ross, standing and offering his hand. "Ross Roberts, and this is Ben Gooding and Mike Dawson, friends of mine from New York. I've told them about the house I'm buying, and they're here to look around the area."

"My sister Dani will be pleased," said Taylor. "She's engaged to one of the developers."

Ben and Mike moved their chairs, so Whitney could join them.

A waitress took orders for drinks, and then talk turned to baseball. Cooper joined in the conversation, demonstrating his knowledge of the game and the players.

JoEllen walked over to them. "Hi. Can I join you? I'm practically family with Whitney and Taylor."

"Not really," murmured Taylor as Whitney rolled her eyes.

But Ben moved his chair over so JoEllen could sit with them.

Sometime later, after drinks and dinner, Taylor rose. "It was nice to see everyone. I'm heading home. I promised Crystal I'd help in the café tomorrow morning, so I'd be trained for the 4th of July weekend if she needs me."

"I'll go with you," said Cooper, getting to his feet.

She faced him. "Okay, but it's such a nice evening, Whitney and I decided to walk."

"Perfect," said Cooper. "I'll walk back with you."

Whitney waved to her. "I won't be too much later." She frowned as JoEllen took Cooper's empty chair, closer to Ben.

As they headed to the front door, Taylor said to Cooper, "Are you sure you want to leave?"

"It's fine. I want this time to say goodbye to you. I'm leaving early in the morning to catch a flight back to New York."

"Okay. It isn't that far, but it'll give us a chance to talk," said

Taylor.

They headed down the sidewalk through town and moved easily together at an even pace, passing visitors browsing at store windows or entering or leaving local restaurants.

"It's been a worthwhile visit," said Cooper, "a productive one, I hope." He glanced at Taylor.

"I haven't made up my mind yet," said Taylor. "I have a lot to think about. But you'll be the first to know. I'm aware how difficult it is to wait for an answer, but I need to decide for myself what I want to do."

They left the town center and headed for the cute neighborhood where Taylor and her sisters had rented a house.

The scene was out of a Hallmark movie as they passed Cape Cod houses with white picket fences or larger Victorian houses with gables, pigeon-breast shingling, and gingerbread trim.

When they arrived at Taylor's house, she turned to him. "It's hot. Would you like to come inside for a drink of water? If you wish, I can drive you back to Jake's."

"A drink of water sounds great," said Cooper. He followed her inside the house and smiled when Mindy rushed forward barking and wagging her tail like crazy. He leaned over to pet her.

Taylor walked over to the refrigerator and pulled out a jar of lemonade. "Would you prefer this? It's homemade lemonade from GG's special recipe."

"That sounds delicious."

Taylor poured them each a glass.

Cooper took a sip of his drink and then set it down and approached her. "I want you to know that I've really enjoyed getting to know you. My feelings have nothing to do with business, and they shouldn't. It's never wise to mix business with pleasure." He smiled at her.

She looked up at him and they stood gazing at one another. Her heart skipped a beat. Was he going to kiss her?

He leaned forward.

She closed her eyes expecting his kiss and startled when his lips met her cheek. Blushing furiously, she stepped back, feeling like a fool.

"Thank you for everything," he said. "I hope we can work together going forward."

"I'll give you my answer soon."

"Hopefully I'll see you here next week." After he'd taken a last swallow of lemonade, he let out a long sigh. "Thanks again."

"I'll walk you to the door." She picked up Mindy to make it clear that she didn't expect another kiss from him.

He turned and gazed at her with hazel eyes that had changed to a warm green. His gaze moved to her lips.

She held her breath.

Mindy squirmed in her arms.

Cooper reached over and patted the dog, accidentally brushing Taylor's right breast.

His cheeks grew pink. "Sorry. Goodnight."

She watched him leave, admiring his cute butt as he walked away, and wondered what had just happened. Was it her imagination or was Cooper not the Romeo she thought he must be? He'd seemed as uncertain as she about how to move ahead with something as simple as a kiss.

Replaying the scene in her mind, she realized it didn't matter. He wasn't about to mix business and pleasure, and she wasn't sure whether she should work with him.

CHAPTER FOURTEEN
WHITNEY

Whitney sat with the others at the table at Jake's and tried to focus on the conversation. She kept comparing an evening like this to those she'd shared with fellow actors in trendy places reeking of Hollywood glitter and glib talk.

Ross smiled at her. "A change from what you're used to, huh?" he said as if reading her mind.

"It's very different, but a healthy move for me," she said. "No matter what you read in the newspapers about certain stars, most of it is exaggerated. This past year has been difficult."

"Oh, yes. I understand. After a while, too much publicity gives you cause to doubt yourself and what you're doing. When it came out that I could no longer play ball, it was a mob scene of reporters throwing questions my way that I honestly couldn't answer. I couldn't even tell my family what I was going to do with my life next because I simply didn't know."

"I might be doing a little better than that. Taylor suggested I open a children's theater group. At least for the summer. I'm looking into it now."

Ross gave her a look of admiration. "If you need a sponsor to help, just let me know."

"I appreciate the offer," Whitney said, smiling at him.

"Hey, Ross, what are your plans for the night?" said Ben. "Mike and I are taking off to a place called Stan's. A band is playing there. Want to go?"

Ross turned to Whitney. "Are you game?"

Whitney drew a breath, giving herself time to think. "Why not? It sounds like fun."

"Okay, I'll take you home afterwards," said Ross. "I know you don't have a car with you."

"That would be nice." Though Ross was friendly, he hadn't made any uncomfortable moves on her. And she found him very attractive with that smile she'd seen on television commercials.

His low-slung, silver sports car had a big engine that roared into life when they pulled out of the parking lot behind Jake's. She observed him as he drove with confidence and obviously was enjoying the car but not doing anything with all that power to show off. It was wise because the road narrowed as they headed into the countryside to go to Stan's.

When they pulled into the parking lot, Whitney stared at the wooden one-story building sitting next to a narrow stream and was sent back in time to when she had come here with Nick and other kids in town her age. In addition to the excellent lobster and clam dishes, Stan's was also known as a great place to catch local bands on the weekends throughout the year or nightly during the summer. Tonight, a sign on the front door advertised a country music singer. Music for the soul, she'd always thought, even if it made her seem uncool compared to others who preferred rock music. But in her teens, she'd won a singing contest with a country song.

Whitney waited while Ross went around the back of the car to open the door for her.

Glad for his helping hand, Whitney swung herself out of the car, stood, and teetered a moment to catch her balance. Ross kept a steady hand on her arm and smiled at her. "Easy there. I forget how difficult it is for passengers to get out of the car."

"Gracefully," Whitney added, laughing at herself.

Inside the building, a bar lined one end of the room with a row of filled bar stools. Tables covered with plastic, red-checkered tablecloths filled the space in front of a raised dais that served as a small stage.

A female and male country duo were testing their guitars and the microphone, preparing to begin their performance.

Whitney had always loved singing and dancing and never tired of hearing new music. Trying to keep her presence low key, she pulled on a baseball cap and headed for a table in the back.

Ross sat down beside her and whispered in her ear, "I'll have to get you a proper baseball cap. You can't be seen with me wearing one for the Red Sox."

She laughed. "GG used to take us to Red Sox games when we were growing up. Once you visit Fenway Park, it's over. You're a fan for life."

He grinned. "I don't think so."

A waitress came over to them. "What'll you have?"

Ross turned to her.

"A seltzer with a squeeze of lemon, please." She was tempted to have a beer, but she couldn't get into the habit of packing on calories that way.

"I'll have one of your IPAs on draft," Ross said.

The waitress gave Whitney a longer look than was necessary.

Whitney pulled her cap down farther on her face and sighed. She was grateful for her success but grew tired of the ensuing scrutiny of her and her life.

"If you're uncomfortable, we can leave," said Ross.

"Thanks, but sooner or later people will find out that I'm living here. I might as well stop fighting it." She lifted the baseball cap away from her face and up onto her head. She smiled at him. "Besides, when I'm with you they won't pay any attention to me."

He laughed. "They're becoming used to me around here, so it's no big deal."

The waitress returned and handed Whitney her water. "Here ya go, Whitney."

Ross and Whitney glanced at one another and laughed.

As the duo performed, Whitney relaxed and hummed along, remembering those years when she'd been so eager to succeed.

After their song ended, the male musician announced, "I understand we have a well-known singer in the crowd. Whitney Gilford, come on up and join us in a song."

People in the room murmured and glanced around.

"Have fun," said Ross, urging her out of her chair.

Whitney stood and walked toward the little stage feeling strangely nervous. But when the audience recognized her, they began to clap and call to her.

She and the duo picked a song they all knew. Soon, Whitney was singing a favorite, one about finding love all over again.

Though the crowd wanted more, Whitney politely declined. She didn't want to ruin it for the couple the crowd had come to see.

Ross was beaming at her when she returned to his table. "That was really good. Now you can relax and enjoy yourself."

She grinned. She intended to do just that. Though she had no interest in a relationship with anyone after dealing with Zane, she was comfortable with Ross.

CHAPTER FIFTEEN
DANI

A couple of days later, Dani sat with Whitney and Taylor on the patio at their house eager to discuss a budget for furnishings and other costs for the cottage not provided for by GG. Though GG's funds would cover the cost of the renovation, furnishings and fixtures weren't included. In addition, they would have to pay any overruns of her budget as extra expenses.

"I need to know how much the two of you are willing to put into the project. Both of you earn more than I do, but I've saved quite a bit of money, so I can do my share."

"The question becomes who is going to live there? Dani, you and Brad will no doubt stay in his house. Right?" asked Whitney.

"As a matter of fact, we're discussing building a house at The Meadows," said Dani, unable to hide the excitement in her voice. "His house is fabulous, but it still belongs to Patti, in a way. We want to make a fresh start."

"That's wonderful news," said Taylor. "I wondered what it would be like for you to live where there must be so many memories for Brad. As for me, I can come and go as I please as long as I have a place to write. I'm open to living at the cottage for at least the required six months, if necessary."

"I intend to live at the cottage for as much time as I can," said Whitney. "My future is up in the air. But I've been thinking of staying in Lilac Lake, and if a role comes up that I want to take, then I'll be on location wherever that might be."

"Okay. We're comfortable we can keep the promise of six months a year?" At her sisters' nods, Dani continued. "We need someone to put together some plans for furnishings. I've saved the dining room table and chairs for restoration, but if we decide not to use them, we can always sell them."

"I'd like to be in charge of interior decoration," said Whitney. "Is that okay with the two of you?"

"Yes," said Dani relieved that she wouldn't have to handle that. She'd promised to spend time learning about the Collister Farm business.

"We need to agree on an overall look," said Whitney. "I'll come up with some styles for us to consider."

Dani smiled. She knew it wouldn't always be this easy. She'd take what she could because progress at the cottage was slower than she'd hoped. Brad was eager to start making wedding plans to make their relationship permanent. But she couldn't even think about it until her jobs at the cottage and in Rhode Island were done.

CHAPTER SIXTEEN
TAYLOR

Taylor headed out of her bedroom and downstairs. The house was empty. She left a note on the kitchen counter telling her sisters where she was going and headed out the door. When she needed to do some soul-searching, there was one place for her.

As Taylor pulled into the driveway of the cottage, she was pleased to see trucks from both the plumbing company and the electrician. With other people there, Taylor wasn't afraid.

She bypassed the house and walked down to the sunning rock where she could ponder how to handle the choice in front of her. Taylor knew she could be stubborn, but she wasn't foolish. To have the interest of Grace Pritchard was both scary and satisfying.

Atop the rock, Taylor sat watching a young boy sailing his Sunfish across the surface of the lake as if he had wings beneath him. She remembered when she and her sisters had done the same. She'd always felt as if she were flying as she skimmed across the water at the helm of the small sailboat. Observing the boy now, the yellow hull of the boat and its red and white striped sail made her think of butterflies fluttering their wings as the wind carried them along.

She lay back against the warm surface of the rock and let her thoughts drift. As worried as she was about working with Cooper, she couldn't deny her attraction to him. She wished she'd been more social earlier in her life and had more confidence discussing with him aspects of romance, love, and her characters' reactions to one another. He'd learn very quickly that his earlier criticism of her was justified. How embarrassing would that be?

But maybe, if she could get past that, they could work well together. He seemed dedicated to the idea. She thought back to when they'd sat on the rock together. They'd been able to be open to one another then.

She left the rock and climbed the hill, pausing a moment to study the cottage. As everyone had said, the bones of the house were good. When the renovation was completed, it was going to be stunning. By then, hopefully, the issue of any ghost living there would be resolved.

Back at the house, Taylor was sitting in her office studying the email Thompson C. Walker, not Cooper, had sent. Knowing the man behind the name now made his harsh words less personal. But no matter how cooperative they became she would never forget the hurt from that critique. She'd have to set up ground rules for working together.

Her cell rang. *Cooper.*

"Hello," she said.

"Have you decided? I really want this book to work, so I hope your answer is yes."

Taylor sighed. She'd had no real choice from the beginning. "Come back. We'll work out our differences."

"Okay. I'll let you know when I arrive."

"Where are you going to stay? It's busy over the 4th of July holiday. It might be difficult to find a room."

"No problem. Your friend, JoEllen, gave me her number when I was there and told me about the River Run Cabins where she's staying. I called her, and she's found a cabin for me to sublet from another renter there."

Taylor blinked in surprise. *JoEllen had given him her number?* Ross had told Whitney that JoEllen had given him her number too. That woman wasted no time with any of the young men in the community.

"That's nice that you can stay there," Taylor said. "How long do you think it'll take us to get the project done?"

"It depends. I was told we must edit this book and agree how the next book will take shape."

"We'll try to work as fast as we can, and then you can return to New York," said Taylor. "I know you love it best there."

"Sounds like it's going to work out," said Cooper. "I'm driving up to Lilac Lake tomorrow. I can't wait to experience a slice of Americana with the celebrations there."

"It'll be fun. You'll see. Just promise me you won't get into our work until after the holiday. It's always been a favorite of mine."

"Deal," said Cooper. "I'll call you when I get in."

"Safe travels," said Taylor. "The roads will be busier than usual with people coming here to the Lakes Region or going to the beaches along the southern coast of Maine."

"Okay, see you later," said Cooper.

She couldn't help wondering if they'd be able to pull off working and living in the same town.

Later, when Dani and Whitney were at the house, they all sat on the patio under the new umbrella Whitney bought to protect her from the sun.

After telling them about the working arrangement with Cooper, Taylor said, "JoEllen found a place at the River Run Cabins for Cooper to rent while he's here. It seems she gave him her information when she met him earlier."

Dani groaned. "JoEllen seems determined to find a guy and live here. Maybe after realizing Brad was never going to marry her, she has a fanciful idea that one of the unmarried men will step in. In any case, she is going to be a nuisance. She's asked Brad on numerous occasions to help her with little things around her cabin. A window was stuck, she needed a ladder to reach the upper shelf in a closet, that kind of thing. But really, I don't think she's given up on him. It's like she wants what her sister had."

"Maybe because she's alone and not dating anyone seriously, she's getting desperate. Especially if she wants a family," said Whitney.

"At least if she ended up with Cooper, she'd be out of town," said Dani.

Taylor stiffened. The thought of JoEllen with Cooper soured her stomach.

Whitney stood. "C'mon, dear sisters. Time to go to town to help with the decorations."

Each year Bob Bullard, owner of the small hardware in town, organized volunteers to tie small American flags to the decorative streetlights with red, white, and blue ribbons, while the fire department strung banners across the street. Crystal had volunteered all three of them to help this year.

Taylor loved being part of the group preparing for the celebrations. Now, and as a young girl, she enjoyed the festivities of any holiday. But the 4th of July at the lake was second best after Christmas. Being at Lilac Lake in New England where many battles had been fought for the country's independence made the celebrations seem authentic.

After the group finished placing flags on the streetlights, they put more of them in the pots of flowers outside the shops and businesses in town. Although the parade wouldn't be until the 4th, the days leading up to it were filled with outdoor festivities, including the annual high school band concert on the lawn of the Congregational Church at the end of Main

Street. It was a moment of pride for the band members and a celebration of families being together.

"I don't know about anyone else," said Dani, "but I say we go to the café for lunch."

Taylor, who'd had only a cup of coffee and a piece of toast, was more than ready. "Sounds delicious. Then I'm going to visit GG."

"Sorry, can't go," said Whitney. "I'm having lunch with Angelica Hammond at the Community Center to talk about theater classes for kids."

"Good luck with it," said Taylor, pleased that Whitney was acting on her suggestion.

"We'll make it a quick lunch," said Dani. "I want to check on the cottage and then go out to The Meadows to talk to one of their prospective buyers about changes to the floor plan they like."

"You really are settling into a new life in Lilac Lake," said Taylor. "I'm happy things are working out for you."

"Thanks," said Dani, smiling at her. "Sometimes I just want to pinch myself to see if I'm dreaming."

"It's so romantic how you and Brad just knew you were meant to be together," said Taylor, emitting a soft sigh.

"We're lucky, but it's hard to step into someone else's shoes. Not that Brad makes it seem that way. But his love for Patti will always be part of our relationship."

"Huh, I hadn't thought of it that way," said Taylor. "But you're right. That's what makes it sweeter." She shook her head. "I still have so much to learn."

Dani gave her a quick hug. "It's not difficult. Just follow your heart. If it's meant to be, it will work out."

"I guess. I just have to get through the next few weeks working with Cooper. Then I can concentrate on meeting new people here and having fun."

The café was busy, as usual. The excitement of the upcoming holiday filled the place with chatter from the people who'd worked together on the decorations and who'd comfortably moved to the café for more socializing and excellent food.

Crystal waved at them as they walked out to the patio, but she was too busy to do more than that.

Outside, they ordered their food and sat back and stared out at the people bustling around.

"I must admit, the town dressed up like this is the perfect setting for the holiday. Remember when Whitney was chosen princess of the parade?" said Taylor.

Dani laughed. "She was only ten, but I think we all knew it was just the beginning of a career for her. She wore that crown until GG finally told her she had to keep it in her room."

"I'm sorry she's had such a tough time lately, but relieved to see she's rallying," said Taylor.

"As GG has always told us, never underestimate the Gilford girls."

Taylor smiled and turned as Nick walked onto the patio, looking around while holding a tray with food. She waved him over. "You can join us if you want. We're not staying long, but we're glad to share the table."

He grinned. "Thanks. I won't be long. The holiday is fun for everyone else, but it's double the work for us."

"We're grateful to you and your deputies," said Dani.

Their lunch arrived, and it was quiet as they all dug into their meals.

Before Taylor and Dani had finished, Nick's cell phone buzzed, and he stood. "Thanks for the hospitality. Sorry to leave in a hurry, but I need to check something out."

After he left, Taylor couldn't hold in a sigh. "I swear he's going in my next book. He's a hero if I ever met one."

Dani grinned. "He's the sexiest cop I've ever seen. With his dark hair, bright blue eyes, and ripped body he could be the hero in any story."

They finished their meal and left the café.

"See you later, I'm off to see GG," said Taylor. She walked over to the town parking lot, got into her car, and drove to The Woodlands, excited to see her grandmother. GG always gave excellent advice.

As Taylor walked down the hall to GG's room, anticipation filled her. She was anxious to tell GG about the latest development in editing her book. Her grandmother had always been a supporter of hers from story conception to release of her books and beyond. She'd been a little hard on Cooper when he'd visited her, but GG was always fair.

As usual, GG was reading a book when Taylor knocked on the door and opened it.

"Hi, darling. Come on in. It's so lovely to see you."

Taylor walked over and gave her grandmother a kiss, recalling the many times she'd done just that.

GG's blue eyes twinkled with happiness when Taylor sat in a nearby chair. "To what do I owe this visit?"

"You're one of my best supporters, so I wanted to fill you in on plans going forward. I've agreed to work with Cooper on my book and to put together an outline for the next one. My agent gave me little choice about getting to know Cooper better, and now I'm willing to try."

"I see," said GG, uncharacteristically quiet.

"My agent, Dorothy, is friends with Grace Pritchard, the head of Pritchard Publishing. They talked the situation over and decided it was time to settle the issue about his critique and for us to get to work. Dorothy reminded me how fortunate

I am to have the support of Grace Pritchard and what it could mean for my business." Taylor sighed. "I know she's right."

"And Cooper? How does he feel about it?" GG asked.

"He's okay with it. In fact, he really wants to make our collaboration successful. He should be arriving sometime today. We'll celebrate the 4th of July holiday and then get started."

"It sounds like a wise plan. Dorothy is right, you know. It's a wonderful opportunity for you." GG's smile was gentle. "I know you have a streak of independence and don't like to be told what to do, but make this work, Taylor. It'll be to your benefit."

"I will," said Taylor. "But it's going to be humiliating for me when he realizes that he was right; I've never been in a strong, deep relationship. I haven't found a man I thought was right for me."

"It's best not to rush into any such decisions about someone," GG said. "Just as when you're enjoying a book, you sometimes have to read between the lines to get a full understanding."

"I know," said Taylor. She stared out the window. Was that why she'd been such a failure at finding love?

"Hello, Ms. Wittner," came a cheerful voice. "And Taylor. What are you doing here?"

Taylor forced a smile. "Ms. Wittner is my grandmother."

"Ah, well, she's a lovely lady," JoEllen said. "I love all my people. Isn't that right, Ms. Wittner?"

GG shifted uncomfortably in her chair but said politely. "So, I've heard."

"Taylor, I'm so happy I had a chance to meet Cooper. He called me, and I helped him find a place to stay at River Run Cabins where I'm living." She beamed at her. "Cooper said he can't wait to spend time with me. You must admit, he's one hot guy."

Even though Taylor felt a little sick at the thought of Cooper with someone like JoEllen, she hid her feelings and nodded because there was no doubt about it, Cooper was hot.

CHAPTER SEVENTEEN
WHITNEY

Whitney left her business meeting regarding the children's theater feeling discouraged. If she were to arrange the theater group as part of the town's activities, she'd be forced to follow so many rules, she'd never get the project off the ground.

Angelica and she had agreed she could rent the auditorium at the community center with the selectmen's approval for an evening production. But she'd need to find a different place for day-time rehearsals because the community center was booked for other summer activities.

She thought of the storage area at the Beckman Lumber Company and decided to drive out there. She'd met Bethany Beckman just once and had found her to be a very pleasant person.

During the drive, she thought if she were given permission to use the space, the float, stored there with the July 4th decorations removed, would make a perfect stage for practicing, putting the space to double use.

She parked the car outside the shop and went inside.

From behind the counter, Bethany waved. "Hi. Nice to see you. I've got some new things in that would be perfect for the cottage."

Whitney smiled and returned the wave. "Terrific. I've been put in charge of decorating the interior, and though we're not ready to purchase anything, I'd love to look at them. Also, I need to ask you for a favor."

Bethany stepped from behind the counter wearing a skirt

that barely showed her baby bump. With streaked brown hair and pretty brown eyes, she was a lovely woman who already had a glow that some pregnant women get.

"Let's go into my office. We can talk there, where I've set aside some items that I thought would be perfect at the cottage."

Whitney followed Bethany. Boxes were piled in one corner, samples strewn on a long table off to the side and one of the chairs in front of the desk was loaded with soft goods, such as kitchen towels and placemats.

Bethany sat behind the desk and faced her with a smile as Whitney lowered herself into the free chair. "What can I help you with?"

Whitney explained about the children's theater program she was hoping to set up and how she would need rehearsal space. "There's room in the area where the parade float is stored. We could even use the float as a stage for rehearsals."

"I love the idea of a theater group. We'd have to check with our insurance agent for any liability issues, but I'd be happy to do that and get back to you," said Bethany. She gazed at Whitney with a look of adoration. "The kids will be so lucky to work with someone like you. I'm a fan of yours. As a matter of fact, I'm feeling a little giddy right now." She shook her head. "I don't mean to gush. Let me show you some suggestions I have for the cottage."

Bethany walked over to where several items were strewn or stacked on the long table. "This is where we unpack boxes to check packing slips. Then the paperwork is given to a part-time worker to input the items into our computerized system. But I promised Dani I'd keep an eye out for things you might want to use at the cottage."

Whitney looked at matching kitchen towels, placemats, napkins, potholders and other items for kitchen and dining room. Bowls, drinking glasses, and cute pictures for the kitchen were in boxes on the floor. The basic kitchenware would come from other sources, but these items would make the cottage their unique home.

After taking photos with her phone, Whitney made a list of things she thought they'd be interested in. "I'll show my sisters and get back to you. If they like them, I'll go ahead and purchase them as a surprise."

"Perfect. I love my job, but Garth is going to kill me if I bring home more stuff. Right now, I'm concentrating on baby items." Bethany cradled her stomach. "We've opted to know the gender of the baby. I can't help thinking how much fun it would be to dress up a little girl. We'll see."

"Either way, I know you'll love starting a family," said Whitney, surprised by the twinge of envy she felt. *Where had that come from?*

They hugged, and Whitney left with a promise from Bethany to call her about the rehearsal space.

CHAPTER EIGHTEEN
TAYLOR

Taylor was washing the dinner dishes when her cell rang. *Cooper.*

"Hello," Taylor said. "Did you make it here?"

"Yes, I arrived a couple of hours ago, got settled in my room, and then I took JoEllen out to dinner as a thank you to her for helping me find a place to rent. The downtown area looks great all dressed up. You weren't kidding when you said it was a big deal here."

"It's a fun couple of days," said Taylor. "That's why we won't start our project until after the 4th, if that's all right with you."

"It is. You mentioned it when I agreed to come back to Lilac Lake. Do you want to meet for breakfast? I need to ease into this life with a friend."

"Sure. Why don't I meet you at the café at nine? I might take a walk before then."

"A walk? I figured you for a jogger," Cooper said in a teasing tone.

She laughed. "Walking is more my style. I have a better chance of thinking and plotting at a slower pace."

"Okay, then. I'll see you at the café at nine. If that's too crowded, I'll treat you to coffee at Beans."

"Perfect." Taylor ended the call and stood staring a moment at the scene outside. The gray sky was streaked with a bright orange color that reminded her of the leaves of trees in the fall. Mindy was racing around the yard barking at a robin who flew to a lower branch of the maple tree and stared down at her. Not one to give up, Mindy barked at it until the bird flew away.

Taylor finished her chore and then went outside to sit on the patio with Whitney. They'd discussed the items for sale at Beckman Lumber, and Taylor loved being able to start over with fresh new things and a different look from her condo.

Whitney was sitting quietly, typing a message into her phone. When she saw Taylor, she stopped and let out a long, sad sigh.

"What's going on?" Taylor asked. Whitney wasn't the same since she'd left California. "Want to talk about it?"

"Not yet," said Whitney. "But thank you. Why don't we walk downtown and see what's happening there? I heard Jake's is throwing a celebration party on their back deck."

"Sounds like fun," Taylor said, suddenly restless.

As Taylor and Whitney drew near to Jake's, music met them in rocking beats. Taylor grinned at Whitney. "This is like college days. C'mon. Let's have some fun!"

They walked around the building to the back deck. The parking lot beyond the deck had been cleared for the occasion, and a local band, Mudd Puddles, was playing music.

People on the deck were moving to the beat with mugs of beer or other drinks in their hands. Those lucky enough to get seats at either end of the long deck were chatting and laughing, trying to be heard above the sound of music.

"This way," said Whitney, tugging on Taylor's arm. She led Taylor up the steps to a table at the closest end next to an open doorway into the bar.

Aaron Collister got to his feet. "Hi, have a seat. I've been saving them for a couple of friends, but they just called to say they weren't going to make it."

"Thanks," said Taylor. Aaron had once explained that he and Brad were half-brothers. When his mother, a Native American, was dying of cancer when he was ten, she'd left him with his father's family. Aaron was a low-key man who hid a gentleness inside his ripped body. She'd always admired him.

"Your friends don't know what they're missing," Whitney told him, sliding onto a stool at the high-top table. "This is fun."

Aaron smiled at her. "There's a lot going on around the region. They found another gig in Portsmouth. What'll you have to drink?" He waved a waitress over and after some discussion, he ordered them the glasses of white wine they wanted.

The waitress returned, set their drinks down, and spent a moment or two flirting with Aaron.

Ross's friends, Ben Gooding and Mike Dawson, noticed them and came over.

"Cool band, huh?" said Ben. He'd played baseball with Ross in high school and college and looked the part of a catcher with his broad, heavy-set body. He settled his gaze on Whitney.

"How are you? Nice to see you again."

Whitney smiled. "I'm fine. Just enjoying some local flavor. I hear you and Mike are staying with Ross. Where is he?"

Taylor perked up. Whitney had had an enjoyable time with Ross the other night.

"Ross is away for the holiday," said Mike. "A sailing trip with other friends off the coast of Maine. That's why we're holding down the fort, so to speak." Mike was a tall, lanky guy with brown hair worn in a ponytail who'd played professional tennis for a short while until he decided to coach instead.

"Oh, I see," said Whitney.

Intrigued, Taylor heard a note of disappointment in Whitney's voice. She was so intent on that conversation she didn't notice Cooper and JoEllen until they were standing before them.

"Hi, everyone," said JoEllen brightly. "This is my date, Cooper Walker." She smiled at Mike and Ben. "Very nice to see you again. Guess you decided to stick around, after all."

As JoEllen continued to talk to them, Taylor studied her. JoEllen was attractive, friendly, cheerful. But there was something about her that she and many others found irritating.

Cooper smiled at her. "Hi, Taylor."

"Hey, Cooper," said Whitney. "Glad you made it back. Guess that means I'll be seeing quite a lot of you if you're working with Taylor."

He grinned. "It's going to be the best book ever." He nudged her with his elbow.

Whitney laughed. "It's going to be really interesting to see how it all works out." She glanced at Taylor and winked.

Taylor couldn't help laughing too. She knew it wouldn't be a simple collaboration.

JoEllen turned to them and frowned. "What's going on?"

"Nothing," said Whitney. "We're just enjoying a laugh."

"C'mon, Cooper. I see a friend from work down by the band. Let's go," said JoEllen.

"You go ahead. I'll wait here," he replied.

JoEllen placed her hands on her hips and glared at him. "But you're my date, and I want to introduce you to her."

Cooper held up his hand. "Wait a minute. I'm not really your date. I thought you were just doing a neighborly thing by offering me a ride."

"You .... You ... bastard! It was no such thing," said JoEllen fighting tears. She turned on her heel and marched away.

Cooper stared at her and then faced them. "That's the second time I've been called that in this town. What gives? I'm just being honest. I'm only here to do my job," said Cooper.

"Be careful. JoEllen is a time bomb ready to shatter someone's life," said Whitney. "Believe me, I've met drama queens like that in Hollywood."

Early the next morning, Taylor walked along the streets of Lilac Lake enjoying the cooler air, the sound of birds chirping cheerfully, and the sights of a town coming to life like a lazy cat stretching.

A deputy sheriff drove his car slowly down the street checking things out. Though Taylor hadn't met the man, she gave him a friendly wave. He waved back.

Taylor thought about the incident between Cooper and JoEllen last night and wondered if it was smart for Cooper to be in town working with her on the book. It was sometimes easier to disagree online than to confront a person to his face. Especially if you were shy, like her. But then, where was the honor in doing that?

As she arrived on Main Street, Taylor saw staff members from Jake's sweeping and picking up trash in front and around the perimeter of the bar. Last night's party had been a lot of fun. Others who'd attended the affair were, no doubt, sleeping in.

Taylor noticed Cooper standing in front of the café and picked up her pace. She hadn't seen him leave with JoEllen and wondered how he'd gotten home.

"'Morning," said Cooper. "It's another beautiful day."

"Yes, it is. We have to hope it'll stay that way for the parade tomorrow."

"Do any last-minute things need to be done on the float?" Cooper asked. "I'm available to help."

Taylor shook her head. "I don't think so, but you can ask Crystal. Let's grab a table while we can."

They went inside, and seeing it crowded there, headed out to the patio where an empty table beckoned to them.

"Perfect," said Taylor. "I love sitting here and watching the action."

Taylor smiled at the waitress approaching them. "Ah, coffee. Just what I need."

They ordered their meal without bothering to look at menus and then sat back sipping their coffee.

"Nothing like the first cup of coffee for the day," said Cooper sighing with pleasure.

Taylor chuckled at the smile of contentment on his face. She felt the same way about coffee, though she seldom had more than the one cup each morning.

"How'd you get home last night?" Taylor asked.

"JoEllen was so busy trying to hook up with someone she didn't even realize I was leaving. Ben and Mike gave me a ride back to my cabin."

"I'm sorry ..." Taylor began.

He waved his hand to stop her. "Believe me, I intend to stay out of her way. Whitney was right. JoEllen's a drama queen."

"I wasn't going to say anything, but she's been a troublemaker between Brad and Dani. They won't let her get away with anything, but just the thought of her trying to intrude is stressful."

"Too bad I'm living at the cabins. She's too close for comfort." Cooper took a sip of his coffee. "What are your plans for the day?"

"I thought I might play tourist and check in on some of the activities," said Taylor. "The Historical Society has a special collection of photographs on display of previous 4th of July celebrations in town. Anything that will give me a deeper understanding of my new home."

He gave her a steady look. "You're really going to move from New York to here? I would think it would leave a huge vacuum in your life to give up all the activities of the city."

"I'm not saying I'd never go back and spend some time in New York, but I'd make my real home here. At least for six months of the year. There are so many benefits to doing so." Even as she spoke the words, Taylor thought of how satisfying it felt. She'd been struggling with finding the best in herself, the one who wouldn't doubt her looks, her ability. There was something about Lilac Lake that grounded her.

"Do you want company?" Cooper asked. "I might as well get to know the town too as long as I'll be here for a while."

"Sure. And you're also invited to our holiday dinner tonight at our house. But, Cooper, I'm still trying to figure out why your publisher and my agent felt so strongly about us working together."

"Your agent, Dorothy Minton, and my mother have been friends for years. I knew once they made up their minds that this is how they wanted things to happen, there was nothing I could say or do about it if I wanted to keep my job."

"Wait a minute! Your mother? Are you telling me Grace Pritchard is your *mother*?"

He made a face. "Yeah. Nobody at work talks about it. She's kept her maiden name and I've been careful not to give it away. She told me she wouldn't play favorites, which is why she's being doubly harsh with me. She knows I've always wanted to be part of the business."

Taylor could feel the angry burn on her cheeks and started to stand. *He hadn't told her about his mother being the publisher? What kind of B.S. was that?*

"Wait!" said Cooper. "Hear me out."

She sank back into her chair but remained ready to walk

away. The situation was totally out of control.

"Listen, I know this is awkward, but it doesn't have to be. We'll keep it simple between us. You want to continue to grow and succeed as an author, and I want to keep my job so I can remain in the family business. It could be a win-win for each of us."

"Why would your mother and Dorothy be so insistent on our doing things this way?" Taylor asked, both confused and irritated at the same time.

"That I don't know. Maybe it's some sort of new sensitivity training thing. All I know is I wasn't given a choice in the matter." He reached across the table and patted her hand. "I like you, Taylor. I'm sure we can work it out."

Shock swept through Taylor's body in waves. She looked down at their hands touching and quickly snatched hers away. The last thing she needed was to let any feelings develop between the two of them. The situation was already weird, and as Cooper suggested, she intended to succeed.

The waitress arrived with their food, and Taylor was relieved to end the conversation for the moment. She needed time to think, maybe set some ground rules between them. But the thought that two important people in their lives wanted them to work it out this way was unsettling. She thought of a comment Cooper made about learning from another one of his authors by working with her. Were she and Cooper supposed to learn from one another? Was that what this was all about? If so, she wasn't sure she was up to baring her soul.

CHAPTER NINETEEN
DANI

Dani was happy to help at the Collister Farm Stand for the holiday weekend. It was a convenient way to pitch in and discover how she might fit into the close-knit family. Brad's parents, Mary Lou and Joe Collister, had warmly welcomed her into the family when she and Brad got engaged. Brad's brother, Aaron, and his two sisters, Amy and Becca, had hugged her with joy at the news. But the day-to-day work of trying to fit in was sometimes exhausting for Dani. She'd always been independent. That, and trying to compete with the memory of Brad's deceased wife, who'd apparently loved cooking and gardening, made it harder.

"You're new here at the stand, aren't you?" asked a woman picking up some fresh vegetables for the weekend. Poached salmon, green peas, and new potatoes were a traditional 4th of July meal in New England, and fresh peas and potatoes were selling like crazy,

"Yes, I'm new," said Dani. "I know Lilac Lake well, though, because my grandmother owned the Lilac Lake Inn for years."

"Your grandmother is a wonderful woman. Too bad she sold it, but I hear the new owners are going to make it even nicer." She smiled at Dani. "Glad to meet you and know some of the family is still in town."

"Thanks." Dani didn't mention her sisters. Their stories weren't hers to tell.

"How are you doing, darling? Did you get the jars of jelly out on display?" asked Mary Lou, beaming at her. Dani returned her smile. "I did."

"Now let's straighten the tomatoes display," said Mary Lou. "Thank goodness for the greenhouse. We have a nice 'Early Girl' crop of tomatoes." She sighed and wiped her hands on her apron. "It's one thing to grow the vegetables and another to sell them. But every little bit helps the farm."

Dani was uncertain how many acres the family owned, but she knew that each bit of land was put to use for something. Chickens and goats were useful too, providing eggs and milk to be made into cheese to sell. Only Pansy, Mary Lou's pet pig, was provided an easy life with no expectations for her to be anything but cute.

People came and went in a steady pattern, keeping Dani busy. For all of Mary Lou's down-home charm, she was a shrewd businesswoman, upselling customers who came in for just a couple of things and left with many more.

Dani was about to leave when she overheard a woman purchasing peas, tomatoes, and potatoes say to a friend, "I understand Taylor Castle is living here now. I just love her books. Someone mentioned on Facebook that she was moving to Lilac Lake. Another one of her admirers."

Shocked, Dani stood still as the women moved on to another counter. Taylor was pretty careful about her private life. Would she want everyone to know she was here?

CHAPTER TWENTY
TAYLOR

Taylor set down the cookbook and stared at Dani after she heard the news.

"This woman knew I was here in Lilac Lake? You know I keep a low profile on Facebook, talking about books and generic things, but keeping my location private. After that famous writer was killed by a crazy fan, I'm careful. I'll check to see what I can find out about the post. First, I need to learn how to poach salmon. If we're going to share a holiday meal, it's got to be delicious."

"Maybe we can work on it together," said Dani. "Mary Lou is such an excellent cook that I'm going to have to learn how."

"Are you sure you and Brad won't mind eating here at the house with Whitney, Cooper, and me for our traditional holiday meal?"

Dani waved away her concern. "It will give me a chance to relax. I love Brad's family, but they are a little overwhelming."

"Okay," said Taylor, relieved. "The more the merrier."

Whitney walked into the room. "What are you two up to?"

"Learning about poaching salmon," said Taylor.

"Telling Taylor about a Facebook post I'm concerned about," Dani said. "A stranger at the Collister Farm Stand mentioned she knew from a FB post that Taylor Castle was living here."

"I'm going to check on it later," said Taylor.

"Why don't we check on it now," Whitney said calmly but with a note of determination. "Everyone needs to be careful on social media, and if you normally don't give out such details, we need to find the source."

"Now you're scaring me," said Taylor, setting the cookbook on the table.

She led her sisters to her office and sat down in front of the computer. After signing in, she checked her Facebook author page. A forwarded photo of Lilac Lake showed up with the question: Is this where Taylor Castle is living?"

She checked the name of the original poster. Someone named JED. She clicked onto the name and found a face all too familiar.

"What the hell was JoEllen Daniels doing posting something like that?" said Dani.

They checked JoEllen's page. She'd posted that same picture of Lilac Lake and then a photo of Cooper with the caption "my new boyfriend." Farther down the page, there were other photos of her with an assortment of people, mostly men.

"Oh my God," said Whitney. "I wasn't kidding when I called her a time bomb waiting to explode. This is someone who's very lonely and insecure."

"What should I do?" Taylor asked wringing her hands.

"Delete the photo immediately. You have a ton of followers, but JoEllen has only a few," said Whitney.

"Do you think Taylor should send JoEllen a warning? Maybe block her?" asked Dani. "I must have agreed to friend her at some point, but I get so many requests, I'm sometimes careless."

"No," said Whitney. "You'll want to be able to keep an eye on her. I'm sorry, Taylor. I know you're upset, but these things happen to Hollywood stars and people in the public eye all the time. You must be careful, that's all."

"I don't think Cooper is going to be happy to be on her

Facebook page, either," said Taylor. "He's now sorry he's renting one of the cabins near her. But it's all he could find."

"Maybe as long as you're staying at Brad's most of the time, Dani, we should offer him your room here," said Whitney, bringing a yelp out of Taylor.

"What? I need space from him," Taylor said. "I already have to work with him."

"Just a thought," said Whitney, giving Taylor a bright smile.

Dinner that evening turned out to be a lot more fun than Taylor expected. Brad brought Aaron and the six of them sat around on the patio with glasses of wine or bottles of beer discussing the parade and other events of the holiday weekend. For Taylor and her sisters, the talk was full of happy memories. For Cooper, the one outsider, it was an education in small-town living.

Leaving the men outdoors, Dani went into the kitchen to shell the peas and scrub the new potatoes she'd brought from the farm. Later, she and Whitney cooked the vegetables and tossed a green salad while Taylor plated the cooked salmon and dressed it up with fresh parsley and dill from the garden.

"It looks almost professional," Taylor said proudly, standing back to view the dining room table laden with food.

The men joined them.

"Looks delicious," said Aaron, smiling at her.

She was pleased by the praise. Maybe cooking for others wouldn't be so bad.

Everyone took seats at the table, and after Taylor thanked them for being there, they dug in.

"We'd better not linger," said Dani toward the end of the meal. "The band concert will begin in a half-hour, and we want to get seats on the lawn."

"Band concert? What's that all about?" asked Cooper.

"It's a tradition," said Whitney. "The high school band plays patriotic music and a few old-fashioned songs and people join in the singing, if they want."

"It's fun in a small-town way," Taylor told him. "There are some fireworks too."

Cooper smiled, but Taylor could tell he wasn't that excited about it.

Later, sitting on one of the blankets they were using for the concert, Taylor turned to Cooper sitting on her right. "Every year, the principal of the high school welcomes everyone. It's a relief that he's doing it and not one of the local politicians who like to talk forever."

Cooper chuckled. "Some traditions are very important."

Taylor laughed. "GG told me that it took some maneuvering to make that change, but people worked together to make it happen."

"Where is your grandmother?"

Taylor swallowed hard. "Back at The Woodlands. We asked her to join us, but she wasn't feeling well. I've promised to give her all the gossip tomorrow after the parade."

Cooper studied her. "I'm sorry. I know you're upset about her not being here."

"Yes, it's hard to think of GG aging, but she's normally in excellent health and promised me it was nothing serious."

The high school principal came up onto the wooden stage and faced them. "Happy early 4th of July, everyone! It's the twenty-third year of celebrating the holiday in the very special Lilac Lake way. For those of you who are new to our celebrations, we encourage you to join in by singing and clapping and enjoying the moment. Now, I turn this program over to the high school band and their leader, Joshua Harding."

The sound of John Philip Sousa's *The Stars and Stripes Forever* began and brought people to their feet, some clapping to the beat. Listening to it and seeing townspeople she recognized from years past brought unexpected tears to Taylor's eyes.

Aaron, sitting to her left, noticed and put an arm around her.

Cooper gave her a sympathetic look and laughed when Brad started marching in place.

Later, after the band completed their show, a hush filled the audience as fireworks began in a field behind the fire station.

Taylor joined others in the crowd "oohing" with pleasure at the sights and sounds of them. At one point, she noticed Cooper watching her and they exchanged smiles.

When the fireworks display ended, Cooper helped Taylor up and held onto her hand a moment longer than necessary.

Sated with holiday cheer, Taylor didn't mind and instead gave his hand a squeeze before pulling away.

"Okay, everyone," said Dani. "We'll meet at the café tomorrow morning. I've arranged with Crystal for us to view the parade from her apartment above the restaurant. That's in return for helping with the float."

"Guess I'd better be going. Thanks for including me," said Cooper. He shook hands with Brad and Aaron and then smiled and bobbed his head at Dani and Whitney before turning to Taylor. "I'll meet you there tomorrow. Thanks for a nice day."

"I think you've had a nice introduction to town, but tomorrow will be fun too. After the parade, we're going to picnic at the cottage. Aaron is bringing his canoe, and we'll have plenty of food."

"Sounds like a plan," said Cooper. "See you."

As he walked away, Taylor couldn't help admiring his physique.

Whitney noticed and winked at her.

CHAPTER TWENTY-ONE
WHITNEY

Whitney stood with others on the deck of Crystal's apartment above the Lilac Lake Café waiting for the 4th of July parade to begin, feeling like a child again. How had her life gotten so complicated, so unfulfilled? She knew how fortunate she was to have secured a role in a successful television series. But had it made her happy? Yes, she told herself. She'd been happy for the first two years of production, and then things had fallen apart in her relationship with Zane. And though she'd told people she had no interest in dating or starting a family for a long time, the truth was she was both intrigued and scared by the thought of something permanent. She'd worked too hard on her career just to let it go too long.

"There you are," said Taylor coming over to her and giving her a hug. "You beat me out of the house. I was going to give you a ride."

Whitney smiled. "I couldn't sleep and thought I'd come down here a bit early. Crystal told me she didn't need any help, so I've been sitting up here with my coffee just relaxing."

"I was all set to help Crystal, but since she hired a couple of new girls, she told me I wasn't needed," said Taylor. "The college girls need the work."

"Where's Cooper?" Whitney asked.

"He's going to meet us here. I offered to pick him up, but he said he'd park at our house and walk over."

"I like him. He seems like a nice guy."

"I know, but I can't let myself think of that and ruin our

business agreement. Did you know his mother is the publisher?"

"What? Then why is she making him come here to help you? It doesn't make sense unless, as I told you, she wants you to improve as a writer and him to improve as an editor."

"Cooper told me he wants to be able to be a legitimate part of the family business. Because of their different names, they've been very discreet about their relationship. But I think she's being really hard on him."

"I'm sure it's all part of a plan," said Whitney. "He's certainly being pleasant about it."

They stopped talking when Aaron, Brad, and Dani showed up.

CHAPTER TWENTY-TWO
TAYLOR

Taylor's mind stayed on Whitney's words as more people entered the apartment. She felt Cooper's arrival before she even saw him. When she turned around, his gaze was on her. He smiled and walked her way. A thought flashed in her mind. His whole career might be tied to how well he could handle a difficult author like her.

She returned his smile and silently vowed to make their working relationship successful. It was to both of their advantages to do so.

"I'm glad you're here," she said. "I can hear one of the marching bands warming up. This spot will give you an excellent view."

"Should be interesting," Cooper said, accepting a cup of coffee from Dani, who was acting as hostess.

"Crystal is working with the girls on the float, making sure everything is set there. And then she'll walk alongside it," said Dani. "We all need to cheer them when they come by."

"Especially because it's all to celebrate Collister Construction's birthday," said Brad joining them. "The girls are tossing out hard candy, beads, and gift cards to the shop at Beckman Lumber."

"Sounds like Mardi Gras," said Cooper.

Brad laughed. "Here in Lilac Lake, it's as big a deal. Oh, here we go!"

As they all moved closer to see, Taylor felt Cooper's hand on her lower back as he helped her through the small group on the deck. She glanced at him, but he'd dropped his hand and was focused on the firetruck leading the parade. Still, she'd liked that fleeting moment of feeling protected.

A marching band from a neighboring town followed the firetruck, led by baton twirlers who threw their batons in the air and caught them just as they reached the spot where Taylor watched. Politicians drove by seated on the back seats of convertibles, smiling and waving to the crowd as they rolled by. Finally, the float for Collister Construction approached.

"Here comes a surprise," said Dani, nudging Taylor.

Taylor grinned as Mary Lou Collister waved to them from the float, where she was standing with a young girl who wore a sash marked Miss Collister Construction. She didn't know who was prouder—the young girl or Mary Lou. The other girls were wearing blue T-shirts with Collister Construction on them and wearing yellow hard hats.

"Hi, Mom," Brad called to her. Both he and Aaron wore proud smiles as their mother waved back. Taylor loved that their family was so close.

The float paused in front of the apartment, and Mary Lou tossed several bead necklaces up to them.

Aaron caught them and then handed one each to Taylor, Dani, and Whitney before putting some around his neck.

Taylor laughed for the pure joy of it as she slipped bright blue and red beads around her neck.

After the last police car had passed by indicating the end of the parade, Taylor went inside with the others.

She turned to Cooper. "What did you think? Pretty cool, huh?"

"It was fun," Cooper admitted. "I see where you get some ideas for your books. There are so many stories behind some of the people. Aaron was filling me in on a few."

"I'm going to help Crystal take care of the float," said Dani.

"I'll come too," Whitney said. "Taylor, why don't you get started on fixing lunch for our picnic at the cottage?"

Taylor nodded agreeably but couldn't help wondering why her big sisters were so bossy.

"I'll help you," said Cooper.

"Okay, it's pretty simple," Taylor said, pleased by the offer.

They left Crystal's apartment and headed to her house in her car. "Wait! Before we go back to the house, let's make a quick run to check on GG. Do you mind?"

"Not at all," said Cooper. "While you check on her, I'm going to call my mother."

"Deal." Taylor was eager to see GG. As much fun as she'd been having, it wasn't the same without her grandmother.

At The Woodlands, she hurried inside and walked down the corridor to GG's room hoping to surprise her.

GG's door was closed.

She tapped lightly on it before opening the door and coming face-to-face with JoEllen.

Taylor stepped back. "What are you doing here? Where's my grandmother?"

"I'm just making sure everything's all right. Your grandmother is in the Tea Room where a special lunch has been prepared."

Taylor fought to control her anger. "You shouldn't be here. I'll wait while you leave before going to see my grandmother."

"I have every right to be here," said JoEllen. "I work here, remember?"

"Your job as a nurse's aide doesn't give you the freedom to be in someone's private quarters if they're not there," said Taylor.

JoEllen flounced out of the room and down the hallway.

Taylor watched her go, troubled by the thought that something else might be going on. She didn't trust JoEllen. Something wasn't right with her. She'd have GG check for any valuables or money. Fortunately, she kept a lockbox for those things carefully hidden away in her closet.

When Taylor walked into the dining room, a smile spread across GG's face. "How nice to see you! Happy 4th of July!"

Taylor gave her a hug and studied her face. "How are you? Feeling better, I hope."

"Yes, thank you. It's nothing to worry about. I haven't been able to sleep well for a few nights, and my system is a little off. I'll be back to normal in no time. Tell me, are you having fun with Cooper and everyone else?"

Taylor smiled. "It's been a fun holiday. We're going to have a picnic at the cottage so we can go swimming and use Aaron's canoe."

"It's a perfect day for it," said GG. "Now, don't let me keep you. Go and have a good time."

Taylor kissed her grandmother's cheek. "Love you, GG."

"Love you too, darling."

As she left the building, Taylor realized she hadn't told GG about JoEllen being in her apartment. She knew GG was careful with her cash and valuables. Still, Taylor would make sure she knew.

Taylor and Cooper followed Whitney, Dani, Aaron, and Brad around the cottage to the front lawn which Aaron had recently mowed. The smooth swath of bright green was inviting as they set down beach chairs and coolers full of sandwiches, fruit, cookies, and assorted drinks. It was a perfect day. The temperature was in the high seventies with a gentle breeze. The sky above them was a clear blue with only the occasional cloud drifting by.

"What a beautiful day," said Dani. "Let's relax and enjoy it." She spread three blankets out on the lawn while Brad carried a couple of the beach chairs down to the shore and set them down close to the rock.

Taylor explained to Cooper, "If it gets too hot on the lawn, sitting in a chair and dangling feet in cool lake water always feels refreshing."

"A voice of experience," said Cooper winking at her.

Taylor laughed. "I'm more of a lawn person for now. Besides, I'm hungry. How about you? Still have room after nibbling in the kitchen?"

He grinned at her teasing and patted his stomach. "Yes, there's room for more."

Taylor swallowed hard. Wearing a T-shirt over his bathing trunks, Cooper's ripped body sent waves of desire through her. Obviously, he worked out but not to excess. At Cooper's age of thirty-two, he seemed very mature compared to some of the men she'd dated. Better yet, he didn't seem to have any idea how attractive he was.

"How about you?" Cooper asked, tearing Taylor away from her inner thoughts.

"What?"

"I thought so. You're not listening to me." He shook his head and clucked his tongue with fake concern. "Is that how it's going to be? You and me forever out of sync?"

"We're talking about lunch not business," said Taylor. "Let's get something to eat now. Then we can swim or take out the canoe, whatever you want." She removed the T-shirt she was wearing over her bikini. "The sun is already hot."

Cooper's hazel eyes brightened as his gaze swept over her, but he didn't say anything before leaving her side to go to one of the coolers.

Taylor let out a sigh, feeling as if she was tumbling back to past years when both Dani and Whitney were grown with attractive bodies while she was a skinny, flat-chested child. Even now, those old insecurities made her wonder what Cooper thought of her. Dani and Whitney were voluptuous compared to her. She had a nice shape, but no one would call her curvy.

Cooper returned holding two paper plates with sandwiches, chips, and pickles. "I've got these. Why don't you grab a couple of drinks for us? I'll have root beer."

Whitney was standing by the cooler filled with the drinks when Taylor approached. "I need a root beer and a diet coke."

Whitney handed them to her. "I think Cooper is smitten with you."

"What? Why would you say that?" Taylor asked. "We're just people working together. That's how it's got to be."

"Says who?" Whitney asked, her gaze boring into Taylor.

"I ... I ... don't know. My agent, I guess," said Taylor.

Whitney laughed. "Go have fun. It's all right. It's a holiday."

Taylor left her and sat with Cooper and Aaron eating lunch, as they gazed up at the cottage.

"Do you still think a ghost lives there?" Aaron asked her.

"A ghost? Really?" said Cooper. "So, it *is* haunted?"

Taylor gave him a sheepish grin. "We don't know for sure, but strange things have happened in the house, and there's an old rumor that the ghost of a woman who used to live there is still in the house. I'm not comfortable being inside and won't be until the cottage is completely renovated. I think with all the changes, the ghost will realize it's time for her to leave."

"It's probably nothing more than a misunderstood spirit from the past," said Aaron, placing a comforting hand on her shoulder. "But I've felt something there, too."

"After we finish lunch, let's go take a look," said Cooper,

almost gleefully. "I've seen a couple of strange lights, but that's all."

"I'm not going," said Taylor. "I'll leave any inspection up to you two. In addition to the story about the ghost, my sisters and I found a storage box with a wedding dress inside, along with assorted baby clothes. It was tucked away on a shelf in the garage as though it had been hidden. GG knows nothing about it. We're eventually going to do some research on it, but none of us has done anything so far. I don't want to start until the renovations are done, and the ghost is gone."

"A troubled spirit will decide on its own when it's time to leave," Aaron said quietly. "But maybe it's best to wait."

"I get it. It's too nice a day to tangle with a ghost," said Cooper.

Taylor glanced at the house, and a shiver traveled down her back. She didn't want to meet up with this ghost or any ghost now or in the future.

They finished their lunch, and then the three of them walked down to Aaron's canoe.

"You two can go ahead without me," said Taylor.

"No, you can sit in the middle. I'll take the stern and Cooper can have the bow," said Aaron. "Let's lift the canoe out into the water."

"Okay, I've done a lot of canoeing at a summer camp before," said Cooper. "It's really cool."

Once the men were thigh-deep in the water, Aaron strode toward her and before she could object, he lifted her in his arms, carried her to the canoe, and set her down inside.

"Okay, Cooper, hop in," said Aaron, holding onto the stern.

The canoe rocked as Cooper stepped inside and settled at the bow.

Aaron's long legs made it easier for him to climb aboard, and then the three of them headed out into the water.

"We'll paddle to the other end of the lake. We might even be able to see The Meadows from the water," said Aaron.

They were well underway when Taylor noticed a big spider crawling up her leg. Holding in a scream, she kicked her leg up and over the side of the boat. "Get away!"

The next thing she knew she was in the water with her wet hair dripping onto her face. The capsized canoe floated nearby as she treaded water.

"What happened?" asked Aaron, reaching for a couple of seat cushions floating nearby.

Feeling foolish, Taylor said, "Sorry. It was an enormous spider." She looked for Cooper but didn't find him. "Cooper?"

"Here," he said swimming around the bow of the canoe. He treaded water and held a hand to his head. "I bumped my head on the canoe."

Taylor swam over to him. "I'm sorry. Let me see."

Both treaded water as she examined his scalp. There was a big bump on the back of his head. "I'm so sorry."

Cooper turned to face her just as she swiveled toward him. Caught inches away, they stared at one another.

Cooper's gaze traveled to her lips. "Thanks for checking it out for me."

"Cooper, we need to flip this boat," called Aaron breaking into the moment, breaking the sexual tension between them.

Cooper turned and swam away.

Whoa! She'd been sure he was going to kiss her. That could never happen if she wanted to continue with Pritchard Publishing. Cooper might be her boss one day.

Later, drying off on the sunning rock, Taylor lay stretched out on a towel. She'd spent many lazy afternoons like this. The sounds of people swimming surrounded her, interspersed with the chirping of birds, the quacking of ducks, and the buzzing of bees and other insects flying nearby. The lapping of the water along the rocky shore added music of its own to the lullaby in her head. Her eyes closed. She felt someone move onto the rock next to her and didn't bother to open her eyes.

"Hey, sleepyhead," came a soft voice. "I don't want to disturb the others, but I'm going to go back to the house to get my portable sun umbrella. Without shade, it's too hot."

"Need help?" Taylor asked in a drowsy voice.

"No, thanks. I won't be gone long. I'll borrow your car. All right?" said Whitney.

"Sure. My keys are in my purse with the rest of the stuff. See you later."

After Whitney left, Taylor rolled over onto her stomach to get an even tan on her back. She thought of Cooper and how he'd almost kissed her and wondered what it would've felt like.

CHAPTER TWENTY-THREE
WHITNEY

Whitney left the cottage feeling lonely. Dani and Brad were so in love they didn't even notice the people around them. And if she wasn't mistaken, both Aaron and Cooper were falling for Taylor. Not that Taylor seemed aware of it. She was relatively innocent in the ways of romance. Maybe that's what Cooper was here to help Taylor with, so her writing seemed more authentic.

As Whitney pulled into the driveway, she could hear Mindy bark a greeting. She hadn't wanted to bring the dog to the cottage for fear she'd end up in the lake. Pirate was constantly in the water, and knowing Mindy, she'd want to be in there too.

She opened the front door of the house. Laughing at how excited Mindy was to see her, Whitney swept the dog up into her arms and accepted Mindy's kisses on her cheeks.

"How's my girl?" cooed Whitney, giving her a last hug before setting the dachshund down on the floor and heading to the patio for the umbrella.

The landline rang, but she let it go. They'd been plagued by robot crank calls lately. If anyone important needed her attention, they knew to call her cell.

She grabbed the umbrella, wrestled it to the car, and left.

Back at the cottage, the group was spread out lying or sitting on the blankets and eating grapes and apples.

Aaron stood. "Here, let me get that umbrella for you. Where do you want it?"

Whitney pointed out a spot next to the blanket nearby and, together, they worked the pole into a soft spot in the ground.

Dani walked over and handed her an apple. "Do you mind sharing the shade? I think I've had enough sun for today, but I don't want to leave the lake."

Whitney patted the blanket next to her. "Have a seat."

"It's been a nice day," said Dani. "It's brought back so many memories of past summers. Have you enjoyed yourself?"

"Yes," Whitney responded. "It feels good to get back to basics. I've needed this time away from California. I feel better, stronger, healthier."

Dani put an arm around her. "I've loved having you here. We lost touch for a while."

"I've felt that loss too," Whitney said. Her cell rang, but Whitney didn't even look to see who was calling. She wanted nothing to interrupt this time with her sister.

Dani's cell chimed with a news release. She stretched to where she'd laid it on the blanket next to them. "Wonder what's going on in the world."

"Don't bother," said Whitney. "Let's not ruin this day."

Dani picked the phone up, studied the screen, and grew still.

"What is it?" said Whitney.

"You're going to want to see this, but first check your phone," said Dani.

"Dani, tell me what's wrong," said Whitney feeling her stomach squeeze with worry. Her sister's face had gone white for a moment.

"It's Zane," Dani said. "He's in a coma from an overdose."

Whitney felt her breath leave her in a rush, making her feel dizzy. "He's alive?"

"Check your phone. You probably have more information than I do."

Whitney reached for her cell, checked for messages, and clicked onto the first of five from her agent. Rather than listen to them, she punched in her number. Barbara Griffith was tough as nails, and in her career, she'd handled the worst of news.

Barbara answered on the second ring. "Whitney, Zane tried to kill himself. But before he did, he sent me a message for you. He's alive, but in a coma. Get here as soon as you can."

Whitney made herself breathe slowly in and out, then said, "Okay, I'll be as fast as I can. When you see him, if you can, tell him I'm coming."

"Will do. They aren't allowing visitors at this time, but I know you'll be among those who can, if it's not too late."

Feeling a chill that had nothing to do with the breeze that had sprung up, Whitney turned to Dani with tears in her eyes. "I have to go to L.A."

Dani listened to Whitney's news and stood. "C'mon. I'll drive you to the house. You can pack while I make your travel arrangements." She turned to the others. "Hey, everyone, Whitney is leaving for California. Zane has overdosed and is in a coma. I'm going to help her pack and make flight arrangements."

Taylor ran over and gave Whitney a hug. "I'm so sorry. Please let me know how I can help."

"Will you take care of Mindy? I can't take her with me," said Whitney, her eyes full of fresh tears.

"Sure. Mindy knows I love her. She'll be okay until you return." Taylor gave her another quick hug.

Then before she could totally lose it because of all the emotions overwhelming her, Whitney hurried to the car. The thing she'd feared for so long was finally happening.

Judith Keim

CHAPTER TWENTY-FOUR
TAYLOR

After Dani and Whitney left the cottage, the fun of the afternoon evaporated.

"Hey, bro, please help me get my canoe loaded into the truck," Aaron said to Brad.

As they walked away, Taylor turned to Cooper. "Sorry to end the day on a sad note, but it's been nice having you be part of the group."

"I had fun. Guess I'll go back to the cabin and take care of a few things there." Cooper smiled at her. "Thanks for including me. I'll see you tomorrow morning at your house so our work can begin."

"Okay. I don't think we can put it off any longer," Taylor said, hating the thought.

After they'd taken care of the food, and Aaron had put the coolers in his truck, Cooper folded the blankets, slipped a T-shirt on over his swim trunks, and said, "I'll carry the blankets to your car and then I'll be on my way."

"Thanks," said Taylor. After he left, she took a moment to look out at the lake. It was such a peaceful setting. In the distance, the White Mountains looked majestic as they overlooked the area like a queen surveying her realm.

She turned and trotted to her car sorry the afternoon had ended abruptly with such horrible news.

That evening, Taylor sat on the patio holding Mindy and

talking to her, attempting to get the dog out of her despondent mood with Whitney gone.

Dani came out to join her. "I'm going to spend the night at Brad's. Pirate will be with me. Are you going to be all right alone here with Mindy?"

Taylor chuckled. "Of course. Go have fun. I'm going to relax with a book. It's been a fun celebration, but I have to start thinking of tomorrow when my work begins with Cooper."

"All the more reason to enjoy a book," said Dani. She waved to Taylor and went on her way.

Taylor went inside, gave Mindy her dinner, and got her electronic reader from her room. She didn't like to read in her genre when she was writing and had several historical books to choose from.

Downstairs, rather than have a meal, Taylor chose a crisp Granny Smith apple to eat as she settled on the couch with her book. Mindy slept at Taylor's side. The dog was snoring softly when her ears perked up, and she sprang to her feet.

"What is it?" Taylor asked. It had grown dark while she'd escaped into the author's fictional world.

Mindy jumped off the couch and raced to the door barking.

Wary, Taylor rose from the couch and followed her, wondering why anyone would come there at this late hour.

She peeked through the peep hole in the door and then opened it. "Cooper! What are you doing here?"

"I can't stay in my cabin," he said. "Can I spend the night here?"

Taylor opened the door wider and stepped back. "Come on in. What's going on?"

"It's JoEllen," he said, shaking his head. "She came to my cabin, asked if she could come in, and then proceeded to take off most of her clothes before I could stop her. I'm not sure what's happening, but I can't be caught in a compromising situation. She could claim anything she wants about me with no observers to confirm the truth."

"You think she'd do that?' asked Taylor, stunned by his words.

He nodded. "She's crazy. That's all I'm saying. She has this idea that she's my girlfriend or going to be. I've got to find another place to stay."

"For tonight, you can sleep in Whitney's room. Then I'll help you find another place to stay while you're working with me."

"Thanks, Taylor. I really appreciate it. Too bad something that seemed good turned out to be so twisted."

"I'm really concerned about JoEllen's mental health," said Taylor. "Her morals, too. I found her in my grandmother's room at The Woodlands when she had no business being there. I'm alerting GG to keep an eye out for her and will ask her to let the staff know if there's a problem."

"Maybe we should tell Brad," Cooper said. "As her ex-brother-in-law, he might be able to defuse the situation."

"I'll talk to Dani tomorrow morning, and she can let Brad know what's going on. It's pretty creepy." Taylor led Cooper up to Whitney's room. Whitney, true to her nature, had left it in order.

"Are you sure Whitney won't mind?" Cooper asked.

"I'm sure of it. In fact, she suggested you take over Dani's room while you're here. Dani spends most nights at Brad's house," Taylor said and then wished she'd kept her mouth closed. Having Cooper around would just complicate their working together.

"If that offer still holds, that'll take care of my problems. I'll speak to Dani tomorrow." He stopped and looked at her. "Is that all right with you?"

Not wanting to be churlish, she said, "If that makes it easier for you, yes. You're not planning to stay in town that long, right?"

"I'm not sure. It depends on you and how quickly we deal with the revisions," said Cooper. He gave her a very un-business-like sexy grin that pulled at something inside her. And then worry filled her. He'd learn soon enough that any relationship she'd had in the past had been brief, probably because she was such a dud at romance.

"Well, okay," she managed to say. "We'll work it out. Make yourself comfortable. I'm going to let Mindy outside and then I'm coming to bed too." Furious at the blush that crept up her cheeks, she turned away. *It had sounded as if she was going to go to bed with him.*

As she left the room, Taylor thought she heard a soft chuckle coming from behind her.

Mindy took her time outside stopping to sniff in a dozen places in the yard before she found the perfect spot. Taylor was grateful for the break. As much as she told herself it was foolish, the reality of a man sleeping in a bedroom near hers made her feel awkward. Thank goodness she had her own bathroom and wouldn't have to worry about that aspect of having Cooper in the house.

When she went upstairs, Mindy at her heels, the light that shone under the door of Whitney's room went out. Taylor entered her room, and closed the door behind her with a sigh.

Mindy waited beside the king bed for Taylor to lift her up onto it. Contrary to every ad about the new comfortable beds that all dogs were loving, Mindy insisted on sleeping on top of a human bed with anyone she accepted. Taylor didn't mind. She liked the company, even if Mindy sometimes snored.

Later, Taylor stared up at the ceiling reliving certain moments of the day. Watching the parade had been fun. She remembered Cooper's hand on her waist guiding her to the balcony and wondered if he'd had any of the same feelings at his touch. Maybe having Cooper here would help her appreciate little gestures like that when she dated again.

She thought of Whitney and hoped she'd make it to California in time to talk to Zane. She wasn't sure of any details, but she suspected Zane was the reason Whitney had been so determined to leave L.A.. She knew for certain that Whitney had fallen in love with Zane when they'd been dating. Her sister had admitted it to her one night over a Christmas holiday weekend in Atlanta a few years ago.

Taylor rolled over and hugged Mindy, who was nestled up against her. Her last thoughts before going to sleep were about maybe getting a dog for herself as soon as Cooper left.

The next morning, Taylor awoke to find her door cracked open and Mindy gone from her bed. The scent of freshly brewed coffee lured her downstairs.

She climbed out of bed, threw a robe on over her sleep shorts and tank top, and headed down the stairway. *Cooper was a houseguest, not someone she had to impress,* she told herself, running fingers through her thick, straight hair. Cut shoulder-length, it was fairly easy to maintain. Nothing fancy.

Mindy ran toward her as she entered the empty kitchen. She poured herself a cup of coffee and, out of habit, headed to the patio.

Cooper looked up from his iPad and smiled. "Hope you don't mind, but I made myself at home in the kitchen. And I let Mindy outside. She was whining at the door."

"Mind? Thanks for taking care of Mindy. And it's fantastic to awake to the aroma of fresh-brewed coffee." She settled in a chair opposite him trying not to stare. Wearing just khaki shorts and nothing else, he looked even better today than he had yesterday.

"I figure we can start all over again with a fresh critique by going over the book by chapter. But before we do that, we might want to talk about the characters, so that I have a better understanding of them. Does that sound okay?"

Taylor moved uncomfortably in her chair, but she nodded. They'd be talking about her characters, not her. "Want anything else besides coffee for breakfast?" she asked him.

He gave her a sheepish grin. "I took someone's hardboiled egg out of the refrigerator. I'll replace it later."

"No problem. That was Whitney's. You'll have plenty of time to do that while she's away." Taylor got up and went inside to fix herself toast with a boiled egg. The protein would be healthy for her. She was beginning to get nervous about the day ahead.

Cooper followed her inside. "If you're okay with my using Whitney's room for a couple of days while I try to find something to rent, I'll go clear out my stuff from the cabin. I've thought about what happened last night, and I want no part of any issues with JoEllen. She's a problem."

"Yes, I'm not sure what's going on with her, but it isn't normal. She'll do anything to change her life but not in a normal way. Even the idea of marrying her dead sister's husband is so weird it's sickening."

"It sure is." Cooper threaded his fingers through his hair and shook his head "I can't get involved in a scandal. That would ruin any chance I have at running the business."

"I never asked, but are you an only child?" said Taylor.

"I have an older sister, Candace," Cooper said. "She's already in training for the role of publisher. We've talked about it, and she isn't sure that's what she really wants, but she wants to prove herself to our mother."

"Well, I promise you I won't involve you in any scandal,

and I'll try my best to work with you." Taylor was pleased to see a look of relief cross his face.

After fixing herself breakfast, Taylor went upstairs to get dressed, amused by Mindy following her every step of the way.

Later, dressed for the day, the two of them sat in the shade of a maple tree in the back yard. Cooper had a notebook with him but set it aside. "Let's talk about the main characters in the book. You have a young woman who is a schoolteacher and loves children and a man who's free-spirited, is a fireman, has many girlfriends, and isn't ready to settle down. Is that it?"

Taylor nodded. "In a nutshell."

"Okay. Let's go deeper. Has the woman, Vanessa, ever had boyfriends, dates as an adult, lovers?" asked Cooper.

Taylor squirmed. She'd done her character studies, of course, but had never been pinned down by hazel eyes boring into her to describe the background of a character. "She's dated and thought one relationship was serious, but it didn't work out."

"Did she and that man have sex? Often? What interests did they share? How deep was that relationship?

Taylor swallowed hard, trying to think on her feet. He wasn't talking about her, she reminded herself. "Well, they both liked to watch baseball and other sports. That's where Vanessa meets Tom, the fireman. In a sports bar when she went there with a friend."

"But what about the relationship before this one?" Cooper asked. "What drew Tom to Vanessa if she hadn't had a deep relationship before, maybe some experience with a man? You know, be a little sexy? After all, he's a hot guy who's popular with women."

"I don't want her to be easy," protested Taylor. "My readers would hate that."

Cooper shook his head. "That's not what I'm after. As your editor, I want to know the why behind the scenes, so the characters have more depth." He studied her. "You know what I'm talking about. Give that experience to your characters. Maybe if Vanessa had a troubled relationship in the past, she'd be unimpressed with Tom, which might provoke his interest. That kind of thing."

"Now that I hear you say it, I know you're right. I'll try to work on her background and make her more interesting, give her more motivation for her actions," said Taylor.

"And what about Tom?" Cooper asked. "What's his story?"

"I created his background of family, friends, interests ..." Taylor began.

"Yes, but we need to go deeper," said Cooper.

Taylor looked at him and sighed. "Maybe that's something you can help me with. I have only sisters, so I need your perspective as a man."

Cooper made a face. "Okay, we'll spend a lot of time together, and I'll explain what's going through my mind, and you tell me what's going through yours, so we can make these characters irresistible to one another. I'm going to make some notes on this, and then I'm going to get the rest of my things from the cabin and check out."

"I'll write up a stronger character description for Vanessa," said Taylor rising. She could hardly wait to get back to the safety of her room and her computer.

"Then, why don't we go to lunch at the café? We can observe others and check our own reactions to what's going on," said Cooper.

"Okay," said Taylor. "That might be helpful."

She said goodbye to Cooper and went to her room. Sitting in front of her computer, she felt like a fraud. How could she write about a strong, sexy romance if she'd never had much of one herself? Research apparently didn't provide all those feelings Cooper was looking for. She thought back to Rob Ellsworth, the man she thought she'd marry after being together for two years in college. She saw now it was a relationship that was comfortable for them both. They'd lived together, studied together, and made love. But there was no burning desire to be together or to make too many plans. It was all so ... easy. Is that why she'd wanted this new book to be better, deeper, more complicated?

CHAPTER TWENTY-FIVE
TAYLOR

The café was crowded when they arrived. Dani was sitting at a table on the patio with Bethany Beckman, who'd taken a break from her store at Beckman Lumber.

Dani waved them over. "Come join us."

Cooper followed Taylor to the table and then stood and helped Taylor with her chair before sitting down.

"Such a gentleman," said Bethany smiling at him.

Taylor made the introductions and then turned to her sister. "What's happening?"

"Bethany and I are talking about some of the decorative items Whitney ordered from her store. She has some other ideas as well. But basically, it's just the two of us having lunch together. How about you and Cooper?" Dani asked, smiling at them both.

Taylor turned to Cooper.

"We're doing some research for the book," he said, smiling at her. "You're both looking great."

Bethany's cheeks grew pink. "Thanks. You're talking to a pregnant woman who is beginning to cope with all the changes her body is going through. So, I welcome the remark."

Dani chuckled. "I'll take a compliment like that anytime."

Taylor studied Cooper's eyes, brightened by the interchange, and realized how attractive he was. She felt the beginnings of jealousy at the way he continued to speak to them, but then she pushed the feeling away. It wasn't part of the research.

Nick walked by in his uniform and waved to them, and she couldn't help smiling. Their town may be small, but it had the sexiest sheriff alive.

"Are you ready to order?" Cooper asked, drawing her attention. A waitress stood nearby.

"Oh, sure," she replied, already knowing she'd order the chicken Caesar salad.

The waitress took their orders and left.

This time, it was Cooper who was distracted as he watched her walk away.

"The waitress sure is cute. Right, Cooper?" teased Dani.

He laughed. "How's the cottage coming? I heard the walls were in and being painted. That's a big step."

"Yes," said Dani, "but it's only one step. There are still many more to go. The trim and the floors need to be done. We're thinking about adding on a sunporch or possibly another room. And nothing has been done with the attic. But that won't happen for some time."

"Because of the ghost?" Cooper said.

"Ghost? What ghost? Do you mean Mrs. Maynard?" Bethany waved away his concern. "That's nothing but an old town rumor. Garth has told me all about it."

Taylor couldn't stop a shiver from racing down her back. It would take several months of living in the cottage before she'd believe it.

"There are still decisions to be made regarding the cottage," said Dani. "But I don't believe there'll be any problem in moving in by the fall." She stiffened as JoEllen walked onto the patio with one of the staff from The Woodlands. They followed a hostess to a corner table.

After they were seated, JoEllen rose from her chair and walked over to them. "Hello, Dani, Taylor." She smiled at Cooper. "I'm sorry to lose you as a neighbor, but we can still be friends." She leaned forward so that her breasts were more visible in the V-neck shirt she wore with her short skirt.

"I don't think so. I'm uncomfortable with what you did," he said pleasantly, but Taylor was aware of the pulsing in his temple, the slight flare to his nose. She made note of those details.

"You need to grow up," JoEllen huffed and stormed off.

After JoEllen left, Taylor turned to Cooper. "You were honest. I like that."

He grinned. "What a piece of work that woman is. She saw me packing up this morning and asked me why I'd consider leaving when we lived so close together?"

Dani shook her head. "She has no clue about the way others perceive her, and she doesn't respect anyone's boundaries."

"Not a healthy combination," said Bethany. "She and I don't usually speak, as you may have noticed. She was after Garth a couple of years ago on a visit, even when she knew we were about to get married. Neither of us was happy to see her back in town."

"We should all keep our distance," said Dani.

Their food arrived and it grew quiet as they dug into their meals.

As Taylor ate, she observed the other customers. Now that she was on the lookout for other people's emotions, she was surprised by the drama around them. Bob Bullard and his wife, Edie, who helped her husband at their hardware store, were having a quiet disagreement, while Estelle Bookbinder, owner of Page's bookstore was deep in conversation with another older woman, breaking into laughter from time to time.

Her gaze caught the attention of Ross's friend, Mike Dawson. At his grin, she felt her cheeks grow hot. She quickly looked away and noticed Cooper's eyes on her. She went back to eating her salad.

When they'd completed their meal, Cooper said to Dani and Bethany, "Thanks for sharing your table. It was nice to meet you, Bethany, and to see you again, Dani."

"We'll have to do this another time," said Bethany. "I don't get away from the store as much as I'd like, but it's healthy for me."

Cooper stood and helped Bethany out of the chair as Taylor watched with interest. He seemed especially gentle with her, no doubt because of the pregnancy. He could sometimes be a real gentleman.

After lunch Taylor and Cooper walked back to the house. She was glad for the opportunity to think things over as they traveled along the sidewalk. Cooper walked ahead, and when he realized she was making no effort to keep up with him, he slowed his pace.

"We're in the country, remember? No need to rush around," she teased.

He laughed. "It's not something I can change right away. Practice. Practice."

She stopped walking when she saw a Monarch butterfly alight on a red geranium bloom in a nearby pot beside a front walkway. "They're so beautiful," she said in a hushed tone. The orange and black creature fluttered its wings and then rose and flew away.

"I forget how much of that kind of thing I miss in the city," said Cooper giving her an appreciative smile.

She remained standing and searched for another.

"C'mon, we've got work to do," he said, taking hold of her hand.

Their magnetism flared, and it felt as if an electric current flowed between them as they stared at one another in surprise.

Her entire arm afire, Taylor pulled her hand away, trying to cover her awkwardness by drawing his attention to another butterfly hovering nearby.

He gazed at the spot she'd pointed out, but she knew he was as shaken as she. She'd written about that kind of scene, but experiencing it with him brought out more than just a shock of attraction. Her whole body wanted to curl into his arms. Stunned by her reaction, she hurried ahead.

He caught up to her. "Hey! Where are you going?"

She turned to him. "I ... I just need to get home." She wanted to hide from her embarrassment, but there was no place to go except home.

She walked ahead at a fast pace.

Cooper kept up beside her. "Look, I didn't mean to make you feel uncomfortable."

"It's not that," she said, lying to him and herself. But she didn't want to address her reaction to him on the streets of her small town. As it was, probably half the people living there already knew Cooper had moved into the house and thought more than friendship was going on. Even that thought made her uncomfortable.

When they arrived back at the house, Dani met them at the door.

"Taylor, would you mind going to the cottage with me? I want you to look at the trim sample for the living room. Whitney picked it out with me, but with her being gone, I'd like your opinion on how it looks in the house."

"Sure, no problem," said Taylor, relieved to think of something else besides the man beside her.

"Would you like to come along for the ride?" Dani asked Cooper.

"Thanks, I'd like that," said Cooper sounding as relieved as Taylor felt.

They climbed into Dani's car and went to check on the cottage.

CHAPTER TWENTY-SIX

DANI

During the drive, Dani felt the sexual tension humming between Taylor and Cooper and smiled. She and Whitney had thought the two of them together were cute, and now she knew it was more than that. Not that either Taylor or Cooper seemed comfortable with it. Most of Taylor's romance had come from books, not from relating to a hot man right beside her.

Dani parked her car at the garage, and while Pirate took off running, she led Taylor and Cooper to the front of the house.

"Ah, I see the sunning rock. Why don't I meet you two there?" said Cooper. "It'll give you a chance to talk privately and me a chance to relax."

"We shouldn't be long," said Dani. That would be one way for him to cool off, she thought, amused by the two of them.

The finish carpenters had set up a table saw on the porch.

Inside, the new walls had been prepped and painted a very pale green that warmed what otherwise might seem a cold interior.

"They started putting the crown molding in the upstairs rooms," said Dani. "Downstairs, we're going for something a little more ornate and wider. Before they do that, I want you to look at it and see if you agree. It will be painted a complimentary color that Whitney chose and will reconfirm."

"I'm sure I'll be happy with anything she chooses," said Taylor. "She has excellent taste."

They climbed the stairs and walked into one of the

bedrooms. A carpenter was nailing trim in place.

"What do you think?" asked Dani.

Taylor studied the simple trim. "I like it. It adds a nice finishing touch to the room."

They returned downstairs and looked at the sample of the molding Whitney had chosen. It was like the molding upstairs, but an additional small, concave section at the top made it a little wider, a bit fancier.

"I like that it's simple. I don't think we need anything formal for this house," said Taylor, more excited about the cottage than she'd ever been. It was coming together nicely. And she saw no sign of a ghost anywhere.

Pleased, Dani stepped outside with Taylor.

Observing Taylor searching for Cooper on the rock, Dani placed her hand on Taylor's shoulder. "Go ahead. Get him. I'll wander up to the inn to give you some time alone."

"Thanks," said Taylor.

Dani left. It was obvious Taylor wanted to talk to Cooper, and there was no better place to do that than on the sunning rock.

CHAPTER TWENTY-SEVEN
TAYLOR

Cooper was lying on the rock when Taylor approached. When he heard her, he rolled over to his side and looked up at her with a smile.

At that sexy grin, Taylor's pulse sprinted, but she hid her excitement at seeing him and sat down.

He sat up and faced her, a look of concern on his face. "I don't mean to make you uncomfortable. We have to make this project work."

"It's not you. It's me," she said feeling like a fool as tears stung her eyes. She blinked rapidly and looked away, studying the lake. She had to get over the uneasiness he caused within her because of her growing feelings for him. The lapping of the water against the rock calmed her.

He put an arm around her shoulder. "I like you, Taylor. We've gotten to know each other a little more. You can tell me anything you want, and I promise it won't go further."

She continued gazing out at the water realizing she'd never had a close male friend before. Women in today's world went after what they wanted. Why did she feel so awkward about expressing her feelings?

"Let's go back and talk some more about the characters. That way, we don't have to get personal." Cooper held out his hand to help her up, and she took it.

For a moment they stood face to face. Cooper, taller than she, stared down at her with a tender expression and cupped her face in his broad hands. "We'll make this work, Taylor. I promise."

She looked up at him. His gaze reached inside her and then he cleared his throat and looked away. "Guess we'd better go."

"Yes," said Taylor, trying to disguise her disappointment. She'd thought he was going to kiss her. But it was for the best that it didn't happen. She couldn't jeopardize her career because she was finding herself drawn to the man who'd made her question her writing ability. It could happen again.

They walked up to the house just as Dani appeared. "Ready?" she asked.

"Yep, thanks, we're all set," Cooper answered and then turned and winked at Taylor.

At home, Taylor went to her office and sat in front of the computer writing up what had just happened between Cooper and her. It wasn't something for others to read but would serve as research for her characters and how she could deepen them. If she got used to the routine of writing down her feelings from time to time, she knew she could do a better job with her stories. It galled her to admit that Cooper's first impression of her manuscript was right. She could go deeper, make her characters more layered.

She'd promised to meet Cooper outside, and as soon as she finished typing, she went downstairs feeling good about the work she'd done.

Cooper was making notes when she approached him on the patio. "I've got a suggestion."

"Me, too," Taylor said. "I thought of it as I was working upstairs. I think we should go through each chapter of the book with you taking the hero's role and me as Vanessa. We'll take notes as we go. That will make the changes to the book seem authentic."

He held up his notebook and chuckled. "Great minds think alike. And it'll be safe because we'll be dealing with the characters, not ourselves. Does that make it comfortable for you?"

Taylor smiled. "Yes. I've already got some additional ideas for Vanessa's background."

"We ought to be able to complete this in no time," said Cooper, grinning.

Taylor hoped so because as exciting as it was to get a better understanding of the characters, it was scary too.

Cooper stood. "I think it might work better if we were in a different setting away from your desk. We can talk more freely then."

"Where do you suggest?"

"Let's go back to the inn. I noticed some signs for walking trails there. Or we could go to Stan's and use the walking trails there. I've heard Stan's has the best lobsters and clams around."

"Stan's is also known because it's an excellent birding place. I'll bring the binoculars our landlady, Margaret, keeps in the kitchen."

"That way, even as we talk, we'll have other things to see, making it less of an inquisition." Cooper smiled. "And we could even grab an early dinner there."

"I knew there was an ulterior motive," she said laughing.

His eyes twinkled as he grinned and shrugged.

Moments later, Taylor sat in the passenger seat of Cooper's silver BMW wagon. She'd figured he'd own something bigger, but he'd explained there was no point when he lived in the city.

"I brought along this bird book too," said Taylor. "I figure we might as well know what we're looking at, though I've learned about a number of them through GG."

Cooper gave her a nod of approval. "The important thing is to get comfortable so we can be honest with one another."

"You mean our characters, not us. Right?"

Cooper chuckled. "Sure. It'll be easiest if we stick to that."

At Stan's, the rustic one-story building was quiet. A few cars sat in the parking lot, but the empty spaces would, she knew, be full later with dinner customers.

They climbed out of the car and stood facing each other with smiles.

"It's so peaceful here," said Cooper. "I've lived in the city so long all the noise seems like low background music as I go about my daily life."

Taylor liked that he noticed things like that. Maybe that's why he'd been so picky about her book. The setting might need strengthening too.

They walked behind Stan's and onto the trail that bordered the small creek. Taylor stood a moment watching the water move slowly, hugging rocks that poked above the surface like an embrace it was reluctant to end. A couple of small sticks floated on the water's surface, adventurers facing the unknown.

Cooper came up behind her and whispered, "Look! A woodpecker."

She looked where he'd pointed, saw the red nape on the black and white bird and said softly, "It's a Downy Woodpecker."

He smiled at her. "Maybe you'd better give me the binoculars. Looks like you might not need them."

She laughed. "Let's go up the trail. They have a series of benches along the path. We can find one and sit and talk."

The creek entered the woods and they followed, coming to a clearing where a wooden bench sat.

"This is perfect," said Taylor. She sat and patted the space next to her.

"Okay, let's talk about Vanessa first. Why is she so unsure about love, herself?" said Cooper giving her a steady look.

"Okay, Vanessa has a younger sister who gets all the attention leaving her to wonder about her place in the family."

"Does she or I should say did she have a boyfriend before meeting Tom?" Cooper asked.

"She had one boyfriend who was serious, but it didn't last. There wasn't enough passion," said Taylor, liking the idea of recreating her character.

"So, she's basically inexperienced?" Cooper asked.

Taylor felt a need to defend Vanessa. "She's popular but shy."

"And she always has that feeling that maybe she doesn't measure up?" said Cooper.

Taylor thought about it. "Yes, I think that's what's keeping her back in the beginning. So that's how we'll show her growth."

Cooper smiled with approval.

"What about Tom?" she asked. "I have him as someone super confident but maybe with a hidden story. What should we do with him?"

Cooper rubbed his chin. "How about if we tie his backstory to his father? We could say his father was successful at everything he did, and Tom wanted to measure up."

"Or we could say his father deserted him and his two sisters when he was just a kid," said Taylor, getting into this game of what-ifs. A sadness crossed Cooper's face and she held her breath. When he didn't speak, she asked softly, "Is that what happened to you?"

Cooper let out a sigh, stood up and walked to the water's edge. He picked up a stone and threw it as far as he could down the creek. When he turned back to her, he said, "It's a short story. My father and grandfather were both killed in a small, private airplane accident along with the pilot, a friend of my father's."

Taylor felt the blood leave her head and gasped. "That's awful. How old were you?"

"Nine," Cooper said and turned away from her again.

Taylor got up and went to him. "I'm so sorry," she said, taking hold of his hand. "What a horrible thing for you and your family to go through. Is that why you're so determined to run the family business?"

"It's more complicated than that," said Cooper. "Being head of our small publishing company isn't like running a family business. We have a board of directors and other people guiding us and sometimes fighting our decisions."

"Was the accident how your mother ended up being head of the company?" Taylor asked.

"Yes, she fought for the position and won because my father had always relied upon her help. It was natural that she took over. She was glad to do it even with having to take care of my sister and me." He dropped her hand. "Sorry, we got off track."

"No, it's good that we could talk about your situation so we can make Tom's situation stronger. We could say Tom's father was a fireman who'd died in a fire and that's why he's so dedicated to the job."

They sat down on the bench and each of them made notes. But as Taylor was writing, she was imagining the pain of a nine-year-old boy losing both his father and grandfather and how it would've affected the rest of his life. She'd been a baby in many ways at that age, still enjoying the steady love and support from both her parents.

After a while, Cooper looked up at her. "I think this system is going to work. Now we need to go a little deeper. What is it that Vanessa wants, the one thing that is important to her?"

Taylor stared out at the creek and heard the song of a cardinal. She could decide to be less than honest but what would that get her? Nothing. Trying to make Cooper believe it was Vanessa she was talking about, Taylor said, "Vanessa wants children. She teaches first-graders and wonders what it would be like to have her own family. Maybe because she wants to share their excitement in learning something new about themselves and the world."

Cooper smiled at her. "I like that. I know from your words that she would make an excellent mother and so will the reader. So, let's use that as her beginning."

"What about Tom?" Taylor said. "What is it that he wants?"

Cooper gave her a puzzled look. "I'm not sure what he wants most of all."

"Does he want a family too?" Taylor asked him and then looked away. It felt like she was asking Cooper that question.

"I think Tom wants to prove that his father would be proud of him," said Cooper quietly. "I would say his father was as kind as he was tough, and Tom wants to be like that."

"I like that. So maybe we show him as tougher in the beginning of the book so that his story has a solid arc to it," said Taylor. She grinned at him. "I'm already liking the changes we're making."

"Me, too," said Cooper reaching for her hand. "I never meant to hurt you. I just wanted you to see that the story had to be deeper. This is only the beginning. But enough for now. We can make notes later. Let's go enjoy dinner at Stan's. I hear the food is terrific."

"Okay," said Taylor, shivering slightly as Cooper continued to hold her hand. The warmth of it frightened her because she realized she was already falling for Cooper.

They packed up their laptops and headed back down the trail toward Stan's.

Inside Stan's restaurant and bar, clients were starting to fill seats at the bar and a few spilled over onto seats at tables.

"Glad we got here now," said Cooper as they waited for the hostess to seat them.

At their table, Cooper held out her chair and waited for her to be seated before settling in a chair opposite her.

"Summertime hours are longer and earlier," said Taylor looking around at the other customers. "Vacationers aren't as worried about schedules."

"In New York, summers are slower, more relaxed because so many residents try to escape the heat. Even if people can't get away for the entire week, three-day weekends tend to happen."

"You mentioned Long Island. Is that where your family spent summers?" Taylor asked.

"Not entire summers, but many long weekends. As kids, though, my sister and I stayed for most of the summer with Mrs. Bidwell, our housekeeper, whom we affectionately called Biddy." The corners of his mouth curved happily. "I still see her from time to time. She's elderly now and living in an assisted living community outside of the city."

"That's nice of you," said Taylor, impressed.

"My mother was always busy, so Biddy was important to us, especially after my father's accident," said Cooper. "Talking about your character, Tom, has brought back some of those memories."

"At the lake, you mentioned canoeing at summer camp," Taylor said, sincerely interested in the man she was getting to know.

"I went for a few summers after Dad was gone, but Long Island days were fun too. We did some sailing, and I had friends there. We all went to a private boarding school in upstate New York. Those of us still left in the area get together from time to time."

"It's nice that you have such close friends," said Taylor. "Most of the girls I grew up with have stayed in the South, but we keep in touch through social media. I have friends in New York and, of course, my writing friends."

Their waitress arrived with a pitcher of water and menus. "What can I get you to drink?" she asked while pouring water into their glasses.

"I'm going to have one of your IPAs on draft," said Cooper. "What would you like, Taylor?"

Taylor chose a glass of pinot noir, and Cooper ordered his beer, and then they spent time looking at their menus.

"I'm changing my mind by the minute," said Taylor. "Everything looks delicious."

"A woman's privilege," said Cooper, chuckling. "Choose whatever you'd like. I'm going to go with old-fashioned Fish and Chips."

"Mmm...sounds tasty, but I'll choose a lobster roll. That makes it a truly special summer day."

The waitress returned with their drinks, and after placing their orders, Taylor sat back in her chair looking around with interest. It surprised her how many details she observed and stored in her mind for story material.

"Thank you," said Cooper, jarring her out of her thoughts.

She faced him. "For what?"

"For participating in this plan to help the book. It's a way to help me too, you know. My mother expects me to take on a role at the publishing house as the head of acquisitions in the future."

"Is that what you want to do?" asked Taylor.

"Yes, finding talent and helping it to grow is a skill set few people can do well. I want to be the best at it." He gave her a sheepish grin. "I know I was clumsy in my approach to you. It was a terrible mistake and I'm sorry."

"Thanks," Taylor responded. He, too, had a lot to learn, but he was trying to his job.

CHAPTER TWENTY-EIGHT
WHITNEY

The flight to LAX was, for Whitney, one of the worst times of her life as she relived both the good times and bad with Zane. It was hard to believe that when they'd both been fresh and new in the business, they'd been so naïve, had so easily fallen in love. True, he was one of the most handsome men she'd ever known, but more than that, he'd had a vulnerable core that was endearing to her. While it lasted, their romance had been special, and then the adulation of his fans became a problem. She knew why, of course, but others had no suspicion how undeserving it had felt to him at the beginning.

Whitney sighed and gazed out the window, tired of holding back tears in fear of bringing attention to herself. Since being back in Lilac Lake, she'd cut her hair a couple of inches shorter and was wearing a baseball cap and sunglasses. Even so, people stared at her. She curled up in her seat and stared out the window at the growing dark as the plane zoomed west on a mission of its own.

After she deplaned at the airport, she went to the baggage claim area as requested and found her agent, Barbara Griffith, waiting for her there with a limo driver. At the sight of Barbara, a take-charge woman with short gray hair in a pixie style that suited her strong features, Whitney broke down in tears, releasing all of those she'd held back on the plane.

Barbara wrapped her arms around her and spoke softly.

"I'm going to get you out of here and to the hospital as quickly as possible. Where are your bags?"

"I have just one. It's turquoise with a turquoise ribbon on it."

"Okay." She turned and gave instructions to the driver, then led Whitney to the car, marching in front of her like a lioness leading her cub.

Whitney followed and gratefully slid into the back seat of the limo, pleased by the darkened windows.

"Is Zane still alive?" Whitney asked in a shaky voice.

"Yes, but it's bad. Even if he wakes up, they're worried about both his heart and his brain." Barbara's eyes filled with tears. "He left a note for you."

"I should've been there for him," sobbed Whitney.

"Don't say that. You did everything you could to help. He knows you loved him. That's what is important," said Barbara. "Believe me, this isn't the first nor will it be the last time when someone gets caught up in drugs. Unless they get help, there's no happy ending."

"That's what I tried to tell him," Whitney said, holding onto her stomach as a wave of nausea hit her.

"You should be aware the press knows Zane left you a note. They'll want to know what it said, but I've told them it's highly personal information, and it's wrong of them to pursue it."

"Fat good that will do," said Whitney, aware of the bitterness in her voice.

"We'll take things one step at a time. My suggestion is to say as little as possible. It's helpful that you'd already stepped back from the show. On the other hand, this drama could be a help in the future when you're seeking more work."

Whitney made a sound of disgust.

"I know that sounds awful," said Barbara, "but it's my job to keep you busy, help make you successful. Besides, this is all for a later time. Not now."

Whitney let out a long sigh, thrilled she'd decided to stay in Lilac Lake for the foreseeable future.

When they arrived at the hospital, a few paparazzi were hanging around the entrance but not the number Whitney had dreaded. She waited for Barbara to get out of the car and then followed her with her head down, following Barbara inside by watching her feet.

Barbara walked past the reception area to the elevators, and Whitney realized she'd spent a lot of time here. But then, Zane was her client too.

On the third floor they were directed to Zane's private room in the ICU.

Seeing Zane hooked up to a respirator and other equipment to keep him alive, Whitney held back a sob. The person in that bed was a far cry from the man with whom she'd fallen in love. A burst of anger inside Whitney caught her off guard. She'd tried and tried to warn him of the dangerous road he was on, that she'd be there for him if he sought help. Now, it was far too late.

A nurse approached Barbara and led her out of the room. Whitney heard them talking and knew it was bad. She walked over to Zane and wrapped her hand around his.

"Oh, Zane, what have you done?" she whispered. "Wherever you are, I wish you all the best. Carry my love with you." When she leaned over to kiss his cheek, a tear fell. As she turned away, she saw that Barbara had come back into the room.

"It's over," said Barbara. Tears rolled down her cheeks unobstructed. "The nurse explained to me that they kept him on life support until you could get here." Barbara turned away from Whitney, her shoulders shaking.

Whitney hurried over to her and then felt her legs grow weak, making her unsteady on her feet. They clung to each other, weeping softly. Zane had been such a handsome man, so full of life, when he and Whitney had first met.

"A few months ago, Zane made me his legal guardian," Barbara said in a trembling voice. "I suspect he knew he might not make it. And now, I'll make sure the hospital follows the Living Will I urged him to complete when he had a lawyer draw up his will."

Whitney rubbed Barbara's back, "He knew you'd do what he wanted. He trusted you."

"Oh, what a sad, horrible mess this is. I've seen a lot, endured a lot, but this is breaking my heart. The two of you together were a dream come true for any romantic. Now, four years later, it's over." Barbara brought herself up straight. "Whitney, honey, what can I do for you?"

"Just be there for everyone who loved him, help them remember the person he used to be. The one I once fell in love with," said Whitney, feeling as if they were talking about a stranger. The one Zane had become.

CHAPTER TWENTY-NINE
DANI

Satisfied with the job that she'd done for Anthony Albono designing an apartment building for him in Providence, Rhode Island, Dani headed north to New Hampshire. She was anxious to see Brad. Though she'd been gone only a couple of days, it had seemed much longer. His presence and the love they shared brought her a joy that filled her being, and when he wasn't around, she felt a loss.

Her cell phone rang. *Whitney.*

Dani punched in the button on her car's console, and Whitney's voice came through. "Hello? Dani?"

"Hey, sis. You're on the car phone. How are you? How's Zane?"

Whitney's sob filled the car. "He's gone, Dani. Gone. There's nothing more I can do for him."

"I'm so sorry to hear this, Whitney. What happened?"

"He never recovered from his coma. The ICU nurses kept him hooked up to life support until I could get there, and then Barbara had to inform them about the Living Will he'd signed recently. It was as if he knew this was going to happen."

"What about the message he sent you?" Dani's heart clenched when she heard Whitney break down and sob.

"The message was that he'd always loved me even when he didn't show it. He also asked me to honor what we once had with all that he was leaving me," Whitney managed to finally say.

"What do you mean leaving you?"

Whitney's voice was shaky as she said, "He's left everything to me."

"Oh," said Dani, unsure whether that was a good thing or not. There would be money but a host of other things to deal with. "Are you going to be all right with that?"

"Yes," said Whitney. "Back in the better days, one of the things we talked about is what we could do with some of the money we were earning. That part will be rewarding."

"What about a memorial service?" Dani.

"Barbara was Zane's agent, too. She and I decided to hold off on any kind of service for a while. He was estranged from what family he had. His mother was a single mom with drug problems, and he had an older sister who left home when he was just eleven, something he deeply resented. But he had both personal friends and those he worked with here."

"Is there anything I can do?" Dani asked.

After a pause, Whitney said in a small voice, "Would you be willing to come to L.A. for a few days while things get sorted out? I feel so lost. I know Mom would come, but you know how she gets if she thinks one of her girls is suffering—like a mother hen protecting her baby chick. And Taylor is working with Cooper, and I don't want to interrupt that."

"Of course, I'll come. I was headed home from Rhode Island, but I'll go to my condo in Boston and fly out to LAX as soon as I can. I'll let you know my flight schedule."

"Thank you, thank you," said Whitney. "I'm on an emotional roller coaster and need your steadying hand."

"You got it," said Dani, pleased to have Whitney's faith in her to help.

They ended the call and Dani called Brad to give him the news.

"I understand," Brad said after they'd talked about it. "I'd want to do the same for anyone in my family. But hurry home as soon as you can. I miss you like crazy."

Dani's lips curved at the affection in his voice. "Not as much as I miss you. I'll call you when I get to L.A.."

She'd remained calm while on the phone with Whitney, but now, as she headed into Boston, Dani realized how shaken she was by Whitney's request. Whitney had always prided herself on being self-sufficient, and she'd sounded like a broken wreck.

CHAPTER THIRTY
TAYLOR

Taylor ended the call with Whitney unnerved by the depth of Whitney's pain and her emotional state. Though, she'd offered to come to L.A., Taylor understood that Whitney wanted her to continue working with Cooper, and that Dani would go to California to represent the rest of the family. It was sweet, in a way, that Whitney was so concerned about Taylor's career. But then, she'd always supported Taylor's desire to become a writer.

Taylor got up from her chair on the patio where she'd been discussing her book with Cooper and walked out onto the lawn to the section where their landlady had planted roses. Sensing movement, Pirate and Mindy, roused from their naps and followed her like the faithful dogs they were.

Needing something so full of life, so real to settle her thoughts on, Taylor leaned over and sniffed a delicate pink rose. The aroma filled her with a sense of wonder. As difficult, as painful as life could be, things like these beautiful roses seemed to balance it. At thirty-five, Zane was only ten years older than she and much too young to die. Like her sisters, Taylor had stayed away from drugs. She wasn't interested in something that could mess with her mind. She already had a vivid imagination and didn't want anything to taint or destroy it.

Cooper came up behind her and placed a hand on her shoulder. "Are you alright? What's going on?"

She turned to him, and he thumbed a tear off her cheek.

"Tell me," he urged showing his concern.

"It's Whitney's co-star, Zane Blanchard. He died. He never recovered from his coma. In fact, they kept him on life support until Whitney could get there. She's taking it badly. I feel so sorry for her. It's such a heartbreaking situation. He was only thirty-five."

"Yeah, that's really sad," said Cooper shaking his head.

"I never got into drugs; I promised my parents I wouldn't," said Taylor.

"I've done my share of weed in college, but now that I'm working in the family business, I stay away from it." He gave her a rueful smile. "I already have enough problems being an editor. I don't need any drug to mess me up more."

They smiled at one another, and then Cooper took hold of her hand. "C'mon. Let's go back to our imaginary people. We're almost done with chapter one."

"Okay." They'd already agreed on the major characteristics and issues of the hero and heroine and were now introducing the characters to the readers. Having known more of their backgrounds, Taylor liked them even better.

Later, they decided to go to the cottage. Aaron had promised to leave his canoe there after using it himself for an early morning session on the lake.

At the house, a contractor's truck for floor refinishing stood in the driveway.

"Looks like the floors are finally being refinished," said Taylor, smiling. "It's getting close to the time when furniture can be moved in. Whitney's in charge of all that, so it'll be a while. There's no hurry. Dani and I rented Marjorie's house through September."

She grabbed the bag with towels and sunscreen, while Cooper carried the small cooler filled with lemonade, fresh fruit, and cookies.

They walked to the front of the house. The porch still needed to be redone, and the exterior of the building needed fresh paint. The decision of adding onto the back of the house was still uncertain, and the attic hadn't been touched.

A sign at the front entrance read: *Do Not Enter! Floors being refinished.*

Cooper let out a soft groan. "Someday I want to go inside the house and see if I can find your ghost."

Taylor held up a hand. "Don't even talk about it. We don't want anything to happen to upset peace in the house."

He laughed and gazed at her with a teasing grin. "You're scared."

"So, what if I am?" Taylor retorted. "I'm not the only one who's uncomfortable inside."

"I'm just teasing you," said Cooper. "Let's hurry and get in the water. It's hot."

Taylor rushed forward. It would feel fantastic to strip her T-shirt and shorts down to her bathing suit and feel the cool lake water on her skin. She liked that she and Cooper were working outside on the book in this hot weather because it made it seem safer to talk about the book without her desk computer staring at her.

Taylor tossed her clothes to one side and began rubbing suntan lotion on her arms and legs.

"Want me to get your back?" Cooper asked.

"Thanks," she replied, handing him the bottle of lotion.

She stood still while he poured lotion on his hands and told herself to relax when his hand touched her back. As he rubbed in the lotion, goosepimples swept across her skin, and it took all her effort not to moan at the effect he was having on her.

"Are you cold?" he asked.

She shook her head. "No, it must be the breeze that came

up," she said, and realized there wasn't even the slightest breeze in the air around them.

At Cooper's soft chuckle, she kept her back to him, certain he'd be wearing a smug look. And why not? She wasn't the only woman who'd fallen for him. He was a handsome man who was much nicer than she'd thought.

When he finished covering her back, he handed her the bottle of lotion. "How about doing the same for me?" He turned away from her, and she stood a moment assessing his body. Neither too thin nor heavy, his muscular body showed the effects of working out from time to time. She poured the lotion onto her palm and rubbed her hand against his back, loving the feel of his ripped body beneath it.

When she finished, she said, "All done," and handed him the bottle.

He turned and settled his gaze on her lips and she noticed his hazel eyes now held a hint of green. Pausing for a moment, he gave her a questioning look before stepping closer, wrapping her in his arms, and kissing her.

Swept up in a cloud of desire, she vaguely heard the sigh that escaped her as his arms tightened around her.

When they pulled apart, Cooper smiled and cupped her face in his broad hands. "Wow," he said softly. "That's definitely something we want to put in your book."

She laughed, happier than she'd ever been. And when he kissed her again, this time deeper, she responded.

A few minutes later, he took her hand, "C'mon, I think I'd better get into that cold water."

She stopped him. "This isn't smart. You and me. We're supposed to be working together."

"I know," Cooper said, meeting her worried look. "My mother won't be pleased. I'm here to do a job."

"Maybe it would be best to just remain friends," said Taylor wanting to cry.

"Too late." Cooper drew her into his arms and kissed her. "We'll keep this our secret for now and continue to work together on the book. If the book turns out right, that'll take care of any other issues."

"Okay," said Taylor quickly agreeing. The thought of not being able to enjoy this romance with Cooper was devastating. She'd certainly been kissed by a man before, but never like this. It was as if this kiss had entered her soul, bringing her body to life in a way that was as meaningful as the lust she felt.

Smiling, Cooper cupped her face in his hands. "Okay, let's relax and talk a little more about the book after we swim and go out in the canoe."

As Taylor stepped into the water, it was cold on her skin, but the heat of Cooper's kiss still warmed her body. Cooper stood at the water's edge with her and then he waded out into it and finally dove head-first beneath the shimmering surface.

When he emerged, his dark hair hung in his face.

She laughed and followed him into the water, striking out in long-armed strokes to reach him.

Treading water, facing each other, Cooper said, "I'm falling hard, Taylor."

"Me, too," she said, leaning forward for a kiss.

Their legs became tangled, and they broke apart.

"Beat you back to the rock," said Taylor. "After I get warmed up, I want to take that canoe ride you mentioned. We need to keep busy."

She didn't wait for him but headed back to the rock swimming in sure, steady strokes.

He met up with her and they climbed atop the rock.

She'd pinned her shoulder-length hair back into a ponytail but loosened the band around it and shook it out.

Lying beside her, Cooper watched. "You're beautiful, you

know."

"Whitney's the beautiful one," Taylor automatically answered. "I'm the shy one."

Cooper frowned and sat up. "Whoa! Don't let anyone categorize you like that. You can be beautiful and shy. You're both."

She let out a long breath. "When I was young, I used to think I didn't belong in the family because my sisters were blonde and beautiful."

"Who did you look like?"

"My father. I knew he was handsome, but I couldn't transfer that to me. It's silly, I know, but that's what I used to think. Lately, my sisters and I appreciate the differences in each of us. Their father was an alcoholic who died in an automobile accident. My father is my mother's second husband. He adopted Whitney and Dani when they were young."

"Then it's understandable that you would be different. But it doesn't make you any less beautiful."

Taylor's lips curved. "Thanks."

He drew her down on the rock and they lay side by side facing the sun until Taylor heard his soft snores, and then she closed her eyes.

Sometime later, she felt Cooper stirring beside her and opened her eyes to find him staring at her.

"Hello," he said, tracing her lips with his finger and then kissing her.

He sat up. "I've decided not to mention anything about you to my mother. The less she knows, the better. Under ordinary circumstances, I'd want her to know about my feelings for you. But I can't let anything put our work in question. Do you mind?"

"No, I understand," Taylor said. "I'll keep quiet about our

relationship too, but it'll be harder because others will see us together."

"I'd hate to stand in your way of further success," said Cooper. "You've proven your desire to do well. Only a serious writer would be open to undergoing an exercise like this."

"Let's not worry about that now," said Taylor. "Let's enjoy the rest of the afternoon. We can go over notes tonight if you wish. I've already thought of some things to add to the book."

"I'm glad we've had this time together. I know how upset you are about Whitney."

Taylor's cell phone chimed. *Crystal.*

"Hi, Taylor. Want to meet up tonight? Sarah Bullard is in town for a few days to be with her parents and help them at the hardware store. She's anxious to see everyone. I called Dani and Whitney but neither one answered their cell."

"There's a reason for that," said Taylor and explained the situation to her.

"How awful for Whitney. She told me once how much she'd loved him. He was much too young to die."

"Yes, it's a shame," said Taylor, hoping her sister would be able to cope with all the paparazzi who were sure to be swarming. She supposed Dani would help keep her clear of them.

"Will you meet up with us at Jake's at six or so? Cooper is invited too," Crystal said. "By the way, how's the work project coming along? Have you decided he's not as bad as you'd first thought?"

"Something like that," said Taylor. "I'll definitely come, and I'll ask Cooper if he wants to join us."

"Thanks. Sarah lives in Florida so doesn't get here that often. We've kept in touch over the years, and I'm thrilled she's back in a town for these few days."

"It'll be fun to see her, though she may not remember me,"

said Taylor. "She's more your age."

"Everybody in town knew the Gilford girls," said Crystal. "She'll be glad to see you. If you speak to Whitney, please give her my sympathy."

"Will do," said Taylor. In the past, Whitney and Crystal's common interest in music and dancing had brought the two of them together. This summer they were happy to renew the friendship.

Taylor ended the call and turned to Cooper. "That was Crystal asking us to join her and a group of friends at Jake's this evening. Sarah Bullard's parents own and run the hardware store in town. She's visiting for a few days, and she wanted to get a group together. I said yes, but you don't have to go if you don't want to."

Cooper shrugged. "I'll join you. I like Crystal. She's fun."

"Okay. Now, let's get to that canoe trip."

Taylor and Cooper walked down to the canoe Aaron had pulled up on shore and turned it over, checking for paddles and life preserver cushions.

"All set," said Cooper. "I need you to grab that end. I'll get the other and walk it into the lake like Aaron did the other day."

Together they managed to get the canoe into the water and then Cooper held onto it while she climbed in.

"Hold on," cried Cooper. He sprung up out of the water and draped his body over the gunwale, wiggling until he made it inside the canoe. "Aaron has a way of making that look easy," he said as he swung his legs around and took a seat at the stern.

Taylor chuckled and picked up her paddle. Kneeling in the bow, she stroked the water on one side of the canoe and then the other, careful to "feather" her paddle as she brought it out of the water to begin another stroke.

From the stern, Cooper guided the boat with several long pulls of his paddle.

A few people were on the water in rowboats or canoes. One couple was in a paddle boat.

Taylor was pleased when they passed them and she had the illusion of being on the lake by themselves. They didn't speak as they headed for the far end of the lake where a construction crew was working on putting in a dock for residents of The Meadows, the housing development owned by Brad and Aaron.

By the time they returned to the cottage, Taylor's arms were aching from all the paddling she'd done, and she realized she normally spent so much time writing that she didn't get enough physical exercise. Cooper hadn't seemed to mind the exercise at all.

Later, as they got ready for the evening at Jake's, Taylor lifted her cell to check on Whitney and was pleased to see that while she'd been taking a shower Dani had left her a message that said she was in L.A., and both she and Whitney would call her tomorrow.

Giving a last look at herself in the mirror, Taylor straightened the white linen blouse she'd put on, along with a pair of tan linen pants, and gave herself a nod of approval.

When she emerged from her bedroom and saw Cooper waiting for her with a smile on his face, she relaxed. It was beginning to seem normal to have him in the house with her. The thought made her happy.

CHAPTER THIRTY-ONE
DANI

During a stressful flight thinking of Whitney and all she'd gone through with Zane for the past four years, Dani was more grateful than ever that she and Brad had found one another. She was especially happy he'd understood her need to be with her sister, interrupting several plans they'd made for themselves.

Dani was aware some people thought that with Whitney's beauty, glamorous job, and association with other interesting people, her life was perfect. But Dani knew how hard Whitney worked and how sensitive she was to others' needs. Spending her summer with her two sisters was a gift from GG that Dani was sure would change their lives forever. It had hers.

Dani accepted a bottle of water from the flight attendant and continued to stare out the window of the plane. She'd met Zane. He was a handsome, complicated man who'd adored Whitney at one point. But later, when drugs had taken over his life, he'd berated her, hurting her more than he'd ever suspect. The television series became the way they interacted most of the time.

Few people knew the real reason Whitney was so anti-drugs. Dani was a toddler when her father was killed while driving intoxicated. But Whitney was old enough to remember the way her father had behaved under the influence of alcohol and drugs. So, while Whitney might have a glass of wine from time to time, she'd never get involved with drugs or with someone using them.

When the flight ended and passengers began to deplane, Dani grabbed her purse and the carry-on bag she'd packed and stood in line, her heart pounding with concern at what she was about to face.

She checked her phone and looked at a message from Whitney stating that her agent would pick her up at the airport and to meet her in the baggage claim area.

Dani followed the crowd of passengers to the baggage claim area and looked for Barbara Griffith. A woman with strong features and short gray hair held a sign that simply said DANI.

Grateful, Dani rushed forward. "Hi, Barbara, I'm Dani Gilford. I'm happy to meet you." She shifted her bag to her other shoulder and held out her hand.

Barbara smiled and held Dani's hand in a firm grip. "So nice to meet you. I'm glad you're here. It's been a rough time. Is that your only suitcase?"

Dani nodded. "I packed in a hurry."

"Come this way. I have a driver waiting for us." Barbara led her to a black limousine.

The driver took her suitcase, and Dani climbed into the backseat of the limo with Barbara, grateful for the tinted windows assuring them of privacy.

"I'm so sorry Zane didn't recover," Dani said, unable to hide a quiver in her voice.

Barbara's eyes filled with tears. "Me, too." Her tears overflowed onto her cheeks. "I tried to talk to Zane about his addiction, even made him draw up a will and a Living Will, as if we knew this was going to happen."

Dani took hold of Barbara's hand and squeezed it. The tough woman Whitney talked about wasn't so tough.

The limo pulled up to a large, one-story, white stucco house with a red-tile roof situated in an upscale neighborhood in

Beverly Hills.

Dani got out of the car and waited while the driver retrieved her suitcase and Barbara paid him. Then she followed Barbara inside the house.

"Hello?" Barbara called.

Whitney came running to them across the tile entryway and flung herself into Dani's arms. "I'm so glad you're here. Oh, Dani, it was so awful seeing Zane like that, knowing he was gone." Whitney cupped her face in her hands, her shoulders shaking. When she looked up at Dani, tears fell steadily in glistening streaks on her cheeks. "I should've done more. I might've been able to save him."

Dani held onto her sister. "You tried your best to help. You can't control someone else. The ultimate decision was his to make. Please, don't blame yourself."

"I know you're right, but it's such a senseless death." Whitney's lips thinned. "He knew he was killing himself with those drugs, that he was ruining his career. He'd already ruined my love and respect for him. I'm furious he didn't listen."

Dani nodded sympathetically, understanding anger was part of the grieving process.

"Let's get you settled, Dani," said Barbara. "You're sharing a guest suite with Whitney, as Whitney wanted. Maybe later, the two of you might want to spend some time with each other at the pool. It's going to be a couple of tough days ahead."

"Thanks so much. That sounds perfect."

Whitney looped her arm through Dani's. "I wanted us to share a room like we used to back in the day as kids. C'mon. I'll show you to it."

They passed the large living room which led out to a pool and garden and entered a separate wing of the house.

After passing a den and a powder room for guests, double

doors at the end of the hallway opened to a large suite that contained a living area, a fireplace, and two full-size beds. Off to the side toward the back, a dressing area with plenty of mirrors and closet space sat beside a huge bathroom with a soaking tub, double shower, and a door with frosted glass that led out to the pool area.

"Barbara must be very successful," Dani said setting down her suitcase and looking around. "This place is gorgeous."

"She's done very well because she's a great agent," said Whitney. "She's been wonderful to me throughout this whole mess." She sighed and her eyes filled once more. "She loved Zane too. But then, when he first started out, everyone loved him."

Dani wrapped her arms around Whitney once more. "What can I do to help? You said Zane left you everything. What does that mean?"

"Well, we'll have to file the will in probate court, cancel charge cards, close out accounts and inform people. Zane wanted to be cremated, so Barbara is taking care of those arrangements. She thinks I should clean out Zane's house of personal items as soon as possible. I have no intention of keeping the property and will put it up for sale when I can." Whitney shook her head. "There are so many things to take care of."

"One day, one thing at a time," said Dani, rubbing Whitney's back. "You can do it. And I'm here to help."

"Thanks. Barbara is taking care of writing an obituary and sending it to the newspaper," said Whitney. "She'll talk to the producers of the show and take care of those issues. I'll take care of his personal information as I mentioned. Tomorrow, I'd like you to come with me to his house to sort through things."

"Where was he when he overdosed?" Dani asked, stepping

away from Whitney and giving her a look of concern.

"At a party. Someone brought him to the emergency room and left him," said Whitney. "How awful is that?"

"Terrible. But having him away from the house makes it easier to take care of it," said Dani, relieved they wouldn't walk into that messy scene.

"Yes," agreed Whitney, looking forlorn as she gazed out the window at the sunshine.

Dani said, "Let's sit by the pool and try to relax. I forgot my bathing suit, but I can sit with you."

"No problem. Barbara keeps a collection of bathing suits on hand for guests," said Whitney.

Shaking her head at the notion of Barbara providing swimsuits, Dani was grateful. After a hasty flight to California, she needed time to unwind.

CHAPTER THIRTY-TWO
TAYLOR

Though Taylor hadn't known Sarah Bullard well as a child, she was happy to be included in the get-together arranged by Crystal. It was this feeling of being connected that made Taylor think she might like living in Lilac Lake year-round.

She and Cooper entered Jake's and headed over to a corner of the restaurant where a large round table held chairs for eight, ten if crowded.

Crystal waved and a woman turned and gazed at her with a smile. Seeing the brown-haired woman with blue eyes, her mind created a younger version of her as a teenager. Heavyset, Sarah had always been pleasant and well-liked by both boys and girls. That same air of friendliness surrounded her now, and when Sarah stood to give her a hug, Taylor easily returned it.

"It's so nice to see one of the Gilford girls," said Sarah. "I hear you and your sisters may live here."

"For at least part of the year, though with Dani marrying Brad Collister, she'll no doubt be here year-round." Taylor placed a hand on Cooper's arm. "I'd like you to meet Cooper Walker, an editor who's working with me on my next book."

"An editor or maybe something more, eh?" said Crystal, bringing a flush to Taylor's cheeks.

Ignoring them both, Cooper shook hands with Sarah. "Nice to meet you."

"Sit down, you two," said Crystal. "Nick's going to stop by, and Aaron said he'd be here. Garth's brother, Brooks, said he might come. Garth and Bethany can't attend. And I've explained about Dani and Whitney."

"It's hard to get people together, I understand," said Sarah. "I'm here for just a few days to help my parents, though it's a vacation for me. I have four-year-old twin daughters, and my husband is giving me a break."

"Twins? How hard is that?" said Taylor. Since falling for Cooper she'd wondered about a future with him. But wondering and being ready for such a thing were miles apart from becoming a reality.

Sarah laughed. "It's double the work but double the fun. But we're thinking of having another baby and then things really will be hard. They tell me three kids are a lot to handle. But, Taylor, how are your books doing? I've read two and loved them. Very enjoyable."

"Thanks," said Taylor, trying not to turn to Cooper with a smug look.

"When's your next book coming out?" Sarah asked. "Or should I ask your editor?"

Taylor laughed at her teasing grin. "You can ask me, though the answer lies with the two of us. We're working on it together. And right after that, I'll begin to work on the next book."

"Won't you miss New York if you decide to stay here?" Sarah asked. "Mom and Dad keep wanting us to move here, but I'm not ready."

"I haven't definitely decided what I'm going to do," admitted Taylor. "I still have my condo in New York, and I don't want to give that up,"

Aaron showed up, and they moved closer to give him room.

He and Sarah stared at one another and then he, still standing, leaned over and gave her a kiss on the cheek. "I hear you're doing well. I'm glad," he said, taking a seat at the table.

"Thanks," said Sarah blushing like crazy, reminding Taylor that as teenagers, Sarah and Aaron had dated.

Cooper's cell rang. He looked at it, turned to Taylor and said, "I've got to take this. It's my sister." He listened a moment, then got up and started walking to the exit.

Concerned, Taylor followed him.

He sat on a bench outside the bar with the cell phone to his ear and a horrified look on his face.

Taylor sat beside him and waited for him to speak to her.

"Okay, if Mom is really doing that well, I'll wait and leave here early tomorrow and drive straight through. That way, I'll have my car. No point in leaving it here. Tell Mom I love her and will see her tomorrow."

As soon as he ended the call, Taylor said, "What's going on?"

Cooper turned to her with a grim expression. "That was my sister, Candace. My mother has had a mild heart attack. She's in no danger of dying but will have to rest and then start lightening her load at work. She wants to meet with my sister and me tomorrow afternoon. They're going to keep her in the hospital for a couple of days and get her on some new routines."

"Oh, Cooper, I'm so sorry," said Taylor. "I hope she'll truly be okay. I know how much you love her. What can I do to help?"

"I'll pack up tonight, so I can leave early tomorrow. I want to get there as soon as I can, but Candace is right. I shouldn't drive at night after I've been out."

"Do you want to leave and go back to the house now?"

Cooper nodded. "Do you mind?"

"Of course not. I know how concerned you are. I'll be right back. Let me tell the others we're leaving."

At the house, the dogs greeted them with barks and yowls of happiness. Taylor patted Pirate on the head and swept Mindy up in her arms wanting something to hold onto while thoughts of spending time with Cooper shattered. Once back in New York and busy with the business, he'd have no time for sunning on a rock in New Hampshire.

Cooper went to Whitney's room where he'd been staying and organized his stuff, packing most of his clothing in his suitcase and packing up his computer, notebooks, and office materials into the cardboard box he'd brought with him.

Taylor sat outside with the dogs, watching them play in the yard, wondering if this is how the relationship with Cooper would end. She scolded herself for being so selfish, but her growing feelings for Cooper were real.

Cooper joined her on the patio. "I'm sorry to leave like this, but I know you understand. We're going to have to finish the book together online. I promise I'll read the whole thing no matter what. And remember, we can text and talk whenever we can. If you like, you can send me one chapter at a time."

Taylor shook her head. "I appreciate all the help you've given me. In my mind, it's already a very different book."

"Glad to hear it," said Cooper crisply. All business now.

Tears smarted Taylor's eyes but she blinked them away. She needed to be a support to Cooper.

He stood in front of her chair and pulled her up into his arms. "This doesn't change how I feel about you. I have no idea what the future holds for me, how the next days, months are going to play out. But I'll stay in touch. I promise."

She gazed up at him and a tear slipped down her cheek. She swiped at it with the back of her hand.

Cooper wrapped his arms around her and gave her a sad smile. "I've fallen hard for you, Taylor. That will never change." He rocked her in his arms while she clung to him. He lifted her face and kissed her.

She closed her eyes, loving the taste of his lips, the smell of him.

When they pulled apart, he said, "Guess I'd better try to get some sleep. I'll leave quietly at the first sign of daylight."

"Do you want me to fix you some coffee? Breakfast? Anything?" she asked.

"No, thanks. It's easier if I just slip out the door. I've never been great at goodbyes."

She understood even as her eyes filled.

He cupped her face in his hands and stared as if memorizing her, then lowered his lips to hers once more.

She allowed herself to be carried away by the passion he aroused in her, storing this moment in her mind to bring out later when she knew how much she'd be missing him.

When they pulled apart, he gave her the saddest smile she'd ever seen and then headed upstairs.

Taylor waited until she was sure he was asleep before she and the dogs headed to her room to spend what she was sure would be a restless night.

Taylor didn't know when she finally fell asleep. It felt like minutes before the dogs stirred and she heard Cooper's car easing out of the driveway. She got up and raced to the front window, but when she looked out, all she saw of the car were the red rearview lights staring at her like a monster's eyes.

Aching with a heartache she'd never known, she crawled back into bed and hugged her pillow, wishing it were Cooper.

CHAPTER THIRTY-THREE
DANI

Dani made her usual morning call to Brad, needing to hear his voice. They'd formed a pattern of sending each other off for the day with declarations of love and support. Facing the day's distressing activities in L.A., she needed it more than ever.

She still had a smile on her face from talking with him when she called Taylor to check on her, GG, and the dogs.

Taylor answered the phone with a listless, "Hello".

"Hi, is everything all right?" Dani asked.

"Not really. Cooper left Lilac Lake this morning to be with his mother. She had a mild heart attack, and he isn't planning on coming back."

"What about your work?" Dani asked, puzzled.

"We'll finish the revisions online and by phone and text. He's promised to read the whole thing no matter what. He and his sister, Candace, are meeting with their mother to discuss how to carry on the business now that she's being forced to revise her workload."

"Oh, I'm sorry," said Dani, sensing the real problem. "You've got feelings for him, don't you?"

Taylor's trembling sigh was an answer before she even spoke. "I've never felt this way about anyone. I know he feels the same way about me, but holding onto control of the family business is more important than that. I get it. I really do, but I don't know if I'll ever feel the same way about anyone else."

"It seems to me you're jumping to all kinds of conclusions. He can help with the business and still maintain a relationship with you," said Dani calmly. "Just as I've been telling Whitney, take it one day at a time."

"How is she?" Taylor asked. "I saw a short clip about Zane's death on a news program. As everyone says, his death is such a shame."

"We're working on the situation, one thing at a time. There are a lot of little items to take care of—closing out accounts and dealing with paperwork. As soon as that is under control, we'll return to Lilac Lake. There won't be a memorial service until after everything has calmed down. The last thing Whitney wants is a media circus."

"That's understandable," said Taylor. "Tell her Mindy misses her, but she's doing fine. So is Pirate."

"We appreciate knowing they are in loving hands. What can I do for you?"

"Thanks, but nothing. Like you said, I need to take one day at a time and keep moving forward. Just saying it, I feel stronger."

"Okay," said Dani. "I can't wait to get back there. Talk to you soon." Dani ended the call and sat a moment. Life certainly had its ups and downs.

CHAPTER THIRTY-FOUR
WHITNEY

Whitney held onto her sister's arm as they entered the house where Zane lived. The house she thought she might share with him one day. The house where her love for him had ended.

His home was a small but adorable bungalow in the Brentwood Glen neighborhood. With three bedrooms and three baths, it was perfect for someone starting out. Owning a home was a huge accomplishment for a man who'd grown up poor. Whitney had always respected his choice. She'd even helped pick out most of the furnishings, working with a decorator with the understanding that someday they'd live there together.

Now, as she stepped into the entryway, it all came back, the love, the drugs, the fights, the disgust.

"It's a mess," said Dani quietly, and Whitney was brought back to the present with a jolt.

Whitney observed the pillows from the couch tossed about, the drinks on the coffee table, clothes strewn everywhere, and swallowed hard. "After we sort through everything and remove personal belongings, I'll get a company in here to give the place a thorough cleaning."

They moved through the rooms in the house assessing the damage. Like Dani had said, the place was trashed. But as far as Whitney could tell, there was no permanent damage to the house itself.

"Why don't I start in the living room and kitchen?" Dani suggested, holding up a couple of trash bags they'd brought from Barbara's house.

Whitney was grateful for the chance to be alone as she sorted through Zane's things in his bedroom. His clothing in acceptable condition would be donated to charity, the rest discarded.

She'd hired a discreet business to pick up things for charity and to dispose of those items they'd thrown away—someone who wouldn't try to take advantage of knowing whose things they were handling.

Working in Zane's room, a myriad of emotions overtook her. Here was the place she'd made love with Zane but was now the place where she'd discovered him with the two prostitutes. Here was a sweater he'd loved, now with burns in it. Memories crashed inside her, but she resolutely carried on, filling bag after bag.

The bureau was the last thing she addressed.

Inside the top drawer, she found a picture of her smiling at him. For her, this was the breaking point. She remembered him taking the photo of her, telling her how much he loved her when they'd first declared their love.

She sat on the bed and wept, telling herself this was the end of everything they'd shared. Although she'd be forced to move ahead, she'd tuck away the memories until she could deal with them.

Sometime later, the doorbell rang.

Whitney stayed back while Dani answered it, fearful of being seen.

Thankful that it was the company she'd hired to take care of belongings and not paparazzi, Whitney stepped forward.

"Thank you for coming. I've gone through things in the master bedroom and have separated them into piles. You can help bag things up there. There's nothing to be taken from any other room. The office is being taken care of."

She watched as the two women from the estate clearing company went to work, quickly sorting items, then loading the back of a large SUV one had driven with bags and carefully placing some of the clothing still on hangers into another car. Later, after the will was probated, they'd return to sell all the furnishings before putting the house on the market.

"It's always a sad time to dismantle a home of its personality," said one of the women placing a hand on her arm. "But your generosity in giving away so many things will be appreciated by many. Hopefully that will give you some comfort."

"Yes, it does. Our proceeds of the sale of furnishings will be given to charity also," said Whitney, thanking them.

Dani came over to her, placed an arm around her, and together they watched the vehicles laden with Zane's personal items drive away.

"I've got boxes ready for the stuff you want to keep for storage," said Dani quietly.

They went inside to finish with their job. Zane's awards, paintings of importance, and personal office items including his computer were things Whitney would keep until she decided what to do with them.

At last, with things straightened enough for the cleaning company to do their work, Whitney and Dani left the house.

Outside, Whitney paused and studied the house, remembering how proud Zane had been to own it. Amazed at how her body could manufacture so many tears, she turned away.

CHAPTER THIRTY-FIVE
TAYLOR

Too restless to work on the book, Taylor cleaned up Whitney's room, washed the sheets and told herself to stop checking the clocks. She'd have to give Cooper enough time to get home and settled before he called.

One of her favorite things to do when she was stressed as a child was to bake cookies. She went to the kitchen, and after looking through the cupboards, decided to bake molasses cookies. Her father had loved them. If Cooper ever got the chance to try one, he might like them too.

She was taking the last cookie sheet out of the oven when her cell rang. She set the hot sheet on the stove and turned to answer it. *Cooper.*

"Hello," Taylor answered, thrilled he'd called from the road.

"Hi. I want to thank you again for spending that time with me working on your book," said Cooper. "I'm glad we ended up as friends and, I hope, even more than that. I don't want you to forget our time together. I won't. That's for sure."

Taylor was quiet. This sounded like a final goodbye.

"Are you there?" Cooper said.

"Yes, I am," Taylor answered, afraid to say more.

"I have no idea what awaits me at home, but I want you to know that no matter what, I have no intention of ending what was happening between us."

Tearing up, Taylor said, "What we had together is very special. I'm not going to simply throw it away because circumstances took you away from Lilac Lake. Just keep in touch. That's all I'm asking."

"Thanks, Taylor," said Cooper, a brighter note to his voice. "I had to know how you felt about me, about us. I wasn't lying when I told you I'd fallen hard for you. I want to see where the future leads us." The sound of blaring car horns filled the air.

"Gotta go," said Cooper. "I'll talk to you later."

"Okay, bye." Taylor ended the call and plopped down into a kitchen chair. The aroma of freshly baked cookies filled the air, but she didn't notice as she became lost in the memory of Cooper's kisses.

She felt a cold nose nudging her hand and automatically lifted it to rub Pirate's ears.

Mindy barked for equal time and Taylor was forced to pay attention to her. But her thoughts remained on Cooper's words. Somehow, they'd make their growing relationship work.

Sitting outside with the dogs, breathing in the fresh air, watching them play together, Taylor felt herself fill with resolve. She went inside and fixed a plate of fresh cookies for GG. She knew she'd be delighted with the cookies. In return, Taylor hoped to get her perspective on the latest developments with Cooper.

GG was outside reading on her patio when Taylor entered her room. Seeing her, Taylor felt a rush of love. Her grandmother had always been a support to her.

"Hi," Taylor called out so as not to startle her.

GG lifted her face from the book she was reading and sent Taylor a smile that warmed her heart. "Hello, darling. It's so nice to see you."

"Thanks. I brought you a treat," said Taylor, holding onto the plate as she bent to kiss GG's cheek.

"Oh, my! Molasses cookies. I do love them," she said.

Grinning with pleasure, Taylor set the plate of cookies down on the nearby table. "Can I bring you something to drink?"

"How about a glass of lemonade? I have a pitcher of it in the refrigerator." GG removed the plastic wrap around the plate and picked up a cookie.

Chuckling at GG's love of sweets, Taylor fixed a glass of lemonade for each of them and then sat opposite her on the patio.

"Delicious," GG exclaimed as she finished her cookie. She took a sip of the lemonade and then said, "How are things going? I talked to Dani earlier. She and Whitney are working hard to get things in order so they can return to Lilac Lake. Dani said it's been a very difficult time."

"It's still hard to believe that someone like Zane, who had so many things going for him, couldn't kick the habit that was killing him. Whitney has taken it hard."

"I'm so relieved you girls have stayed away from drugs," said GG.

Taylor made a face. "Mother told us some of the things that went on with her first husband and warned us over and over again about the trouble it leads to. Luckily, we all listened to her."

"I'm glad to hear it," said GG. "What's going on with you?"

Taylor took a sip of lemonade and sighed. "It's Cooper. GG, I've fallen hard for him, and he says he feels the same thing about me. But I'm not sure how things are going to work out for us." She fought to keep her voice strong. "Cooper left early this morning to go back to New York. His mother just had a mild heart attack. She's going to be fine, but she must make some changes in her life. Cooper and his sister, Candace, will have to take on more responsibility at their small publishing company."

"What about the book you were working on together?" GG asked.

"We're going to talk and text and converse online. But I've been thinking about some changes of my own," said Taylor, straightening. "I'm a good writer and I'm willing to work hard to become a better one both now and in the future. I've already learned so much working with him. But it's important for me to protect my creativity, keep it as my own."

GG gave her a thumbs up. "I'm pleased to know that. It tells me you're a professional, ready to listen to advice, but strong enough not to lose yourself and the reason readers love your work. It's been helpful for you to work with Cooper. He's a forthright man. He's been very honest with you, and that counts for a lot."

"I love him, GG," said Taylor, suddenly overcome with feelings. Tears stung her eyes. "I've never felt this way about any man. It's kind of magical. You know?"

"Oh, yes, indeed. I do know that feeling." She smiled sadly. "Or perhaps I should say I remember that feeling."

"Had you and Grandpa known each other for long when you got married?" Taylor asked. She'd seen a photograph of GG and her groom but didn't know much about him other than he'd died in the Viet Nam war not long after they married, leaving GG pregnant.

GG shook her head. "We knew each other for less than six months. It seems that when a woman in our family decides someone is right for her, she moves quickly."

Taylor laughed. "I know. Think of my mother and father and now, Dani and Brad." She grew serious. "I'm not sure about Cooper and me. He's so different from what I thought he'd be, and now his role is changing."

"Maybe that's for the best," said GG. "Let the days unfold.

If it was meant to be, things will work out. In the meantime, you have work to do on your book. That will help."

"Yes, I already understand how I can add things between the lines that will make my books stronger. No matter what, I will always be grateful to Cooper for that."

Taylor was talking to GG about activities at The Woodlands when a knock sounded on the door and JoEllen walked in.

"Mrs. Wittner? I came to check up on you, but I'll come back when you don't have company," she said.

"It's all right. There's nothing that can't be shared with one of my granddaughters."

"Hello, JoEllen," said Taylor.

"Hi, Taylor. I'm glad to see you. I tried calling Cooper, but he didn't answer. I think I might have left something in his cabin."

"He's been moved out of that cabin for some time. You might want to check with the office there," said Taylor trying not to grit her teeth. That something was probably a piece of underwear she'd taken off to try and seduce him.

"Oh, well. I'll talk to him another time. Now, Mrs. Wittner, have you had any difficulty breathing today?"

"No, I'm fine. I told you yesterday that it was just my allergies kicking up. That's all."

"You know to call the staff anytime that happens. Right?" said JoEllen.

"Yes." GG's smile didn't reach her eyes. "Thanks for stopping by. As you can see, I have company."

Left with no choice, JoEllen waved and left.

"That woman is so annoying. JoEllen told one of my friends she was saving for a new car and would be glad to accept any donations from her. She called it a Go Fund Me. Never heard of such foolishness in my life," huffed GG.

"Just be careful with your belongings," said Taylor. "I don't trust her." She rose. "I'd better get back to the dogs. They're demanding more and more of my attention because they miss Dani and Whitney. I'll be so happy when they're back in town."

"We all will," said GG. "I'm getting spoiled with having the three of you here in Lilac Lake."

They smiled at one another as Taylor bent down to hug GG goodbye.

CHAPTER THIRTY-SIX
TAYLOR

At home, Taylor felt better about her work. Discussing motive and backgrounds of her main characters had given her new insight into how she could strengthen the book. She didn't need Cooper to look over her shoulder. This book was her third. She'd work on it as much as she could by herself while Cooper was handling family problems. Then, she'd show it to Cooper.

After making that decision, she went back to Chapter One and began to edit, pleased her imagination was flowing again.

She was hard at work, almost ready to take a break when Dani called.

"Hi, how's it going?" Taylor asked her.

"We're close to coming home," said Dani, "and I can't wait. Whitney will be able to take care of a lot of business from New Hampshire. She's going to form a foundation in Zane's name to help children and teens with mental health issues. And she still wants to do something with theater for the kids. In fact, she may tie some of the projects together. But she'll have plenty of time. It takes months, sometimes a couple of years, for a will to be probated."

"Lots of things to handle," said Taylor, aware of the work ahead of Whitney.

"Yes," said Dani. "I have something I need you to do for me. Will you go to the cottage and take some photos of the floors on your phone and send them to me? I want you to make sure they all look fine, especially the kitchen and upstairs hall bathroom. If so, we can go ahead and have some other work done on the interior."

"Oh, Dani, you know that house frightens me," Taylor said. She heard a whine in her voice but was unable to stop it.

"Taylor, we all agree that nothing is there to harm us, that Nick saw no sign of intruders, and the workmen haven't complained about anything untoward. Do this for me. Please."

"Okay. When do you need the photos?"

"Can you go this afternoon?"

Taylor sighed. She'd just gotten her groove back with her writing. But she heard the plea in Dani's voice and realized she wouldn't have asked if it wasn't important. "All right, I'll leave now and send you photos."

"Thanks, I appreciate it," said Dani. "Talk to you later."

After the call ended, Taylor got up from her desk chair and stretched. It felt good to move. If she were lucky, she'd be in and out of that house in a matter of minutes.

Taylor went downstairs and called to the dogs. They trotted to the front door eager for a chance to get out of the house.

She loaded them into her car and drove to the cottage.

Pulling up to the garage, she noticed that though no other vehicles were there, the overgrown bushes next to the house had been removed, something that needed to be done before the house could be painted. When the painting was completed, they'd put in new shrubbery.

"C'mon, Pirate and Mindy. You're coming with me," said Taylor, glad for their protection.

Both dogs jumped out of the car and bounded away, no doubt happy for the freedom.

When she called them back, they came, but as she approached the front porch, they sat on the lawn and wouldn't move closer, even with the promise of treats.

Feeling uneasy, Taylor found the key hidden underneath a

rock close by and opened the door. The smell of stain and urethane hit her nose. Bending over, she touched the floor of the entryway. It was shiny and dry. Leaving the door open, she walked through the living room and into the kitchen. The old linoleum flooring there had been ripped out so the wooden floors of the newly added powder room, laundry area, and eating nook would all be the same. Taylor took several shots of it, appreciating the work that had taken place. If she were lucky, she could quickly take photos of the rooms upstairs and leave.

Swallowing hard, she climbed the stairs and told her pounding heart to slow down. She photographed the hallway, the sub-flooring in the bathroom awaiting tile, and went into the master bedroom. All seemed well. She took a few photographs there and hurried downstairs. Though the house was torn up now, the project was moving forward and would be beautiful. She knew from the schedule Dani had drawn up that in addition to the wooden flooring on the main level, the bathroom floors would be tiled, the laundry room floor would have a waterproof surface, and the bedrooms would be carpeted.

Taylor hurried to the front door and heaved a sigh of relief when she closed it behind her.

She called the dogs and sat down on the porch steps waiting for them to come to her.

Seeing the sunning rock, memories of her time there with Cooper flooded her mind. He'd kissed her tenderly and then with more passion. She hadn't imagined the rush of emotions between them. You can't fake something like that, she thought, wondering what she'd do if it turned out to be nothing but a brief summer romance. That thought tore at her.

She lowered her head in her hands and tried to draw in

soothing long breaths. A warmth enveloped her, then a feeling of contentment filled her. She had to believe that something so wonderful wouldn't simply disappear. She lifted her face and found the dogs sitting and staring at her.

She called to them, but they wouldn't come closer.

Shaking her head at them, she got up and moved toward her car at the back of the house.

Before she drove away, she sent the photos to Dani, then she headed home, hoping Cooper would call.

Later, Taylor was sitting in her office when she got a call from Dani.

"Hi," Taylor said. "You got the pictures all right."

"I did," said Dani. "Did you look at them?"

"No. I didn't think I needed to. Why?"

"Just wondering," said Dani. "Whitney and I have booked a flight for tomorrow. We should be there sometime tomorrow evening."

"It'll be great to have you home. Should I plan dinner?"

"No, but thanks. See you tomorrow sometime between nine o'clock and ten."

Taylor ended the call pleased to think her sisters would be back in Lilac Lake. Like GG, she was becoming spoiled by having her sisters close by.

She finished rewriting the scene and went downstairs. Time to feed the dogs and have a glass of wine to reflect on where she was going with the rewrite.

It wasn't until she was sitting on the patio with the dogs happily fed that she took out her phone to look at the photographs she'd sent Dani.

There were some clear shots of the kitchen, powder room, and laundry.

She scrolled through a couple more until she reached the

ones in the master bedroom.

She'd taken photos of the floor and then a few of the room.

Her heart bumped to stop as she studied the two of the room. In each one there was a shadow. Taylor told herself dust had gotten onto the camera on her phone, but after holding the phone closer and enlarging the picture, she could clearly see the nebulous shape of what looked like a small person. Her stomach heaved with the acid that rushed into it. God! Had a ghost been watching her the whole time?

She wrapped her arms around herself, so cold she thought she'd never get warm.

CHAPTER THIRTY-SEVEN
WHITNEY

Whitney looked at the pictures on Dani's phone and turned to her. "I see the same thing you do. But Taylor said she didn't feel or see anything strange?"

"I didn't mention anything, just asked if she'd taken a look at them. When she said no, I let it drop. She's already frightened by the house. We can't let anything stop us from going forward. GG promised her father she'd hold on to the family property, and we're going to help her fulfill his wish."

"When I get settled back home, I'll do some investigation of my own," said Whitney. "The box with the wedding dress and the baby clothes has to mean something."

"We can all do our own research. Once we find an answer, the ghost won't have any reason to stay." Dani shook her head. "So far, the ghost or spirit or whatever it is, hasn't objected to our renovating the house."

"You're right. That says a lot," said Whitney. She finished putting her paperwork into an expandable file and added it to her suitcase. "I'm just glad to be going home. I shouldn't have to come back here for a while. Not unless there are legal issues that can't be handled for Zane's estate from New Hampshire."

Barbara walked into the bedroom suite Whitney had been sharing with Dani. "How are you two doing? You know, I'm going to miss you. As sad as the circumstances are, I've enjoyed having you share my home during this time."

Whitney walked over to Barbara and hugged her. "You're so much more than my agent. You've become such a wonderful friend."

"Not many people would say that about me in this tough business, but I'm glad you feel that way. I've always admired you, Whitney, but never more than now. You've taken a bad situation and are turning it into something positive for the future. Zane was right to leave his estate to you. He knew he could trust you."

Though Whitney felt the sting of tears, she blinked them back. Zane would be pleased with her plans for a foundation. It made her happy to remember the early times when she'd loved him, and they'd planned something like this together.

"I'll be in touch," said Barbara. "I know it's too early to ask you to consider any dramatic roles, but the day will come when you'll be interested again. I'm sure of it."

"*I'm* not so sure about that, but I'll try to keep an open mind," said Whitney, stepping aside as Barbara embraced Dani.

"You're a great sister, Dani," said Barbara. "Thank you for coming to California. I know how busy you are with the renovation of the family cottage. Good luck with that and that handsome contractor fiancé of yours."

"Thank you. You'll have to come to Lilac Lake one day," said Dani.

"You never know. Maybe I will," said Barbara, then turned to Whitney. "The limo is waiting for you. I'll walk you to the door. Goodbyes aren't my thing. Besides, I have a meeting. I hope you understand."

"Of course," said Whitney. She didn't like goodbyes either. Especially after dealing with this one.

After they'd deplaned in Boston and were heading to Dani's car, Whitney felt the tension that had gripped her for days slowly ease. She couldn't wait to get back to Lilac Lake and the comfort she always found there. Besides, one little dog needed a hug or two.

They loaded up Dani's car and then Dani, with the skill of years of driving in Boston, got them out of the city and on the way north on I-93 to New Hampshire. Whitney leaned her head against the headrest of the passenger's seat and closed her eyes.

Less than three hours later, Dani shook her. "Wake up. We're home."

Still sleepy, Whitney stepped out of Dani's car and, laughing, picked up Mindy and hugged her tight.

"She's so glad to see you," said Taylor, squeezing in a hug. "So am I. It's nice to have you home. I'm very sorry about what happened to Zane and all you've been through. Now, you can rest here."

"You have no idea how much that means to me," said Whitney returning Taylor's hug while Mindy pranced at her feet.

Taylor hugged Dani. "Glad to have you home. Pirate is too, I see."

Dani laughed and caressed the dog's shiny black ears before turning at the sight of Brad jogging toward her.

He swept Dani into his arms. "I missed you, babe."

"I missed you too. We have lots to talk about," said Dani.

"Come with me," said Brad in such a way that caused Whitney to exchange sighs with Taylor. Dani and Brad were perfect together.

"See you later," said Dani to Whitney and Taylor. "I'll check in with you tomorrow morning." She and Brad walked away, arm-in-arm, toward Brad's house with Pirate at their heels.

"Guess things are back to normal, huh?" Whitney said.

"Not exactly," said Taylor. "I've discovered a ghost in the

cottage. I'll show you later."

Whitney didn't speak. She needed a moment to herself. Being back in Lilac Lake was the beginning of letting go of all that had happened in California. Zane, the love they'd shared, and his painful end would always be a part of her, but now, she needed to let the beauty of Lilac Lake do its magic on her.

As if she knew Whitney's thoughts, Mindy lay her head on Whitney's shoulder as they entered the house and went out to the back patio to watch the stars twinkling in the night sky above them.

CHAPTER THIRTY-EIGHT
TAYLOR

Later that night, Taylor lay in bed relieved to have both her sisters home. Whitney was normally a cheerful person, and to know what she'd been going through tugged at Taylor's heartstrings. Whitney had returned to Lilac Lake looking shattered.

Taylor automatically reached out to pat Mindy's head and, finding that space empty, wondered if it was time to get a dog for herself. But that decision would have to wait. She had to figure out what was happening with her career before she could take on the challenge of a dog.

When she awoke the next morning, Taylor tiptoed down to the kitchen, fixed herself a cup of coffee and went out to the patio. After a restless night, she'd ended up sleeping late. Whitney was still asleep.

Taylor gazed out at the roses Margaret had planted and thought of all the changes life brings. She hadn't heard from Cooper since his call from his car, and though she'd wanted to reach out to him, she was waiting to give him time with his family before phoning. Still, the lack of communication bothered her.

As if her thoughts had conjured him up, her cell rang. *Cooper.*

She snatched the phone, and calming herself, waited a couple of seconds before answering. "Hello?"

"Hi, Taylor. Sorry I haven't called earlier but things have been crazy here. In fact, against my wishes, my sister has assigned another editor to you. Lucille Dumont is excellent at her job. I think you'll like her."

"I'm getting another editor?" Taylor asked, feeling as if she'd been stabbed.

"I'm not happy about it but I have no choice but to go along with what Candace is proposing for the business. After I get things sorted out with her, I'll be in touch. Regardless of what she says, I'd still like to work with you, even long-distance. Just give me time."

Rather than speak, Taylor ended the call and covered her mouth with her hand to stifle the wail that rose within her. She'd thought what she and Cooper had shared was special, had even dreamed of a life with him.

Was it her?

Was that why none of her relationships seemed to work out?

No, she reminded herself. She'd been the one who'd ended most of the relationships after feeling there was no future with the man she was dating.

Taylor covered her face and took several deep breaths, trying to understand what just happened. Shock and surprise once more turned to anger. She punched in her agent's number.

Dorothy Minton was an older woman who was both gentle and tough. She'd always been kind and encouraging to Taylor.

"Hello?" Dorothy answered crisply. "Taylor, how are you?"

"I'm angry. I just got a phone call from Cooper Walker telling me his sister is assigning a new editor to me. Someone named Lucille. Following his mother's heart attack, Cooper is too busy to do the work."

"All right. What is it you want?" Dorothy asked. "We can try to declare your contract with Pritchard Publishing null and void. But I'm not sure the real issue is your editor. What aren't you telling me?"

Taylor emitted a long, painful sigh. "Cooper and I were beginning to work very well together. I learned a lot from him. But, Dorothy, I'd already decided that I was going to continue working with him on my terms. You know I'm always willing to listen to advice, but I need to protect my creativity."

"Yes, I agree. What happened with you and Cooper? That's the real issue."

Taylor took a moment struggling to find the right words. Finally, she blurted, "I fell for him, Dorothy. And he told me he felt the same way."

"And then you got the call. No word from his mother on this?" Dorothy asked.

"No. Why would I? She's sick," said Taylor. "Cooper and his sister are trying to run the business while their mother is recuperating."

"I suggest you keep working on your book alone. When you get it close to done, call me," said Dorothy. "You're more talented than you think. I've got to cut this short. Talk to you soon. I'm late for a conference call. Sending hugs your way."

After the call ended, Taylor sat a moment going through the conversation in her mind. Something was going on. Dorothy wasn't concerned. In fact, she seemed to love the thought of Taylor completing the revisions on her own.

Taylor was still frowning as Whitney appeared.

"Thanks for letting me sleep in," Whitney said as Mindy trotted out on the lawn to do her business. Whitney stopped and stared at her. "Hey, what's wrong?"

Taylor shook her head. "I'm so confused." She told Whitney about both conversations and gave her a look of concern.

Whitney sat down in a chair beside her and gave her an encouraging smile. "I saw you and Cooper together, and what

I saw makes me feel that your relationship with him isn't over. He needs time to find his place in the family business. Sounds like Candace is trying to run the show. Time will take care of a lot of things. But it can't finish the rewrite of your book. Only you can do that with or without an editor."

"That's pretty much what my agent said." Taylor straightened with a determination to show Candace, Cooper, and their mother that she could do exactly that.

Seeing the smile that spread across her face, Whitney laughed. "That's the sister I know."

Dani joined them. "What did I miss?"

Taylor and Whitney filled Dani in and then they sat together.

"We need to talk about the cottage," said Dani. "Now that the floors are done, baseboards can be added. Also, Whitney, have you made final choices on the light fixtures?"

"Yes, I'm going with what I showed you, and I spoke to the salesman. We should have them soon," said Whitney.

"The bathroom floors are scheduled to be tiled this week and the flooring for the laundry room installed. As soon as they are, the finish carpenters will take care of all the baseboards. Then carpeting can be installed in the bedrooms," said Dani, looking at a checklist.

"How are we doing with the furnishings?" Taylor asked Whitney.

"We've already agreed on a general theme, and the living room couches and rug have been ordered. You each must pick out your own bedroom furniture. That's where we've agreed to spend our own money."

Taylor and Dani glanced at each other and nodded.

"The rest is something I'm still working on. Kitchen and bathroom counters, cupboards, and cabinets have already been chosen. We'll want bar stools and the kitchen table to be compatible. I'm going into Boston sometime this week to meet with a decorator."

"Sounds promising," said Dani looking pleased. "The dining room table will be refinished unless you find something we might like better."

"Furniture orders can take a long time to fulfill. So, I'll try to get on it as soon as possible," said Whitney. "I'm still decompressing from the trauma of the past several days."

"Understandable," said Taylor, admiring the strength Whitney was showing. "There's one thing we still need to discuss. And that's the photographs I took the other day. Something is showing up in them that makes the thought of a ghost more real." Taylor couldn't suppress a shudder.

"I wondered if you'd noticed," said Dani. "I thought I'd speak to someone at the historical society to find out more about the Maynard family."

"If necessary, I can ask Crystal about her friend who's done some spiritual cleansing of houses. She might be able to encourage the ghost to leave. He or she is friendly, so that's a plus," said Taylor.

"Right now, I can't get involved. I'm dealing with a ghost of my own," said Whitney.

"When you're ready to talk more about your time in California or anything else, I'm willing to listen," said Taylor.

"Thanks," said Whitney, blinking rapidly. "I'm going to be fine, but I'm still coping with everything. Or trying to."

Dani stood. "C'mon, group hug."

Taylor jumped to her feet and as her sisters' arms came around her, she felt their love and sent hers to them.

After Dani left and Whitney went to her bedroom, Taylor fixed herself a glass of ice water and headed up to her office. It was time to prove herself. With or without Cooper, she'd continue to be successful with her work.

CHAPTER THIRTY-NINE
DANI

Dani put Pirate in her car and headed out to the cottage curious to check the progress and to see if she could see any evidence of a ghost in the house. The image in Taylor's photograph was undefined. It could be that she and her sisters were trying to envision something that wasn't there. There'd been enough talk about a ghost to skew their perception.

As she pulled up beside a couple of trucks in front of the garage, she thought about the box they'd found hidden inside. That was another mystery they'd have to solve. But for now, she needed to concentrate on renovation of the house. Also, Brad's mother, MaryLou, was asking when she and Brad were planning to be married, and where. Dani needed time before deciding. She'd been enjoying every day of being engaged, even flashing her ring to herself to confirm she and Brad were official. It still sometimes seemed a dream.

She let Pirate out of the car and stood a moment studying the yard. With the overgrown shrubbery removed, the house looked bigger. She ran her fingers over the clapboards. The paint that hadn't peeled was easily flaked off with her fingernail. She'd chosen a warm gray to paint over the prepped surface.

The new breakfast nook added light to the kitchen and an interesting dimension to the back of the house. French doors that were part of that addition would eventually lead outside to a wooden deck. Renting Margaret's house had given her an understanding of how useful a deck or patio could be even though winters could be long. That, and the front porch facing in another direction would provide outdoor living for several months. Now that she and Brad had decided to build at The Meadows, Dani was taking advantage of testing ideas at the cottage before embracing them for her new home.

Dani was grateful Brad had suggested the idea of a new place. His house next to Margaret's was tasteful and well done. But Brad having lived there with Patti while she was slowly dying of cancer left a ghost of a different kind—painful memories of all Brad had lost.

She walked around to the front of the house, climbed the porch steps, and went inside. As she crossed the threshold, she murmured "We wish you no harm", as Brad's brother, Aaron, had once suggested. He didn't believe in ghosts but respected spirits of the past. She was willing to go along with that.

Upstairs, she went into the hall bathroom and watched a man lay the floor tile. "Hello," she said cheerfully, making the man startle. "Sorry. I didn't mean to scare you."

"That's all right. I'm getting used to it," said the man looking up from where he was kneeling on the floor.

"What do you mean?" Dani asked.

"It's nothing serious. Someone told me the house was supposed to be haunted and I can't get it out of my mind. My kid and I watched a weird movie last night on Netflix. No worries. I haven't seen anything, just thought I felt something."

Dani looked around but didn't see or feel anything unusual. "You're doing an excellent job. Have you done the master bathroom yet?"

"Yes. The tile you picked is easy to work with. I should be able to work on the powder room downstairs this afternoon."

"Thank you," Dani said, aware that talented craftsmen

were sometimes hard to find. Thank heavens GG had arranged for her to work with Collister Construction on this project. It made things like finding skilled people easier.

She walked into the master bedroom and on a whim stood in the stream of lemony light pouring through the windows and whispered, "We wish you no harm."

She turned away to go into the master bath and felt a swish of warm air cross her face. Surprised, she stopped and looked around, then realized a breeze had come up and was moving the air in the room.

CHAPTER FORTY
TAYLOR

Taylor sat in her desk chair and faced her computer with new resolve. She'd go all the way back to Chapter One to make sure she hadn't missed an opportunity to make something her own by rewriting as needed. Then she'd continue editing the book to prove to herself and others that she could do this.

She thought of the time spent with Cooper and how she'd felt a deep connection to him. She'd opened up to him in a way she'd never done with a man before. It was that, more than anything else that frustrated her with the decision for him to step away from working jointly with her.

Pushing aside those grim thoughts, she went to work. Taylor found it easier to write about her character, Vanessa, being dumped now that she felt she herself had been. She was deep in her revisions when her cell rang. *Pritchard Publishing.*

"Hello," Taylor said politely though fresh anger threatened to choke her words. "This is Taylor Castle," she said, using her pen name.

"This is Candace Walker. I understand you've been working with one of our editors, Thompson C. Walker."

"Yes, though I prefer to call him Cooper," said Taylor uncharacteristically bold.

"Even so, I've assigned a different editor to your book. The one you're revising." Candace sounded cold, reserved.

"Actually, I'm completing my project, and then Thompson C. Walker will look at it. He promised he would." Taylor controlled her frustration and decided she had nothing to lose by being firm.

"I see," said Candace, with a note of surprise. "For the time being, we'll continue with that arrangement. But if you need assistance doing those revisions, Lucille Dumont will be happy to help you. I'm sending along her information as we speak."

"Anything else?" Taylor asked, determined to be strong.

"No, that's it. Due to family circumstances, we're getting in touch with our authors to make sure they're moving forward." Candace's voice softened. "Thank you, Taylor."

The call ended. Taylor was shocked by her boldness but then she broke out laughing. Damn, it felt great to speak up, to be the one in control.

When she went back to work, she felt a new positive energy and later, when she looked over her work, she liked it.

That evening, Taylor was surprised by a call from Cooper.

"Hi. I didn't expect to hear from you," she said, her heart racing.

"I heard you talked to my sister earlier today," he said. "I don't know what you said, but she told me not to interfere with your work. Is that true?"

"Not exactly. I told her I'd work on this book on my own and then present it to you as promised."

"Oh," said Cooper. "I was worried you didn't trust me."

"I trust your work," Taylor said.

"But not me?" He sounded hurt. "I'm sorry if things have gotten messed up. But we'll work it out. Why don't we continue to do what we've always done and talk each day."

"I know you're under pressure right now and don't know when you'll return to Lilac Lake. I get it. I do. But it makes me wonder if there's a chance for our relationship to grow."

"Understandable," he said. "But, Taylor, I need you. Right now, I'm fighting for my life here at the company. Candace thinks she's simply going to walk into my mother's position. I'm trying to work that out, but it's going to take time. I have an appointment to see my mother tomorrow at the rehab center she's assigned to for lifestyle changes. She has to lose some weight, change her eating habits, come up with a different work schedule, and learn to relax by pacing herself. She's not happy about it but she's going forward with the program."

"I'm pleased for you that your mother is doing well and is committed to making changes," said Taylor.

"Me, too. My mother is driven to do her best, and my sister has inherited all of that. But I won't allow Candace to shut me out, us out."

"Of course not," said Taylor. "Besides, you're an excellent editor."

"Thanks for your confidence," said Cooper. "I needed to hear that. We'll work things out, Taylor. Trust me. Okay?"

"All right," said Taylor. "But remember, you must trust me too." Pride filled her when she realized she was sounding more like her sister, Dani.

"Don't give up on us. Gotta go. Talk later," Cooper said and clicked off the call.

Taylor stood and gazed out the window. Seeing a cardinal, her spirits lifted at the sight of the red bird whose music made her smile. Somehow, she and Cooper would work things out, wouldn't they?

The next day, Taylor was working at her computer when Dani called up the stairs to her. "Taylor, come on down. I have news!"

Taylor saved what she was working on and hurried down the stairs and into the kitchen where Dani was sitting with Whitney. "I went to the local historical society to see what I could find about our ghost." She pulled out pages from the notebook she'd become accustomed to carrying and faced them with a grin.

"Josiah Maynard arrived in the area in the early 1700s and was a minister to a small non-denominational church as well as a being a farmer. One of his five sons became owner of a local store, and others worked at various jobs in the area. By the time the 1900s arrived, the Maynard family was well-established in almost every facet of living in the area. Milton Maynard married his wife, Addie, in 1958." Dani gave them a sly smile. "But get this, Addie, our Mrs. Maynard, was his second wife. His first wife died just a year earlier under suspicious circumstances—a fall down the stairs."

Taylor's mind whirled possibilities. "Was there an investigation?"

"No, because Milton's brother was chief of police and the family concurred that she had mental health issues. They believed she killed herself after the death of her baby boy."

"Oh my God. Was the box of items we found in the garage hers?" said Whitney wide-eyed.

"I don't think so," said Dani. "The items seemed too new, too stylish to be hers. And then how could we tie the birth and death certificates to her? They were dated much later than that. I do know from reading through the files that Milton, Addie's husband, was a minister here in the area in a non-denominational church like his ancestor Josiah. And though not much is said about Milton, several people credited Addie with helping them through life's troubles. Not Milton."

"This is interesting news," said Whitney, "but I'm not sure how it ties into the ghost at the cottage. I think I'd prefer to let things rest. Poking around in that family's old business may cause unforeseen problems for us."

"I agree," said Taylor, relieved to know she wasn't the only one getting bad vibes from what Dani was telling them.

Dani shrugged. "Okay, I'll let it drop for now. But sometime this information might come in handy."

"Thanks," said Whitney. "I'm not ready to deal with that family's tragedies. I'm still coping with Zane's death."

"I'm sorry," said Dani giving Whitney a hug.

"We're here for you," said Taylor. "What do you say we go to the lake and try to relax there?"

"It's a perfect day for visiting the rock," said Dani. "Let's go."

Though a threat of a thunderstorm hung in the air, they packed up towels, suntan lotion, and bottles of water and headed to the cottage.

As they approached it, Whitney said, "I see some of the old landscaping has been removed. It looks so much better. What's going in its place?"

Dani turned to Taylor. "Are you up for talking to the landscapers about it?"

"Sure," said Taylor. "That will help keep me busy."

Dani frowned. "Any news from Cooper?"

Taylor gave them an update. "For the time being, I've decided to work on my book alone, and when it's ready, I'm going to New York to present it to him, not some new editor."

"Sounds like a plan," Dani said. "Good for you."

They got out of the car and headed to the water. The air was sticky and humid, prompting them to move quickly at the promise of the cool water on their skin.

Taylor's thoughts flew to the afternoon she and Cooper had been here and how she had reacted to feel his skin under her hand. Even now, thinking of it, desire settled deep inside her, making her wish things were different. She'd bragged about her new sense of independence, but she would do anything to go back to the time when she and Cooper were working together and falling in love, unaware of any family issues.

CHAPTER FORTY-ONE
WHITNEY

Whitney sat atop the sunning rock with her sisters, grateful for their company. Since Zane's death she was uncomfortable being alone. She knew it was wrong to blame herself for his death, but she couldn't stop wondering if she'd done enough to try and get him healthy.

Barbara had called her this morning to see how she was doing, and it took all of Whitney's will power not to break down into the tears that lingered inside her.

"Hey, sis, c'mon! I'll race you to the Inn's dock," said Dani.

Whitney shook her head. "You go ahead. I'm going to stay right here. Don't go far. It's going to storm soon. I can smell the rain coming."

"Okay, I'll be right back," said Dani.

Whitney watched Dani take off. Of all three of them, Dani was the most athletic. It was one reason Whitney thought Dani and Brad made such a cute couple.

She lay back on her towel on the rock thinking back to her early relationship with Zane. It hadn't been as easy, as natural as it was between Dani and Brad. Even Cooper and Taylor seemed right for one another in a way that was different, maybe healthier than what she'd shared with Zane. She knew she was right to break up with him. If she'd only been able to help him more.

CHAPTER FORTY-TWO
TAYLOR

Taylor sat up and looked at the horizon. A sheet of rain was falling at the far end of the lake. She nudged Whitney. "C'mon! We've got to run! The storm is coming."

A flash of lightning in the distance streaked through the darkening skies like a warning finger. They got to their feet, called to Dani swimming toward them, grabbed the towels, and headed for the cottage.

Just before they reached the porch, rain pelted them in pounding waves. Laughing, Taylor ran past Whitney and ran up the porch steps. Standing there, she watched Dani jog towards them, flinching at the sound of thunder rolling in the sky above her.

With the three of them clustered together on the porch, Taylor wondered if this was what the future held for them, finding solace with one another as they faced life's storms.

One of the living room windows rattled behind them. Taylor whirled around. Whitney grabbed her arm. "It's just the storm. No reason to worry."

"Especially now that we suspect that the box and certificates that we found are not associated with Addie Maynard," said Dani.

"If not her, who?" Taylor said.

"That, dear sister, is another story. One I'm not going to delve into today," said Dani. "The house is getting close to being done, and I want to enjoy it without worrying about a ghost. We don't believe in them. Remember?"

"Speak for yourself," said Taylor.

The rain stopped as quickly as it had come. Taylor followed her sisters to Dani's car, stopping for a moment to envision new plants. She didn't know enough about landscaping in New England to know what would do well there, but she did know what she liked. What she liked even more was Dani's and Whitney's trust in her.

At home, Taylor showered and shampooed her hair and then got ready to do more revisions. She'd found she was thinking of her characters more and was anxious to get back to them. She'd been working for an hour or more when her cell rang. *Cooper.*

"Hello, there," Taylor said. "What's up?"

"Hi, Taylor. I just finished meeting with my mother at the rehab hospital. She was very interested in knowing what was going on in the office and with you. Your agent called her."

"She did?"

"Yes," said Cooper. "My mother wants to meet you so we can all come to an agreement about going forward with your book."

"Oh, I'm surprised. I thought she was staying away from the business," Taylor said.

"So did I," said Cooper. "She's promised not to go into the office, but she's keeping an eye on things. She was upset when I told her what was going on at the office with Candace. Others have told her a few things about her overbearing behavior, too."

"When am I supposed to meet with your mother?" Taylor asked, suddenly nervous.

"At the end of the week. Is that pushing you too much? You'll want to have the revisions done by then. Wish I could be there to help, but you can still call me with questions or to get my suggestions. I've missed being with you, talking to you on a regular basis."

Taylor swallowed hard. "Me too. Don't worry, I'll get it done. Tell me where you want to meet, and I'll be there."

"You still have your condo in the city, right?" Cooper said.

"Yes. As a matter of fact, I think I'll drive down to the city tomorrow and work from there. Knowing I'm within reach might make things easier."

"It will," said Cooper. "If you need any input, I'll be there to help. I'd like to see you anyway. Send me your address, and I'll make time to stop by."

"I'd like that," said Taylor, giving him the information. Maybe being close to one another would help them decide if what they shared in New Hampshire would work in the big city.

Taylor went downstairs to tell Whitney about her decision to leave in the morning.

Whitney listened and then said, "Do you think you can get the revisions done before meeting Cooper's mother?"

Taylor shook her head. "I don't know, but I'm going to try. Right now, I'm going to pack so I can leave first thing in the morning."

Upstairs, Taylor began to pack her clothes and realized most of those she'd left in the city would do just fine. She'd always gone for classic styles. It seemed like yesterday that she'd brought suitcases to New Hampshire wondering if she'd like a new life there. Now, she was anxious to spend time in the city with Cooper.

Early the next morning, Taylor went quietly downstairs hoping not to disturb Whitney or Mindy. Outside, she breathed a sigh of relief that she'd made a clean escape. From next door, Brad and Dani, early risers, waved.

Taylor went to her car, eager to be on her way. She wanted to arrive in the city in plenty of time to get settled and then begin work on the book.

The five-hour drive gave her an opportunity to add some thoughts to those she'd already jotted down. Being under pressure to complete a book was something all authors understood. Schedules could easily be changed causing unexpected deadlines. This, she told herself, was no different. But she knew she was lying to herself. The owner of the publishing company was involved, and so was her son. Her daughter, too, if you wanted to account for the confusion at the office and how it might affect her book.

On a whim, she called Cooper.

His voice mail came on. Disappointed, she left a message telling him she was on her way.

He called back a short while later. "Great news! It's raining here and I've heard it's a big weather system in the northeast. Drive carefully."

"It's raining here, too. I'm not sure when I'll get there. After living in Lilac Lake, I've forgotten what driving in heavy traffic is like."

He laughed, and she recalled how his eyes crinkled at the corners when he did so, sending longing through her.

A truck whizzed by her on the Interstate and then cut her off. She slammed on her brakes. Shaken, she said, "Gotta go" and ended the call.

The moment Taylor opened the door to her condo, she felt a sense of homecoming. She loved being in Lilac Lake, but she also loved New York. She supposed it would always be that way.

She looked at the ivy plant that had dried up to shriveled

brown ropes and wondered how Dani could trust her to help with the landscaping at the cottage. But that was something she'd promised to do, and she'd squeeze it in.

Taylor quickly unpacked and settled in her office. This was the most important aspect of being back home, this comfort in her office where everything seemed familiar.

Quickly, before she could forget, Taylor typed up several of her thoughts about changes she wanted to make or additions to scenes. As she typed, she could envision the strength these ideas gave the story.

Once she got them down, she decided to check her cupboards and refrigerator. She needed to stock up on food and drinks for the next week. Normally she nibbled at both breakfast and lunch and then did something special for dinner either by going out to a restaurant or ordering food in from the many choices around her.

She made a list of things she needed and went to a neighborhood grocery store. She was amused as people rushed by her so different from life in Lilac Lake. She purchased what she needed, loaded up her canvas shopping bags, and was on her way back to her condo when she saw a familiar figure walking down the sidewalk toward her.

"Cooper!" she called.

Grinning, he trotted toward her.

She lowered her shopping bags to the sidewalk and went into his open arms laughing and crying at the same time.

"What's this?" he said, pulling back and giving her a look of concern. He thumbed her tears away and looked down at her, his hazel eyes turning green as they'd done before when he was about to kiss her.

She lifted her face to his, and his lips came down on hers, sending a trembling of happiness through her.

When they stepped away from one another, Cooper's grin

was as wide as Taylor's felt.

"I thought I'd stop by to see if you were settled. Any chance I could talk you into having dinner with me tonight?" he asked.

She beamed at him. "You might be able to. Especially if it's someplace that offers Chinese food."

He laughed. "I can manage that. I know Lilac Lake doesn't have that kind of restaurant."

"Exactly," she said. "Want to help me carry these groceries?"

"Sure." He picked up both bags. "I'm happy you're in the city. It'll give me a chance to spend some time with you." He grinned at her. "I've really missed you."

She returned his smile. "Me, too. But I need to concentrate on my writing before I meet your mother. I want to have the revisions done by then."

"I agree," said Cooper. "I'm happy to check pages as you go."

"Thanks, but I've decided to wait until the book is finished and then have you look at it, pages or chapters at a time. Does that work for you?"

"Absolutely. By the way, my mother has had a talk with my sister, and Candace is backing down on a lot of her decisions. But you're right. You want to be in the best position possible when you meet my mother. Don't get me wrong. Everyone loves her. But she has high expectations for herself and everyone else."

"I'm afraid of her already," said Taylor trying without success to cover up her old insecurities.

Cooper put an arm around her. "You have nothing to be worried about. She'll love you."

Later, sitting in a restaurant, Taylor couldn't help groaning with pleasure over the tasty Chinese food. If she moved to Lilac Lake permanently, she'd definitely have to make trips back to the city for a taste of more diverse foods.

Wearing an air of sophistication, Cooper was more attractive to her than ever. Yet, she'd never forget the sexy image of him in swim trunks at the cottage.

He smiled at her. "It's good to be back, huh?"

"Yes, but now my home is in both places," Taylor said honestly. "I've already decided if I move to Lilac Lake, I'll return here as often as I can."

"So, you're keeping your condo?" Cooper asked, raising his eyebrows in surprise.

"Yes. I wasn't sure about it but now I am," Taylor said.

"I'm trying to decide what I'm going to do," said Cooper. "A lot of my work can be done out of the office, but I need to be there to help run things. Right now, everything is up in the air until my mother is back on the job. She swears she'll return in a month."

"I'm glad she's doing so well," said Taylor.

"Me, too. Ever since my dad died, she's been busy at the office but never too busy to spend time with my sister and me."

"That's so important. I want to be a mom like that."

Cooper gave her a searching look, one that pulled at her heart. "I've always wanted a big family of my own."

Taylor couldn't help the blush that crept across her cheek at the thought of making babies with Cooper.

As if he read her mind, he reached across the table and gave her hand a squeeze. They were still smiling at one another as the waiter approached and asked them if they wanted anything more.

"No, thanks," said Cooper, pulling a credit card out of his wallet.

She smiled. He seemed as anxious to leave as she was.

They left the restaurant and walked to her condo. One of the things Taylor liked about her condo was that numerous restaurants were available within a few blocks. She especially liked it tonight because she was as anxious as Cooper to spend some time alone with him.

Having thought she might've lost him, Taylor turned to him with an anxious look. "You'll come up to my condo?"

"If you're sure, I'd like to," he answered and those fascinating eyes of his glowed a warm green.

They reached her building and entered the elevator. Her condo was on the twelfth floor.

At the door, Taylor's nerve endings did a tap dance at what was sure to come. She went ahead and unlocked it and then stood aside to allow Cooper to enter.

"How about a cold glass of water? I'm always thirsty after eating Chinese food." Taylor knew she was stalling, but she couldn't help it. She knew what they both wanted to happen, but she was unsure how to proceed.

"Water sounds great," said Cooper, following her into the tiny galley kitchen.

She fixed two glasses of ice water and they went into the living room.

Cooper sat and patted the empty space on the couch next to him.

Taylor handed him his drink and sat beside him.

"Here's to us," said Cooper, lifting his glass. "I hope this evening is the first of many to come, sharing meals and enjoying one another."

"I'll toast to that," said Taylor raising her glass and tapping it against his.

Cooper reached over and tugged her closer.

Taylor set down her drink and snuggled up against him,

loving the feel of his strong body wrapped around her.

"I'm really happy you're here in the city and want to remain part of the life here," said Cooper. "That means a lot to me."

"And what about the time I'm away in Lilac Lake?" said Taylor, challenging him.

"I like it there too. It's a nice place and the people are friendly. We could have the best of both worlds."

"Hmmm," Taylor said and met his lips with hers.

In his embrace, their surroundings melted away and the issue of having two different homes disappeared. Nothing, Taylor reminded herself, was more important to her than the love they shared. She'd waited all her life to find it.

When it became apparent that they each wanted more, Taylor and Cooper went to her bedroom.

Feeling nervous and awkward, Taylor stood there.

"Relax," murmured Cooper. "It's going to be fine."

She leaned into his kiss and then as things progressed, she learned he wasn't exactly right. It was much more than fine.

Later, they lay together and talked about their childhoods, their dreams for the future, and how they could work out more time together.

But when Taylor started to get carried away by their plans, she pushed those thoughts away. First things first. She had to get the book done and make it through a meeting with Cooper's mother without destroying her future at Pritchard Publishing.

CHAPTER FORTY-THREE
TAYLOR

Taylor awoke the next morning and rolled over to face the spot where Cooper had been last evening. Their coming together was spiritual, so much deeper than physical. The way they'd connected gave her a strong sense of commitment to work things out with him both professionally and personally.

It took her a moment to register the note on the very top of the pillow. She lifted it and smiled when she read the single word "LOVE". It said so much more than a lot of words skirting around the issue.

Though she wanted to linger in bed awash with the memory of their lovemaking, she got up. She had only a few days to get those revisions done, so she'd need to work quickly. Fortunately, she'd already plugged in her ideas for strengthening scenes.

She was in her pajamas in front of her computer when Cooper called. "Hey, sleeping beauty. Sorry to slip out without saying goodbye, but I knew we both had to get up early. You were sleeping too peacefully for me to disturb you."

"I realized you'd left sometime in the night, but I appreciated your note. Now, I'm busy working on the book. But if you're free for dinner, we can order in this time. I thought I'd give you a section of the book each night before we meet with your mother. Are you game to do it that way? The pages would be for you just to read, not critique, unless you see some glaring issue."

"Sounds like a plan. That way I'm not adding input, just

commenting, if necessary." Taylor could hear the smile in his voice when he said, "I like your independence."

Pleased with her plan, she ended the call and went back to work.

At five o'clock that afternoon, Taylor got up from her chair and stretched like a lazy cat. A third of the way into the book she had the characters well-established with their goals and an introduction to some of the problems that might hinder them.

Pleased with her progress, she hurried into the shower and got dressed. She'd have time to zip out to the store to buy dinner—fresh sushi, fruit and a bottle of white wine. Cooper had mentioned he liked sushi, and there was a place that sold it two blocks away.

Taylor had just returned to the condo when Cooper called to say he was on his way, that he was using his work with her as an excuse to leave the office at a reasonable time.

"I've got food for us and several chapters for you to read."

"I'll get through them as fast as I can because I've got other things on my mind."

Taylor felt a thrill go through her even as she laughed with him. Though she'd told him she'd fallen for him, she hadn't yet told him those three special words. But she knew the time was coming when she'd be more comfortable saying it.

She'd just finished straightening the condo when he arrived.

At the doorway, they smiled at one another and then she rushed into his arms. Laughing, he hugged her to him. "I thought about being with you again all day long."

Nestled against him, she said, "Me, too. But I was able to

get my work done. It really helps that I'm able to think of Vanessa as me and Tom as you."

He kissed the top of her head and stepped away from her. "Candace and I had a frank talk about what we each wanted going forward. I want to stay on the creative side of things while she likes the business side, overseeing sales numbers, contracts and all the things that bore me. We decided there was no need to be at odds. It was a perfect blend of talents."

"That must be a huge relief for you," said Taylor. "What does your mother think of that arrangement?"

"It's something we've talked about before. You've helped me change my thinking by seeing life in Lilac Lake. I want flexibility to do my job when and where I want, not be stuck in an office all day. With more and more people working from home, businesses have learned the work can still be done well, maybe even better, when people have that kind of flexibility. I love my job, have a commitment to my family and above all else, want the chance to spend more time with you." His gaze bored into her. "Is that all right with you?"

Taylor returned his steady look. She'd never had this strong connection with a man before. "It's more than all right with me. I want to spend as much time with you as possible," she said boldly. "And not only now, but in the future too."

Smiling, he wrapped his arms around her. "I like that new sassy attitude of yours." He bent down and kissed her, sending promises of more days like this by the way his kiss deepened.

When they pulled apart, Taylor said, "Have a seat in the living room. I'm going to bring you a glass of wine and a few chapters to read."

"Okay." He took off his tie and laid his blazer on one of the living room chairs. "Ah, that feels terrific. That's another thing. I'll be able to work in casual clothes away from the office."

"No one dresses for work in Lilac Lake," said Taylor, teasing him.

"I've already thought of that," he said grinning at her.

Taylor handed him a glass of wine and the bundle of pages she'd completed. "Just let me know if there are any glaring omissions. That's all."

While Cooper read, Taylor wiped down counters in the kitchen and straightened the silverware drawer, trying to keep herself busy so she wouldn't hang over Cooper's shoulder as she wanted to.

After he'd read the pages she'd given him, he set them aside and smiled. "I really like what you've done. The characters are better drawn and the plot thicker. Keep going. It's going to be your best." He gave her a teasing grin. "Now, can I have another glass of wine?"

Taylor burst out laughing. "Sorry, I was so nervous about whether you approved the changes that I forgot to offer you one. Let's relax. I've got some fresh sushi and a few other treats for dinner."

"The only thing I'm waiting for is dessert," Cooper said, wiggling his eyebrows and giving her a playful look.

She grinned, liking the idea herself.

At dinner, they spent some time talking about the publishing industry's struggles to keep up with the changes in the market and he listened to her as she told him about the challenges of some of her friends who were Indie authors.

Taylor liked that they could disagree and still carry on their conversation. And later, when they were lying in bed together, she found a whole different way to converse.

The routine of meeting in the evenings, sharing a meal, and having Cooper do a quick read-through of revised material continued for the next two nights.

Finally on the last night before she was to meet Cooper's mother, it was time for the final pages to be handed over. Taylor hadn't realized just when her story began to mimic the relationship between Cooper and her but now, after finishing the book, she could see it clearly.

She sat back from her computer satisfied she'd done a satisfactory job with the story. Readers wanted happy endings. She hoped she and Cooper would have the same one.

Cooper arrived, looking dapper in his work clothes. "Are we ready for tomorrow?"

Taylor smiled. "I think so."

She handed Cooper the last fifty pages of the novel with trembling fingers. His opinion meant much more to her in a different way than before. Early on, they'd worked together on ideas. But this book, this ending was her own.

"Okay," Cooper said, giving her an encouraging smile. "Let me sit down and read them now."

He took the pages and lowered himself onto the couch in her living room.

Taylor could tell he was as anxious to read them as she was. She closed her eyes, wishing with all her heart that he would like them. It meant so much to her,

He'd only been reading for fifteen minutes, when she couldn't stand it any longer. She got up from her desk chair, walked into the room, and gave him a hopeful gaze.

Cooper didn't even look up to acknowledge her.

Defeated, she went back to her office and began pacing again.

After another fifteen minutes went by, she peeked in at him. "Would you like some water? A glass of wine? Anything?"

He shook his head and waved her off.

Her nerve ends tingling, Taylor went back to her office and

stared at the empty page on her laptop. It was just a machine, she told herself. The stories came from her. Sometimes with the help of a friend, someone she trusted, but mostly from her. No one could take that away from her. Writing a story was as much a gift as being able to sing and dance like her sister. Without the ups and downs and a lot of practice, a story couldn't be written. She'd certainly had her trials with this one.

Taylor had no idea how long she'd been staring at the computer when she heard Cooper call to her. Her heart pounding, she left the office and went to him.

He looked up at her and to her horror, his eyes filled.

"Oh, no! What do you think?"

"It's beautiful," said Cooper setting the papers down and getting to his feet. "A perfect ending."

Taylor threw herself into his arms. "That makes me so happy. I ... I ..." she stopped. The three words she wanted to say to him were part of the story. Their story. "I love you."

Cooper smiled at her, his eyes shiny with emotion. "I love you too, Taylor." He cupped her face in his hands before lowering his lips to hers.

Taylor stretched on tiptoes to meet him and responded with all the love she felt for him. Sometimes words were not enough. You had to read between the lines to find the love you'd been waiting for all your life.

Now, no matter what the next couple of days brought, she knew this was enough.

CHAPTER FORTY-FOUR
TAYLOR

The next day as Taylor waited for Cooper to pick her up to meet his mother, she fussed with her hair, her skirt, her blouse. In an effort to look professional when she met Grace Pritchard, Taylor had pulled her hair into a bun at the back of her head, giving her a more classic look. She wanted to make a favorable impression on so many levels.

At the sound of the doorbell, Taylor hurried to answer it.

Cooper's eyes widened at the sight of her. "Wow! You look beautiful. So ..."

"Professional?" she asked.

"That and more. Nice of you to dress up to meet my mother."

"And my boss," said Taylor, beaming at him.

He waited while she locked up and then they left to go to the Uber driver waiting for them.

"Where are we going? The rehab hospital?" Taylor asked, sliding into the backseat of the car.

"No, my mother is now at her condo while continuing some classes at the rehab center. She likes this routine much better, but she's still under the watchful eye of the staff who check in with her every day to make sure she's exercising and eating properly. They know patients rest better at home, but they won't let her get away with anything."

"I'm happy for her. There's no place like home."

Cooper grinned. "Even if you have two?"

She laughed. "Yes, as long as you love them both." She'd

thought about it and had decided she was comfortable with the thought of living in both places. She'd do her share to cover the use of the cottage and didn't think her sisters would resent the time she spent in New York. With Dani living in Lilac Lake full-time, it made things easier for all of them.

They pulled up to a handsome building on 57th, one of the toniest areas in the city. Taylor knew his mother had a large apartment, and Cooper was temporarily bunking in with her after recently moving out of a bachelor pad he'd shared with two other men for the last few years.

"Here we are," said Cooper. He helped her out of the car, and they headed inside.

Taylor's hands went cold and for a moment her stomach clenched.

Sensing her discomfort, Cooper draped an arm around her shoulder. "Nothing to worry about. Remember?"

She forced a smile. She knew it was silly to place so much importance on this one meeting, but it meant more to her than even Cooper knew.

They took an elevator up to the thirty-sixth floor, and when they got off, they faced a series of double doors. Cooper led her to one entrance and knocked before opening it.

The marble entranceway led to a living room lit in part by the windows along one wall that showcased the city scene outside. A large, pale-blue Oriental rug was the centerpiece of the room, tying together two plush tan-leather couches and two wing chairs covered in a stunning blue, tan, and cream woven fabric. A wood and glass table sat between the two couches facing one another, holding a pile of books. The room was formal and yet it had enough of a lived-in look to be comfortable. The tension in Taylor's shoulders eased.

Grace Pritchard strode into the room, her gaze switching from Cooper to her. "Hello, Taylor. I'm happy to meet you at last."

Taylor shook her outstretched hand and smiled. "I'm pleased to meet you too."

"And how are you, my darling boy?" Grace asked, kissing her son on the cheek.

"It's nice to see you looking so well, Mom. You had us all worried for a bit."

"I'm tough," she said, smiling and waving away his concern. "Shall we sit?" She moved to one of the couches.

Taylor and Cooper sat on the couch facing her.

Grace settled her gaze on Taylor. "I've been wanting to meet the woman behind the books I've fallen in love with. Did you know Dorothy Minton and I are longtime friends?"

"I didn't until recently," said Taylor.

"Well, there's more to the story than that. Dorothy and I shared a friend, a woman by the name of Sherrie Blaine. She's passed on now, but years ago after a horrible divorce, she was wiped out financially, left to live on the street. A certain woman named Eugenia Wittner stepped in to help her and gave her a start in setting up her own editing business. Is the name Eugenia Wittner familiar to you?"

Taylor's eyes widened with surprise. "Yes, that's my GG. We know she's done kind things for other people, but she never talks about it."

"Well, when Dorothy and I were discussing her clients' books one day, your name and background came up tying you to Lilac Lake. I was curious," said Grace. "After a little research, I realized you were Genie Wittner's granddaughter. Dorothy and I thought it only fair that you be given a chance to prove yourself with Pritchard Publishing. Neither one of us was surprised by the lovely response your books receive. They're very special. So, it seems you've proven that one good deed deserves another."

Taylor let out the breath she hadn't realized she'd been holding. "GG is a special woman. I'm very proud of her."

"As you should be," said Grace. "Now, let's talk about the book you're revising."

"I've just finished with it. I think you and others will be pleased. It's a much stronger, deeper book."

"But still has your special kind of sweetness?" Grace said, leaning forward, her gaze boring into Taylor.

"Yes, I think so."

"Even though I didn't oversee the rewrites, I think so too," said Cooper. "Taylor wanted to do this on her own, and after completing a quick readthrough, I'm happy to say it couldn't be better." He lifted Taylor's hand and gave it a squeeze of encouragement.

Grace gave them an approving smile. "Do I detect something else going on between the two of you?"

Taylor couldn't stop the rush of heat to her cheeks.

Cooper glanced at her and then faced his mother. "We've fallen in love."

"Ah, that's so lovely to hear," said Grace. "Dorothy and I suspected that might happen." She turned to Taylor. "Dorothy is Cooper's godmother, so she knows both of you quite well."

"Does my grandmother know about all this?" asked Taylor, not sure how she felt about this kind of manipulation.

"No," said Grace. "We didn't know how things were going to work out and wanted things to happen naturally." She got to her feet, walked over to Taylor, and held out her arms. "May I?"

Taylor stood and was embraced by Cooper's mother.

"This is the first of many, I hope," said his mother, stepping away and smiling at her. "I loved the way you handled Candace. She told me about your phone call and your insistence on doing things your way when it came to your book. That's the kind of spirit I admire."

"Writing is a very personal thing," said Taylor. "I couldn't let anyone take that away from me."

"Nor should you," said Grace. "Is it all right if I plan a quiet dinner tonight for the two of you with Dorothy, Candace, and me?"

Cooper looked to Taylor.

Taylor felt happiness radiating from her curved lips. "That would be very nice."

"Thanks, Mom," said Cooper.

Watching them hug, Taylor knew everything would be all right. Cooper was a terrific man who was unafraid to show his affection, not the cold, heartless person she'd first thought.

She turned to him now. "Why were you so harsh in your first email to me?"

He shook his head. "I'm sorry about that. I guess I was disappointed that after reading your first two books, I wanted more between the lines. You know?"

She nodded. He'd been right about the story all along. It wasn't until she was falling in love with him that she recognized it.

His mother smiled with satisfaction. "There's more power in action, not just words."

"In that case," said Cooper with a teasing grin. He swept Taylor into his arms and kissed her to prove it.

That evening Taylor and Cooper returned to his mother's apartment for the quiet dinner she promised.

"I'm so happy with the way things are turning out," said Grace, greeting her. "I suggest we have a champagne toast for our guests to celebrate a new romance and a new book."

"Great minds think alike," said Cooper and as they smiled at one another, Taylor could see the resemblance.

The moment Dorothy appeared at the door Taylor hurried over to her. "You've been keeping secrets from me. I didn't know you were such a matchmaker, but I love you for it."

Dorothy laughed. "An agent's job is to help her client have the best outcome possible."

"Spoken like a true pro," said Grace, kissing Dorothy's cheek. "The two of us have done a spectacular job with these two."

Dorothy laughed. "Spoken like a true doting mother."

They walked away, arm-in-arm.

Cooper joined Taylor, holding a silver bucket filled with ice and a green bottle of champagne. "Seems like the family is here except for my sister, Candace. She's always a little late. But you'll like her." He turned as the door opened.

Candace, looking a lot like her brother, smiled at her. "Hi, Taylor. I'm Candace. Welcome to the family."

"Thanks," Taylor managed to say, shocked to see Candace's nose ring and the tattoo on her arm after meeting their conservative mother.

"A lot goes on between the lines," Cooper said into Taylor's ear.

Taylor couldn't stop the laughter that bubbled out of her. "I'll say."

They each took a seat in the living room, and then Cooper opened the bottle of champagne, tasted it, and poured some in each glass. Grace's glass contained only a tablespoon of the bubbly wine, but she still lifted the tulip glass with the others.

"Here's to the magic of words and love," said Grace. She turned to him with a sad smile. "Your father would be so proud of you."

"What about me?" asked Candace, sounding like a typical sister.

"You, too," said Grace, chuckling. "I'm proud of both of

you. There were a few missteps with the two of you with me away from the office, but I'm learning that the business is in excellent hands. It will be a relief for me when the two of you take on bigger roles."

"So, when are you going to retire?" asked Candace.

"Retire?" The shock on Grace's face was telling.

Taylor joined in the laughter, pleased to know she and Cooper would have time to work things out between them.

After a quiet but tasty meal accommodating Grace's new diet, Taylor and Cooper headed to her condo.

"What a great day," said Cooper as they sat in an Uber car avoiding the rain.

"The best," Taylor agreed. "I really like your mother. Your sister too."

"Thanks," said Cooper.

The driver let them out at her condo, and Taylor hurried to the front door to avoid the raindrops.

After paying the driver, Cooper followed her.

Upstairs, Taylor stood at the window and gazed at the city lights below. The rain on the glass pane blurred the view making it look like a painting. She and Cooper had talked about getting a place in the city together sometime in the future, but for the time being, this was the perfect place for her.

Cooper came up behind her. "Any idea how much I love you?"

She turned to him with a smile and then gasped when she saw the ring box in his hand.

He got down on one knee and looked up at her. "Taylor Gilford, will you marry me? I love you in a way I didn't think possible. In such a short amount of time, I've realized that you're the part of me I've been missing. I want to share the rest of my life with you, have a family together, and support one another as we meet life's challenges. I promise to be there for you every step of the way. I love you so much."

Tears blurred Taylor's vision. She couldn't have written a better scene. She clasped her hands together. "Yes, Cooper, I'll marry you."

He rose and hugged her to him. "You've made me so happy." He cupped her face in his hands and lowered his lips to hers. Taylor leaned into him loving his strength, his tenderness.

When they pulled apart, he opened the box. Inside was a round diamond surrounded by deep blue sapphires.

"It's gorgeous," said Taylor as Cooper slipped the ring on her finger.

"Did you know sapphires are said to be the wisdom stone, stimulating concentration, enhancing creativity, and promoting purity and depth of thought?" said Cooper, giving her an impish grin. "How could I choose any other ring for a writer like you?"

She looked at the glittering diamond on her hand and laughed. "I assume you read that somewhere."

"Of course," he answered, kissing her once more. "I wanted it to be perfect, just for you."

CHAPTER FORTY-FIVE
TAYLOR

Two days later, Taylor headed back to Lilac Lake. She was a far different person from the one who'd gone there a couple months ago thinking her stay was just for the weekend. So much had happened to her and her sisters. She and Dani had found love while Whitney had said farewell to a man she'd once loved. There were still things to decide, but like GG had hoped, life at Lilac Lake was proving to be the catalyst for changes in their lives. Of the three of them, Whitney was the one most uncertain about her future. But no matter what life handed her going forward, she and Dani would be there to support her.

Her thoughts turned to GG. She was a treasured woman who'd been given the opportunity to change lives with gifts like the Genie she was named after. After years of knowing her love, Taylor wanted to be there for GG as she grew more in need of care. Just thinking of the time when GG might not be there for her and her sisters, Taylor's eyes filled.

Her thoughts turned to Cooper. In addition to her own family, Taylor had the promise of a new one with Cooper's mother and sister. Seeing Cooper with them, she understood his desire to hold his own in the business and silently applauded him for it.

Taylor's cell phone rang. *Dani.*

She picked up the call smiling. "Hi, what's up?"

"Just checking up on you. I talked to GG this morning and she told me the most amazing story."

"What did she tell you?" Taylor asked. She'd told her parents the happy news, but she'd told her mother she wanted to tell GG in person. Had Cooper's mother talked to GG?

"First of all, did you know Cooper's mother was friends with your agent?" Dani responded.

"Oh, so you know everything?" said Taylor, starting to laugh.

"Everything," said Dani. "GG's invited us to tea so she can hear the story all over again. She told me to tell you that the best things happen between the lines."

Taylor laughed, thinking of Cooper. "I think so too." She caught a flash of sunlight on the diamond in her ring and felt a rush of happiness. Life was sure to hold many surprises in the future, but together she and Cooper would meet them all.

She and Dani talked for a few minutes more, and then Taylor headed home to Lilac Lake.

# # #

Thank you for reading *Love Between the Lines*. If you enjoyed this book, please help other readers discover it by leaving a review on your favorite site. It's such a nice thing to do.

Sign up for my newsletter and get a free story. I keep my newsletters short and fun with giveaways, recipes, and the latest must-have news about me and my books. Welcome! Here's the link:

https://BookHip.com/RRGJKGN

Enjoy an excerpt from my book, *Love Under the Stars*. Book 3 in The Lilac Lake Inn Series:

CHAPTER ONE
WHITNEY

On a bright August day, Whitney Gilford sat on the sunning rock she and her two sisters had used since they were kids spending time at Lilac Lake in the Lakes Region of New Hampshire. It was the best place she knew to gather her thoughts.

Too upset to sit still, she jumped to her feet, picked up a nearby stone, and threw it as hard as she could into the water, observing the spray of water it created with little satisfaction.

"Dammit, Zane! Why wouldn't you let me help you? Or help yourself? You could've had such a wonderful life." Her voice carried across the lake in angry waves, scaring several birds from their perches in trees sprinkled along the coastline.

Breathing hard, Whitney unclenched her fists and sank back onto the rock, letting tears of frustration and sorrow escape onto her cheeks. Then, angry again, she swiped them off. It was time to get to work, time to try to clean up his mess and make things right.

She knew on an intellectual level she wasn't to blame for Zane's death, but she'd gone into an emotional tailspin after hearing it. And then, when she found out he'd left her his house, his money, and everything he owned, she'd filled with remorse for not succeeding in getting him into rehab. Now, she was dealing with anger at his decision to end his life like that.

Almost a month ago, she'd received the shattering call telling her Zane Blanchard, her co-star on the television series, *The Hopefuls*, had died of a drug overdose. She and Zane had fallen in love soon after the series began four years ago, but it hadn't lasted long. Even when drugs changed the nice guy Whitney loved into someone she detested, they'd tried for the sake of the series to pretend they were still together. But after repeated failures to get Zane into a rehabilitation center and the cruel changes in his behavior toward her, Whitney ended the relationship.

At one time, back when she and Zane were dating, they'd discussed different ways they could use some of their earnings for charity. Whitney knew exactly what to do with the inheritance Zane had given her. She'd set up a foundation to help children with mental health issues. Heaven knew, there were plenty of kids of all ages needing that kind of assistance.

She gazed out over the lake and listened to the water gently lapping at the edges of the rock, smothering it with soft kisses. She watched as ducks glided in the water nearby, and smelled the aroma of the evergreen trees that dotted the shoreline helping to soothe her soul.

Here at Lilac Lake, Whitney often relaxed on the patio of her rental house at night, sitting under the stars, staring at their glittering beauty, finding solace in the continuity of life.

"Hey, Whitney. I thought I might find you here," said her

sister, Dani, walking toward her across the front lawn of the cottage the three sisters owned and were renovating. At thirty, Dani was the middle sister and a talented architect. She had agreed to marry Brad Collister, one of the two brothers who owned a local company, Collister Construction, which the new owners of the Lilac Lake Inn had hired to do a complete renovation.

Whitney waved, and Dani joined her on top of the rock. "Now that the interior of the cottage is complete, minus furnishings, we'd better talk about attacking the attic. We've put it off until now, but we need to decide whether to leave it or take advantage of the workmen available to us to turn that into a unique living space."

Genie Wittner, their grandmother, whom they lovingly called GG, had sold the Lilac Lake Inn to new owners, who'd agreed to leave the family cottage and three acres of the property out of the deal as long as the three sisters renovated and then used the cottage for at least six months of the year. If that didn't happen, the new owners of the inn had an option to buy the cottage at a fair market price.

GG had done her best to keep the entire property in the family, but with her age and financial issues, this was the best solution for her to honor her father's wishes. Now it was up to Whitney, Dani, and their younger sister, Taylor, to keep that promise.

The cottage they'd inherited had been left in poor condition. With her architectural expertise, Dani had agreed to supervise its renovation. Even with the attractive work already done on the house, there remained a major problem— the belief that the house was haunted.

Taylor, especially, was bothered by the presence of a spirit. Neither Whitney nor Dani could deny feeling something amiss inside the house. They, along with Taylor, had agreed to follow through on investigating what facts they could find about the ghost, whom townspeople thought was Mrs. Maynard, a woman who'd lived there twenty years ago.

"Let's keep the attic as it is for the time being," said Whitney, "but I'll try to investigate and resolve the issue. We know only a little bit about Addie Maynard and her husband, but we know nothing about the box that held a wedding dress along with baby clothes. I believe it's connected in some way to the mystery of the ghost."

"Yes, and the envelope holding birth and death certificates for a baby named Isaac Thomas might play a part, too," said Dani.

"What are you two up to?" asked Taylor, joining them. The youngest at twenty-five, Taylor was a successful author who'd recently become engaged to her editor. With her dark hair and brown eyes, she was physically different from Whitney and Dani's blonde looks, but she had the same Wittner family spirit, as GG liked to say.

"We were talking about the need to finish the attic," said Dani.

Taylor held up her hand to stop her. "We have to take care of Mrs. Maynard first. But that's not why I'm here. I heard something disturbing that I think you should know about, Whitney. Some fans on Instagram are blaming you for Zane's death. One of them threatened to confront you and make you confess to ruining his life."

"I don't like the sound of that," said Dani, frowning.

Whitney held up her hand. "It's just talk. Don't let it concern you." She didn't want to go there because she still blamed herself for not preventing his tragic death.

"Yes, but with Dani spending time with Brad and me going back and forth to New York City, I'd feel better if we asked Nick to keep an eye on you." Nick Woodruff was the police chief of Lilac Lake, and though people admired him for his dedication, there wasn't a female under 80 who didn't also admire his sexy looks. He'd been one of the summer gang of kids back when Whitney, Dani, and Taylor spent summers visiting GG. After an amicable divorce from Crystal, Nick showed no signs of being interested in anyone.

"I don't think we have to go that far. People say hurtful and nasty things like that on social media all the time, but it's only bravado," said Whitney. "Zane's drug habits are well-known."

"Taylor may be right, though," said Dani. "We'd feel better if Nick was aware of the situation."

"Look, I don't want him checking on me unless the situation escalates. I've tried to keep a low profile in Lilac Lake," said Whitney. "After dealing with the details of Zane's death, I'm finding my footing and don't want people hovering over me."

"I understand," said Dani. "But at the first sign of trouble, I'm going to ask Nick for help."

"Deal," said Whitney. "In the meantime, I'll do some investigation into our ghost. Dani, you said Addie Maynard married Milton in 1958 after his first wife died a year or so before. After Milton died in 1997, Addie took up GG's offer to live at the cottage. That was almost twenty years ago."

"Yes, she died in 2002," said Dani.

"The house was empty for that time?" said Taylor. "Why would GG let the house go empty for so long?"

"I'm not sure she did," said Dani. "Let's ask her. I'll call and see if we can join her for tea." Their grandmother was now living at a nearby assisted living facility called The Woodlands, which Brad and Aaron Collister's construction company had built with GG's backing.

The women stretched out on the rock, basking in the sun, as they used to do when they were younger. Then as now, it was a soothing place to be.

Dani popped up. "Okay, I can't stay any longer, but it was great to catch up with the two of you."

Taylor got to her feet. "I'm taking a short break, but I need to get back to work. Being here gave me a new thought for a plot twist."

Whitney waved to her sisters and lay back against the granite rock allowing her thoughts to drift. The last two years of growing conflict with Zane had taken a toll on her. She needed quiet time to heal.

That afternoon, Whitney joined her sisters in a visit to GG. Their grandmother had always been a huge emotional support to the three of them. Their mother, a valuable supporter of causes in Atlanta, Georgia, where she lived, wasn't the warm person GG was. Maybe because her first marriage was to an alcoholic who died in an accident while driving drunk, and though their union had produced both Whitney and Dani, it had also been filled with a lot of heartache and self-doubt. Her second marriage was, thankfully, a happy one and had created Taylor.

As Whitney exited the car and headed inside to GG's apartment at The Woodlands, her heart beat a little faster in anticipation of seeing her grandmother. GG had a way of always making things seem better, and Whitney needed that now.

When they entered GG's apartment, they found her sitting in her favorite chair reading a book. She noticed them, and a wide smile softened the wrinkles on her face.

"There they are. My lovely girls," she said, holding out her arms to them.

Whitney lined up to give her grandmother a hug and a kiss on the cheek.

"What are you reading?" asked Taylor.

"Something you might like. *Breakfast at The Beach House Hotel*," said GG. She set the book down. "Now, let's enjoy one another. After Dani's call, I had lemonade and cookies delivered to the room. But first, tell me why you're here. Dani mentioned my giving you some information."

"Yes," said Whitney. "I'm starting to do some investigation into the mysterious box we found in the garage at the cottage."

"We're trying to get to the bottom of the rumor about a ghost living at the cottage," said Dani. "We know that Addie Maynard died outside the cottage in December 2002. Has the cottage remained empty ever since? We know you'd moved to the inn by then."

"When we were here in the summers, it was unoccupied," said Taylor.

"After Addie used the cottage, I allowed people in the community to house refugees there on a temporary basis, along with other people, mostly women in need of a safe space. But I was saving the cottage for you girls, so I never rented it out to a family on a permanent basis." GG shook her head. "Then when taxes and other expenses of running the inn began to become unwieldy, I simply tried to keep things going while I decided what to do. After being caught in that financial scandal in Boston, I had no choice but to sell the inn, keeping the cottage for you girls to enjoy with your families in the years to come. Sadly, it was the best I could do to keep my father's promise to hold onto the land."

"We're going to honor your wishes and keep the cottage in use," said Whitney, taking hold of her grandmother's hand and squeezing it.

"I know you will," said GG. "That makes me very happy. I remember summer days when you girls visited. It was always such a pleasure, something I looked forward to all year."

"What do you know about Addie's daughter, Carolyn?" said Dani.

"I remember her as a pretty girl, a bit on the shy side," said GG staring into space. "I don't know what happened, but there was a painful rift between Carolyn and her mother, and she left town in the early fall of 2001. I never heard anything more about her, but others may have more knowledge than I."

Taylor was busy writing down notes, but she looked up at GG and said, "There's got to be a story behind it. We want to know what it is before we decide to work on the attic."

"How is the cottage coming along?" asked GG.

"We're getting ready to put the last few finishing touches on it. The outside needs to be painted," said Dani. "Once that's done, we'll complete the landscaping around it. For the time being, we're holding onto the funds we have before making any other decisions."

"We can't wait for you to see it. We're having a celebration when it's all done," said Taylor.

"There are going to be some nice surprises for you," said Whitney. She was in charge of decorating the house and was using some of the family portraits and photographs they'd recovered from the inn to decorate walls inside the cottage.

"How are things going for you here? Has JoEllen Daniels come into your room uninvited recently?" Dani's nostrils flared with anger. "Brad's trying to stay away from her, but she too frequently calls him to come fix this and that at the cabin she's renting."

"That woman is such bad news. When you think about her believing Brad would marry her to fulfill his dead wife's wishes, it's ludicrous," grumped Taylor.

"It's really a twisted belief," said Whitney. "But she's desperate to marry someone."

"And in the meantime, she's annoying," said Dani. "I try

not to say much about it to Brad because he gets so frustrated with her that I don't want to add to it."

Just then, there was a knock on the door. A tall, thin, blonde stuck her head inside. "Good afternoon, Ms. Wittner. I'm checking to make sure you're all right. Is there anything I can do for you?" She looked everywhere but at GG.

"No, thank you, JoEllen," said GG in a tone of dismissal no one could ignore.

"Okay, then, I'll be on my way. I knew you had company and wanted to make sure." JoEllen smiled at Dani.

After JoEllen left and closed the door behind her, Dani seethed. "JoEllen told Brad she'd be here in town to check up on him, and now she's doing that to me too. It makes me furious."

"It's best to ignore her," said GG. "You and Brad will be living out at The Meadows someday, and that will make it easier."

Dani's frown disappeared. "It *will* be nice, but it won't happen for some time. Customers take precedence over us." Dani and Brad had decided to build a house for themselves at the development.

"And how are you doing, Whitney?" GG asked, giving her a penetrating look.

"Better," Whitney said. "But it's going to take a long time to get over the anger and sadness I feel. I'm starting to work on structure and ideas for the foundation I'm setting up in Zane's name. That helps."

"Yes, keeping busy is wise," said GG smiling at her.

Whitney's heart filled with love for her grandmother. GG had been a comfort to four-year-old Whitney after her father died and before that when fighting was a constant in her parents' home. Luckily, a couple of years later, her mother met a good man, married him, and gave birth to Taylor.

"You're going to be fine," GG said to Whitney, squeezing her hand.

Whitney gave her a weak smile. She wouldn't worry GG by telling her about the crazy social media talk that she, herself, was the cause behind Zane's death.

# # #

About the Author

A ***USA Today* Best-Selling Author**, Judith Keim, , is a hybrid author who both has a publisher and self-publishes, Ms. Keim writes heart-warming novels about women who face unexpected challenges, meet them with strength, and find love and happiness along the way. Her best-selling books are based, in part, on many of the places she's lived or visited, and on the interesting people she's met, creating believable characters and realistic settings her many loyal readers love. Ms. Keim loves to hear from her readers and appreciates their enthusiasm for her stories.

Ms. Keim enjoyed her childhood and young-adult years in Elmira, New York, and now makes her home in Boise, Idaho, with her husband, Peter, and their lovable miniature Dachshund, Wally, and other members of her family.

While growing up, she was drawn to the idea of writing stories from a young age. Books were always present, being read, ready to go back to the library, or about to be discovered. All in her family shared information from the books in general conversation, giving them a wealth of knowledge and vivid imaginations.

"I hope you've enjoyed this book. If you have, please help other readers discover it by leaving a review on the site of your choice. And please check out my other books and series:"

The Hartwell Women Series
The Beach House Hotel Series
Fat Fridays Group
The Salty Key Inn Series
The Chandler Hill Inn Series
Seashell Cottage Books
The Desert Sage Inn Series
Soul Sisters at Cedar Mountain Lodge Series
The Sanderling Cove Inn Series
The Lilac Lake Inn Series

"ALL THE BOOKS ARE NOW AVAILABLE IN AUDIO on iTunes and other sites! So fun to have these characters come alive!"

Ms. Keim can be reached at **www.judithkeim.com**

And to like her author page on Facebook and keep up with the news, go to: **http://bit.ly/2pZWDgA**

To receive notices about new books, follow her on Book Bub:

https://www.bookbub.com/authors/judith-keim

And here's a link to where you can sign up for her periodic newsletter! **http://bit.ly/2OQsb7s**

She is also on Twitter @judithkeim, LinkedIn, and Goodreads. Come say hello!

Acknowledgments

And, as always, I am eternally grateful to my team of editors, Peter Keim and Lynn Mapp, my book cover designer, Lou Harper, and my narrator for Audible and iTunes, Angela Dawe. They are the people who take what I've written and help turn it into the book I proudly present to you, my readers! I also wish to thank my coffee group of writers who listen and encourage me to keep on going. Thank you, Peggy Staggs, Lynn Mapp, Cate Cobb, Nikki Jean Triska, Joanne Pence, Melanie Olsen, and Megan Bryce. And to you, my fabulous readers, I thank you for your continued support and encouragement. Without you, this book would not exist. You are the wind beneath my wings.